OBSOLETE

CT FRENCH

ISBN: 0989464113
ISBN-13: 978-0989464116

Spring Creek Press
Hendersonville, NC

DEDICATION

I have been surrounded by strong women all my life (one reason I love to write these characters) and this book is dedicated to a very important one, Sherry Jo Cannon, my beta reader and best friend since high school. A friend who shares my dream of opening a rescue for abandoned dogs and whose positive persona brightens each and every day.

ACKNOWLEDGMENTS

There is no one I would rather share this journey with than my sister Cyndi Hodges (aka Caitlyn Hunter – read her books, they're great!). Although we had a rocky start (I admit it, I was jealous of her beauty and sunny personality), I have found in her a kindred spirit and an author whose lyrical prose inspires me. Thank you, Gik, for always being in my corner, cheering me on and offering great insights re; my WIPs. I am honored to co-author the Appalachian Journey series with you.

Thanks to my family for their love and continued support and to my readers who motivate me to keep moving forward. I am so blessed…

CHAPTER 1

I stood on the ridge above the small valley, far enough away that the stench was not so bothersome, watching flames lick wickedly toward the sky. From this angle, the huge pit resembled an ugly pockmark upon the dark-green grass, the stiff arms and legs of the bodies jutting at odd angles, some reaching upward as if seeking salvation, others resembling discarded dolls thrown into a trash bin. I watched the burial crew retreat from the pit, black smoke trailing them like a death shroud, carrying smoldering cinders and minute bits of cloth and flesh. The smell would be horrendous as they waited for the fire to finish its cremation. Afterward, they would dump lime into the pit and, if there was room, add more bodies tomorrow. Remembering the gauze mask, I ripped it away and threw it to the ground. I eyed it, thinking to pick it up, but decided, who would notice? A small bit of trash among a country full of dead bodies and animals. Even so, I should have thrown it into the fire before leaving.

My horse nickered behind me, nudging my back with his muzzle. I stumbled forward a couple of steps then turned to him. With a smile, I placed my hand on his neck and stroked beneath his coarse mane, breathing in the comforting, alluring smell of horse.

Leaning my forehead against his, I could sense his restlessness and gave him one last pat before whispering, "Okay, Boomer, we'll go." I threw myself over his broad back and settled into the saddle, giving Boomer the lead, trusting him to find his way home as he picked his way delicately down the far side of the ridge, away from the plume of smoke behind us. I relaxed my knees, once more in awe that a woman closer to one hundred pounds than two could so easily control a creature outweighing her by tenfold. The saddle creaked comfortably as I swayed with its movement and, not for the first time, I thought this was not such a bad thing to come out of the mess visited upon the world. By men, no less. No wonder Katherine was so set on their continued destruction and demise.

We had come through a cold and dreary winter and now the natural world was waking up. But so were the smells which kept us occupied of late disposing bodies of animals and humans alike. Unlike Biblical prophecies of fire and damnation and ultimately Armageddon, humans had been felled by their own pious hatred in the guise of an entity too small to be detected by the human eye. The blue pox, as it had come to be known, swept through the world in early fall and by the beginning of winter had done its damage, killing off 99.99 percent of the male population and 99.95 percent of females, the greatest portion being those under fifty. At least, according to figures circulating within the scientific community before most of them were obliterated. As were animals. I had spied a few snakes lately, one creature I would love to have seen removed from Earth forever. Spiders were in abundance as were birds and bats. With the advent of summer, we would know more about the effect of the blue pox on insects and such. I would just as soon not see fleas or ticks or mosquitoes return, and horse flies, the worst of the lot. Their bite could draw blood, not only upon horse but human as well.

I leaned back in the saddle, noting the pregnant dogwood buds ready to burst into flowers resembling the cross. The flaming redwood trees added bright color to the woods, the Bradford pears already alight with crisp, white blooms. Here and there wildflowers struggled to thrive above the sodden fallen leaves muffling our movement. I breathed in deeply, the musty smell of rotting vegetation underlying the bite of damp, cool air within the confines of the woods. Leaning my head back, I studied the cloudless sky, a color of blue I had never seen before. Already pollution was receding from our planet, leaving in its wake fresh, clean air and gorgeous skies.

Cleared land lay at the bottom of the ridge, and as we made our way through a rambling field, I noted the earth had already begun to reclaim what had been taken. Vines snaked up sheds and houses, the grass grew tall and green, blowing in the slight breeze, hiding the rank ugliness of civilization.

I wiped my face on my sleeve. Without the protection of trees, the air was hot and still and I hated to think what summer would bring. Although we utilized generators for electricity in our small commune, some of the niceties of civilization were sorely missed. Gone were the days of steamy showers and hot baths. Long, leisure meals with friends at nice restaurants or a quick bite to eat at fast-food joints with drive-thrus. Attending live sports events, plays or concerts. Downloading bestselling ebooks, watching movies with mind-blowing special effects. Televisions and radios would turn on but produced nothing but static, limiting our news sources to word of mouth. And worst of all, the internet no longer existed. As something of a computer geek before the pox, that was probably the hardest of all for me to get used to being without. With a sigh, I placed a barrier in my mind. Chances were I would not see another television program or hear another radio broadcast or turn on another computer in my lifetime and possibly never have another hot shower. No new books would be written, no movies made. No mind-boggling inventions to make my life easier. In another hundred years perhaps. If our children survived, that is.

When I drew near our camp, I made a sound in my throat and Boomer stopped. I leaned over and put my arms around his neck, hugging him tight. Horses also died during the pandemic but my steed, like me, had withstood its onslaught. I wondered for the thousandth time what made us different, what secret armor we held in our body strong enough to keep us well. And would I come to regret this fact as survivors died off from accident, illness or old age? The youngest in our commune, my greatest fear was that I would be the last one left. My stomach tightened in a knot, remembering the days after my mother and father died when I wandered the streets alone and lost, crazy with grief, praying I was not the only one left alive. Boomer nickered, bringing me back to the real world. I patted his flank, grateful for this horse that had saved me from that world of madness, and thought, no use worrying about what was to come. Only the future would tell.

I straightened, watching our encampment, noting the armed deputies patrolling the perimeter, a small group of women using gas-powered machines to till soil in the acreage set aside for gardens. We had come together on a small college campus in East

Tennessee and now there were just over five hundred of us. The influx had slowed to a trickle over the winter but Katherine expected more to make their way toward us once warm weather settled in for good. Soon we would be too large for this small campus and I wondered what she would do about the overflow.

My gaze traced the quadrangle of the university grounds, simple in its design, with dormitories and buildings standing neatly side by side along its four sides. My brief stint at a large, well-known college in Georgia gave me an appreciation for campuses not large and sprawling and confusing to maneuver. We were lucky to have found this place, a prototype for future ones, utilizing underground springs and a reservoir to distill water throughout the buildings, with solar panels on roofs and windmills dotting the hill behind the football field for additional power. From pictures, I knew the landscaping had at one time been picturesque with rolling lawns and blooming flowers and shrubs and large, stately trees shading the streets. I hoped we could honor its beauty with our hands but we were limited only to perennial plants already in the ground waiting for Earth's signal to rise. Already, tulips and daffodils and crocus were popping up but their span was short and they would be gone before long. I sighed. I had always loved snapdragons and moss rose and periwinkle, plants that bloomed the summer long. Maybe they grew wild somewhere, maybe I would find a greenhouse that had survived the winter or a garden center with seeds and bulbs that had not been ransacked. I could only hope.

Taking the reins in hand, I clucked my tongue and Boomer lunged ahead. I leaned forward, close to his head, molding to the American saddle horse, enjoying the sense of freedom and speed. His gait was smooth, much like sitting in a rocking chair, and of the few bright moments in my day, this I cherished most.

I raced through the meadow and onto the campus, steering Boomer clear of the asphalt streets, still clogged with automobiles and motorcycles but now free, thank God, of rotting corpses. Women called out to me and I lifted my hand as we flew by. Without guidance, Boomer headed toward the barn and fresh meadow grass after a rubdown.

At the stables, I dismounted and quickly unsaddled and unbridled the horse. He stood expectantly as I fetched brushes and a cloth. I talked to him in a low voice as I performed this chore, sure Boomer knew every word I spoke. He would roll his eyes at me from time to time as if to say, yes, I quite agree, please do go on.

I had just released him into the pasture when a woman's voice hailed me. I glanced around and smiled at Katherine, a tall woman, loftier than my five-seven, with a firm, sturdy body, heavy breasts and hips. Dressed in jeans and a t-shirt, her long auburn hair blew around her face, her dark-gray eyes framed with fine lines the only giveaway she was well into middle age. The first person I found alive after my family died, my family now. An anthropologist in her former life, Katherine was a natural-born leader and our small community looked to her to guide us through the tragic days following the pox. She easily stepped into the role of chief and the rest of us passively became her loyal subjects.

After we hugged, she stepped back, eyeing me. "I always wonder why you like to ride so much, but looking at you, I can see why. You're absolutely glowing."

I shrugged the compliment aside as we fell into step and began the trek back toward the student building, the central point of our community.

Katherine glanced at me without turning her head. "How'd it go?"

I felt my face fall, my mind called back to that horrific scene. "Fine. Pretty macabre but it has to be done."

"You don't have to go with them, you know."

"I'd rather be out there than stuck inside with you greeting newcomers and deciding what to do with the...the others."

We fell silent on this topic, one I had a problem with but did not wish to confront Katherine about. Not yet.

"Something exciting happened today." She smiled, a glint in her eye. "We have a pregnant woman among us now. Suzie says she's due any day."

My heart quickened. Our future rested on this woman giving birth. If the baby should die, would this mean all babies were doomed to this fate? We would not know until another pregnant woman joined us. But if the baby lived, the human race would go on, hopefully until Mother Earth decided it was time to end her own reign in our small galaxy. A slight thrill chased up and down my spine when I realized this would save the others' lives as well. Well, at least the healthy, virile ones.

"Does she look well? Can she handle it? And is there anyone here that can deliver the baby?" My voiced edged with worry.

Katherine gave me a reassuring smile. "We have a CNA and veterinary tech among us but only Suzie, a nurse practitioner, has witnessed a baby being born. She says it isn't that complicated an issue. Besides, the mother does most of the work, at least according to Suzie." She put her arm around my shoulder and gave me a slight squeeze. "Don't worry, Madison, I'm sure it will be fine."

We stared at one another, Katherine who had never borne children, and me, just eighteen years old and never even having considered it. Much less performed the act which brought it about.

"Where is she?"

"Suzie's got her settled in the infirmary. She was tired from the trip, her ankles swollen over her shoes. It's a wonder she made it here."

"I'd like to meet her."

"Come along then, I'll take you to her."

"Was anyone with her?"

"Yes." She hesitated. "One of the others." Katherine grimaced. "She became upset when we took him away. Apparently they had grown quite close. Things got hairy for a moment. He was armed, after all. But when he saw we outnumbered him, he grew passive fairly quickly."

I didn't want to hear this. Sometimes I wondered if we had not gone back in time or perhaps slipped into another dimension, to a more barbaric place where women ruled and men were outcasts. Through stories told by women who joined us or passed through and from what limited information we gleaned via our ham radio, we knew there were other communities out there. Some ruled by women who turned men away from their camps, others of a more democratic nature where men and women lived and worked side by side. So far, we had not learned of any like us where the men were detained for what I felt could only be nefarious reasons. Katherine, encouraged by Callie, our unofficial police chief, imprisoned the healthier males for labor and, with an eye towards the future, procreation purposes should the need arise. As for what was done with the others, I tried not to think about that but had a deep suspicion, one I did not voice. Although Katherine and Callie told us they sent them on their way, in my ramblings across the countryside, I had found several male bodies dead not from the pox but from a neat bullet hole in their forehead. But deepening my skepticism, Androk, the name Katherine chose for our small community, and the way she referred to the women as Androktones. I wondered how many realized this was what Herodotus called the Amazon women, meaning killers of men.

I often speculated, if there had not been a breakdown in electrical power and frozen semen had been available to us, what would they have done then? Obliterated them altogether?

CHAPTER 2

The infirmary was in the basement of one of the buildings which originally held classes dealing with the sciences, biology and chemistry and such. Katherine and I pushed through the glass doors into the cool, brick building and traveled down two flights of rough, concrete steps to reach the small sickbay. Lisa, the certified nursing assistant, moved busily about, seeing to the few in-house patients. I recognized Cora, an elderly woman, lying on a bed, her face pale, eyes closed. I grew alarmed at her disheveled hair and wrinkled clothing. In this new world where most women no longer bothered to cut or style their hair, put on makeup, or even shave their legs and under their arms, our Cora held steadfast to the Southern genteel woman of the past. She refused to be seen without lipstick coating her lips, her hair tamed into a bun at the nape of her neck, her clothing impeccably clean and pressed. I looked upon Cora as one would a distant relative with enough eccentricity to find them intriguing and had gained her favor by raiding the campus drugstore of its meager supply of lipstick, promising to provide more if the need arose. I crossed over to her and took her hand, saying a small prayer against the blue pox. Although we had seen no sign of it for months, fear lingered in the back of my mind that the killer bug lay in wait, like an ogre under the bridge, ready for some mysterious signal to spring into action and eradicate the rest of the world.

Cora opened her eyes and smiled at me. "Hello, dear," she said in her soothing South Georgia accent.

I squeezed her hand. "Are you all right, Cora?"

She nodded but made no move to rise or squeeze back. "It's that infernal rheumatism. I'm afraid it's got me flat on my back with pain."

I brushed her soft-as-cotton, white hair off her face. "Is there anything I can do for you?"

"No, dear. All I can do is ride it out. Suzie's given me a pain medication which she assures me will help quite remarkably." She closed her eyes once more.

"Makes you sleepy, huh?"

She smiled without opening her eyes. "I'll be fine," she said drowsily. "Just got to wait it out."

I tucked a blanket around her then turned back to the room, searching for Katherine. I could barely see her behind a curtained receptacle and walked that way, listening to her muffled voice, trying to discern what she was saying. I stepped around the curtain and my gaze fell on the bed where a very pregnant young woman reclined, her stomach so huge, from the angle of my position, I could not see her face. I moved around to the side of the bed for a closer look. She rolled her head toward me and offered a wan smile. She was young, close to my age, but seemed so very old and tired. The skin around her eyes appeared bruised, her blond hair clung to her scalp in greasy clumps, and red patches splotched her pale face.

I returned her smile, thrilled to see someone under the age of thirty. "Hello. Welcome to our community."

Suzie, busy inserting an IV into the back of the young woman's other hand, glanced up and smiled. "Hello, Madison. This is Sarah with an H."

Another change in this new world. No one in our commune ever went by their full moniker, we were all simply known by our first names or chose new ones. "Hi, Sarah. How are you?"

"Tired," she said in a weak voice. Her eyes teared and she turned her face to Katherine. "Why'd you have to take Seth away? He helped me. I wouldn't have made it this far without him."

Katherine made comforting noises as she brushed at the blanket, tucking it under the edge of the bed. "We'll talk about that later. Don't worry, we didn't harm him. He's quite well. It's just our policy here that no men are to partake of our community."

I listened to Katherine murmur her comforting words and not for the first time thought the word *propaganda*. When I first met Katherine, she made it clear she had no use for men but at that point had no agenda other than to form or become part of a community of women. Since Callie joined us, Katherine's views had changed drastically and we had all fallen for their spiel, every last one of us. Men were bad, men had brought the blue pox on the world, men did not deserve to be part of what they had destroyed. Women were rulers now, this was a woman's world, we were in control and would make a better world than the one man ended. And the way Katherine spoke these words created an exhilarating sense of empowerment, of well-being, of being part of a community, belonging with and to one another.

Suzie rested her hand on Sarah's stomach. "It won't be long now, sweetie. You need to rest, try to get some sleep. We want you strong for the delivery."

"Will my baby live?" Sarah said, stirring to alertness. "Will he be all right?"

My eyes met Katherine's. *He.* What would she and Callie do with a male child?

"Your baby's just fine," Suzie said in a soothing voice. "It has a strong heartbeat, seems to be a very healthy baby."

Katherine squeezed Sarah's forearm. "Listen to Suzie. She knows what's best. It's important you have a healthy, safe delivery. I'll be back later to see how you're faring." She pushed aside the curtain and strode away.

I patted Sarah's leg in a comforting manner. "Get some rest, Sarah. I'll come back soon and see how you are."

I caught up with Katherine on the staircase. "Did you hear what she said?"

Katherine cast a sideways glance at me before returning her gaze to the steps. "Yes, I heard."

"And?"

"And what?"

"A boy child. You can't ban a boy child, Katherine. He'll need to be fed, cared for, for years."

She hesitated, each foot on a separate stair. "I don't know," she said, more to herself than me. "We hadn't thought of that. I suppose I need to meet with Callie to discuss some sort of protocol."

I placed my hand on her forearm. She cocked an eyebrow my way. "Promise me you won't..." I hesitated. I couldn't say the word *kill,* not to her, not at this point "...ban him, Katherine. At least promise me that."

Her lips pursed. "We don't even know if he'll survive the birth, much less the blue pox. Let's wait and see what happens." She resumed her climb.

"Katherine, if the baby lives, that will tell us babies can survive."

"Yes, that's one reason we're so anxious for this birth."

"And if he does survive? What then?"

She frowned back at me. "Like I said, let's wait and see what happens. There's no use to get ahead of ourselves, Madison."

"I'm talking about procreating. I know you and Callie have discussed it."

Her eyes lit. "Oh, yes, of course. Callie and I have been talking about this, quite a bit. This is one reason we keep the healthy males. If the baby lives, then we'll assign young women to the men and have them mate."

I made a strangled sound.

"The world must go on. Yes? And since we don't have the facilities for artificial insemination, we're forced to the more, shall we say, primitive method."

"And who will decide who mates with whom, Katherine?" I asked, unable to mask the indignant tone of my voice.

She reached out and stroked my cheek. "Don't worry, darling, we've got that worked out already." We had reached the door to the lobby and she pushed through it, me on her heels. She put her arm through mine and we strode toward the outer doors in a chummy manner. "And no need to fret," she added. "You're young, you won't be required to mate until you're ready."

As I made my way home, I thought about our conversation. At eighteen, of course, my thoughts centered on sex a great deal. At times, I wished I had succumbed to the many temptations that had arisen during high school and my first semester of college. To know what it felt like to lie with a male, to please him, be pleased by him. But I stubbornly held onto the romantic notion of my first time being with a man I loved and now chances were that would never happen. I hated the thought of having sex with one simply to become impregnated. How cold and capricious that would be. And when they decided I should participate, would I be paired with one man until pregnant or would they send me to different ones? What if I wasn't attracted to the man chosen for me? What if he was too rough or smelled?

I sighed. What if, what if. There would be time to worry about that later. For now, I needed to concentrate on the tasks at hand. Freeing the campus of the rotting corpses, both animal and human, unclogging the streets with the stalled cars and motorcycles. But a lingering thought slid into my mind in a nasty way, sending a shudder through my body. When did I stop being me and become part of a large we?

CHAPTER 3

I spent the next morning with the burial crew loading bodies onto a dump truck, riding Boomer as I followed the truck to the burial site. A mask over my face, rubber gloves on my hands, I turned away as the truck's bed tilted toward the sky, depositing the gruesome corpses into the pit, sending up puffs of white lime which lay over gray ash. When the truck lumbered away, I glanced back at the pit, trying to see the bloated, decomposed bodies as dolls, mannequins, anything but what they were. But the horrific smell served as a stark reminder that these were not artificial beings but people who had once loved, laughed, cried. Who did not deserve the death they received. Before I could look away, I spied a very perfect, very small form among the bodies and was glad I had not eaten breakfast that morning. Would I ever grow used to death, I wondered, stepping away from the grave.

Heads pivoted and murmurs began. I glanced up, noted Katherine strolling toward us, Callie by her side, and thought ironically that anymore, it seemed when you got one, you got the pair. Callie was a large woman, broad through the shoulders and thighs. A prison guard in her former life, she had an authoritative, condescending air that intimidated some, garnered respect from others. Callie never appeared without a firearm holstered on her side and her utility belt strapped around her waist from which dangled handcuffs, mace, a monkey fist and sap.

Katherine smiled as she passed the women and came to stand by me. She cast a quick look at the pit before turning back to address the workers. Callie, I noted, stood apart, her eyes darting over the assemblage as if checking for anything out of the ordinary.

Katherine waved a hand at the pit. "This," she said, with a grimace, "is the result of our former world, a world ruled by men. This was caused by men, covered up by men, and ended with men. We've been offered a second chance at a new world, a world wherein we, women, will make our own decisions, live our own lives, be our own people without the influence or domination of the male population. We will have a better world, a world not ruled by testosterone." Applause broke out and she paused to acknowledge this. She raised her voice when she spoke next. "Remember this, remember what man sowed and what he reaped. Remember who is here to clean up man's ultimate destruction of his world. He will have no place here in our world, he will not be given the opportunity to destroy our world. If not for the fact that his only use will be for procreation, he would be considered obsolete."

Cheers went up at that. Women nodded at one another as they clapped, smiles on their faces. I watched them, thinking once again, *propaganda*, and how easy it was to fall under its malevolent spell. And at once felt guilty for having such a betraying thought. Katherine had saved me, kept me with her as we made that awful trek through a ruined countryside to find this place. She was my family. I owed her my life.

Katherine smiled at me and I forced my lips to turn upward. She tilted her head toward me, giving me a curious look. "Is this too much for you?" she asked with concern.

I shook my head.

"You're so young, just a baby. You shouldn't be dealing with something like this."

I hugged her, glad to know someone cared for my well-being. "It needs to be done. Besides, I can't stand to do nothing and it's such a beautiful day. I love being outdoors, you know that." I glanced at Boomer, idly grazing along the outer boundary of the clearing.

Katherine followed my gaze and smiled. "And a chance to ride that glorious steed, I would guess."

"Exactly."

She squeezed my hand. "When you're finished, come see Sarah. She's been asking about you."

"Me?"

"I think she connected with you, which is to be expected. After all, you're almost the same age. I'm sure she hasn't seen another young woman since before the pox."

"Sure. I'll go see her as soon as I get back." I wrinkled my nose. "Well, after I get cleaned up."

Katherine flashed a smile my way then strode off toward Callie, who was watching her. The thought occurred to me that maybe the two were lovers but I quickly nixed it. Katherine had been married before our world as we knew it came to an end. I wondered if she had loved that man in that former time, lived with him, shared her life with him. Or had he in some way influenced her bias against the male gender by planting a cancerous seed that blossomed into a dark reality impugning all men for whatever he had done to her?

The pit was filled by mid afternoon. We shoveled lime over the bodies for the last time, watched as a woman who worked construction before the pox wielded a Bobcat to dump dirt over the lime. Finished, the pit resembled one large, freshly filled grave. I stuffed my gauze mask in my pocket as I strode toward Boomer, who neighed as I approached. "You ready to go home?" I asked. He snorted in answer. I threw myself on his back, glad I hadn't put a saddle on him that morning, wrapped my hands in his mane, and let him take the lead. As he streaked toward the barn, I leaned close to his neck, imagining myself one with this magnificent, powerful creature.

After grooming Boomer, I released him into his paddock and went to my small apartment, on the bottom floor of a large, brick home converted to living quarters for married students when there were such things. Although Katherine had made it clear I was welcome to live with her, I needed a place of my own where I could grieve the loss of my family and former life in private without having to listen to Katherine's pontifications of a better world. So I suggested we reside in the same house but in separate apartments and Katherine surprised me by agreeing to this arrangement.

I washed up then headed toward the infirmary to see Sarah.

Wearing a gray-checkered hospital gown with white socks on her feet, she sat in a chair by the bed reading a book about natural childbirth. When I entered her cubicle, she put the book aside and smiled at me. "Madison. I was hoping you'd come visit me." She looked better than she had the day before. Rosy patches glowed on her cheeks and her swollen ankles no longer resembled overstuffed sausages. Her dark-blond hair had been washed and was tucked neatly behind her ears.

I sat down in a chair near the curtain. "I'm happy to. I was wondering how you're feeling but you look much better."

She smiled, a dimple forming in her left cheek. "Oh, I feel much, much better. They're taking good care of me." She glanced at the curtain and whispered, "Who's out there?"

I peeled the curtain aside and peered out. Shelly, a lab technician in her former life, was at the other end of the room tending a woman who looked to have cut herself. I turned back to Sarah. "Shelly but she's pretty far away."

Sarah scooted her chair close to me. "What's going on here?"

I blinked in surprise. "What do you mean?"

"I came in with Seth and all these women with guns immediately surrounded him and took him away." Nascent tears formed in her eyes. "I don't know what they've done to him. I've asked and asked and they just pretend not to hear me. Have you seen him? Do you know if he's all right?"

A pang of guilt raced through me. The least I could have done was check on the man she arrived with so I could assure her of his safety. But Callie and her deputies had them working at clearing buildings on campus and I had been in the field. "I'm sorry, Sarah. I've been out at the...I've been off the grounds today. I haven't seen any of the oth—men."

She swiped at her eyes. "It was horrible. He had a gun but they had more guns and they threatened to kill him if he didn't give his up. Why would they take him from me? He's the reason I made it this far. He helped me." Her voice rose and I sensed she was close to hysteria.

I put a hand on her arm and glanced over my shoulder at the curtain. "Shhh. Don't let them hear you. Listen, I'll check around, see what I can find out. Don't worry. I'm sure he's okay. This is a women's camp and it might have scared them when they saw he had a gun. Please, Sarah, don't worry about this. You need to rest, take care of yourself and the baby."

She nodded and I could see it took great effort to compose herself. "I'd appreciate it so much if you'd make sure he's all right and let me know."

I tried to instill confidence in my smile. "He's fine, I'm sure. So don't worry. I'll find out what I can and come back in the morning. How's that?"

She leaned over and hugged me. Startled, I froze before returning her embrace. It had been a long time since anyone other than Katherine had touched me in this way.

"Thank you, Madison. Thanks so much."

I stood to go, patting her on the shoulder. "Hang in there. It's not as terrible as you're thinking. You'll see him soon, I'm sure." I felt guilty for the lie but Sarah needed to stay strong at this point. She didn't need to be concerned with anything other than herself and the impending delivery.

She nodded as she sniffed her nose and wiped her eyes. We heard Shelly's footsteps and I chose that time to make my exit.

Shelly smiled at me as I passed. "How's our patient?"

"Oh, she seems great. She looks so much better, doesn't she?"

"She was a bit dehydrated when she came in but she stabilized fairly quickly. The baby seems strong. I don't think it's going to be too much longer."

"Shelly, promise me you'll let me know when she goes into labor."

She gave me a curious look.

"I'd like to be there. She seems to need someone to be close by her. We're the same age and I'd like to help her if I can."

"Oh, sure, honey. I'll let you know." She touched my cheek. "What a sweetie you are."

I left feeling apprehensive and defeated. What had they done to Seth? Would I find his body out there, a bullet hole in the forehead like the others? Or had they decided to keep him for whatever purpose they felt they needed him?

The next day, I found Seth working with a crew of women and seven of the others clearing buildings of dead bodies and animals. I joined the group, an eye on Callie's deputies who watched the men with steely eyes and nervous hands hovering around their guns. Seth was there, his face puffy and bruised, his lip split. I noticed he walked with a limp and wondered why things had to be this way. His demeanor was angry and frustrated and I felt sorry for him but there was nothing I could do for him.

During the lunch break, I sat behind Seth and when no one was looking introduced myself to him.

"What do you want?" he growled, turning and glaring at me.

Sandra, one of the deputies, snapped her head up at that, looking around to see who had spoken.

"Shhh," I said in a low voice, trying not to move my lips. "Keep your voice down." I watched his shoulders slump with defeat as he faced forward and noticed Sandra watching him.

It sounded like he muttered, "Crazy eyes," as he gave her a defiant look.

Once her gaze turned away from us, I said, "I've seen Sarah, wanted to let you know she's all right."

He straightened at that but did not look at me. "Thank God. I've been worried about her."

"And she's been worried about you. I told her I'd find you, make sure you're all right."

He snorted. "I'll live, I reckon. For how long, though, that's the question, isn't it?"

I didn't have an answer to that. "You should escape if you can," I said after a few moments.

His head snapped up. "I won't leave without her. You'll tell her that for me? That I won't go unless she's with me?"

"Yes, I'll tell her," I whispered, thinking how much he must love her to face danger here in order to be with her.

At day's end, I watched the deputies parade the others down the street, headed toward the building set aside for them, a dormitory that had been converted into a prison with barred windows and doors, wishing I could do something but knowing I was one against this community of women.

Katherine called one of her community meetings that evening, an event she used from time to time to address issues within the commune, reiterate the policies she and Callie had set forth, and to deliver news from the outside. At the end, she spoke of Sarah but did not mention Seth. The women seemed excited at Sarah's pregnancy and there was much deliberation as to the survival rate of her baby. When I was finally able to break away, I stopped by the infirmary to tell Sarah about Seth but she was asleep so I decided I would wait until the morrow to relay the news. As I left, I prayed her baby would be female and would not have the pox but knew chances were slim either way.

CHAPTER 4

As it turned out, Shelly wasn't in the infirmary when Sarah went into labor the day after my conversation with Seth. Suzie was present and she and Darlene, a veterinary tech in her former life, assisted with the delivery. I had been afield all day, riding Boomer beyond the campus as I did at least a couple of times a week, searching for survivors, taking notes for Katherine as to anything unusual outside our little world. Apprehension tingled along my spine as I rode, wondering if one day I'd find Seth's body out there. When I asked Katherine about her plans for Seth, she assured me he would be fine and had found his place with the others. Whenever she said this word, she gave it a malevolent twist, and this grated on my nerves. They were only men and had nothing to do with the pox and, in my view, should not be penalized for their gender. But Katherine, with prodding from Callie, had become a fanatic on this subject and could not be convinced otherwise. I had learned to keep my mouth shut, for any sort of protest or controversial comment on my part produced hours of lectures and platitudes for her cause.

I rode in, dusty and tired, my notebook filled with graphs and sketches of the small community that bordered our campus to the north, placing dead bodies and animals, stalled cars, and sources for food and fuel. I groomed Boomer, fed him his sweet feed treat, and released him into the paddock. Walking toward my apartment in hopes of a shower that would not be ice cold, I sensed an underlying excitement as I passed members of our community. Curious as to the cause, I stopped Melinda, a tall, bony woman in her early 60s who worked as an accountant before the pox. "What's going on?" I asked.

Her expression was a mixture between happiness and apprehension. "She had the baby. It's a boy."

A boy. Fear traced along my spine. "Is it alive? Was it born alive?"

"Oh, yes, but Suzie doesn't think he's going to make it. He has the pox already." She wrung her hands with agitation, glancing around as if the virus lurked nearby. Her demeanor reminded me of those horrible days after the pox became the killer it was, the panicked looks on people's faces, the escalating violence as they demanded treatment for themselves or their loved ones, the increasing number of healthy persons murdered by others who thought they were infected. Her voice pulled me back to the present when she said, "Oh, I thought it was gone but the germs are still around." She looked at me, her eyes widening with alarm. "What if it mutates or becomes stronger? We could all die."

Panic pricked my brain but I forced myself to remain calm, saying in as reasonable a voice as I could manage, "If we were going to die, Melinda, we would have done so by now. I'll go see how Sarah and the baby are. It may be that the part of him that is from his father is dealing with the pox. He may live if he's strong enough."

She nodded then hurried away, to commiserate with some other worrier, no doubt.

I ran to the building housing the infirmary, pounded down the steps, and pushed through the door. A throng of people surrounded Sarah's bed and I shoved my way through. Katherine stood at the foot, a thoughtful look on her face.

Sarah held the baby to her breast, tears streaming down her face. When she saw me, she began to cry harder. "He won't eat. He's sick. I don't think he's going to make it."

And maybe that would be best for him, I thought, but did not state. I pulled the blanket away from his face, tried not to let my horror show when I noticed the blue cast. "Give him time, Sarah. He has your genes and that may very well save him."

She grasped my hand. "You think so? You think my baby will live?"

I glanced at Katherine, now in conversation with Callie. "There's a chance. Hold on to that."

Sarah smiled through her tears. "Thank you, Madison. I'm so glad you came."

The other women began to drift away, murmuring to one another. I pulled a chair over and sat near Sarah. The baby seemed too weak to move. His eyes were closed, his little hands fisted. I smiled at his bright red hair as I reached out and smoothed it down. "His daddy must have been a redhead."

Sarah shook her head. "His hair was dark. I guess his is a combination of the two of us."

"Have you decided what you're going to name him?"

"Travis, after his dad."

I studied her for a moment. She seemed to glow with life. Her cheeks were a lovely color of pink, her blue eyes sparkled. "Were you married, Sarah, or was he your boyfriend?"

"We were going to marry. When he found out I was pregnant, he insisted we had to marry before the baby was born." She reached down, cupped the baby's head with her hand. He stirred for a moment before returning to sleep. "But that didn't happen." Tears rolled down her cheeks.

"I'm so sorry." I watched her, wondering what it would be like to love a man enough to cry for him.

She glanced at the women huddled together near the door, and lowered her voice to a whisper. "They're going to take him from me, aren't they?"

I startled. Surely not this soon. "No, Sarah. He needs his mother. When he's able to, you need to breastfeed him."

"Oh, Madison, I tried but he won't latch. He's too weak to suck."

"He's fighting the pox. Give him time." I stood and leaned over the baby, pulling the blanket back, staring in awe at those tiny hands and miniature feet, his toes curled. Rusty-colored lashes rested against dusky cheeks, his tiny auburn eyebrows perfect arches above eyes which I knew would be blue. "He's beautiful."

Her face glowed at this.

I could not help but smile back. "I better go, give you a chance to rest."

She reached out her hand toward me, whispering, "Stay with me. At least for a bit."

I sat back down. "Of course, I'll stay."

Sarah leaned closer. "Have you seen Seth?"

After I noted Katherine wasn't within hearing distance, I nodded. When I spoke, I modulated my voice to a near-whisper. "I check on him every day. He's fine, Sarah. They've put him with a work crew going through buildings, clearing them of dead bodies."

"Did you talk to him?"

"Yes, once. Yesterday. I told him you were doing well and he seemed pleased to hear it." I glanced around at Katherine, in deep conversation with Callie. "He said to tell you he won't leave without you."

Sarah's eyes widened. "You won't tell them he said that, will you?"

"Of course not. You have the right to leave or stay."

"But does he?"

I fidgeted in my chair. "He should. I have no idea why they're keeping him here." A lie but what could I tell her?

"They don't have the right. They shouldn't have the right to keep him here."

I didn't know what to say. This was true, after all.

Her hand grabbed mine with fierce intensity. I looked into her eyes, clear and glittering. "Tell him to go, Madison. Tell him to leave here."

If only he could. "I already did but he said he won't leave without you."

She tilted her head for a moment, studying me. "They won't let him leave, will they?"

"I'm sorry, Sarah. I wish I could do something about it but it would be me against the whole community."

She said, "I understand," but her eyes belied this.

I watched as Sarah put the baby to her swollen breast once more. He rooted for a brief moment but this seemed to tire him out and he closed his eyes. "Maybe if we pumped your breast milk, you could feed him with a bottle or use infant formula if that doesn't work."

Sarah looked at me through tear-skimmed eyes. "He needs to eat, Madison. He'll die if he doesn't."

"I'll be right back." I looked around, spied Suzie now in conference with Katherine and Callie. I walked toward them, listening intently to their sibilant whispers. Their voices were so low, I couldn't make out what they were saying but knew it could only be about the baby. "Excuse me," I said as I stepped into their midst. "Suzie, have you thought about pumping her breast milk and feeding the baby with a bottle?"

Suzie glanced at Katherine.

"My aunt's baby was premature and that's what they did. He didn't know how to suck so she pressed the bottle's nipple against his upper mouth and he took milk that way."

Callie raised an eyebrow at me. "I say, if he's meant to die, let him die. He's a male, after all. We don't need him."

"But we do. We do need him."

Katherine studied me for a moment. "And why is that?"

"Because he will tell us if we can survive this pox. Besides, Sarah's milk will contain the antibodies he may need to fight it. Isn't that right, Suzie?"

Suzie nodded. "Right now all she's producing is colostrum which is filled with the antibodies he needs. If he doesn't get that, I'm sure he'll die. If he survives, then maybe we will live past this."

Katherine turned and regarded Sarah for a long moment. She held her baby tightly against her chest, watching us. I knew she couldn't hear what we were saying but suspected she knew, nonetheless.

"Katherine, you can't let him die like this. We have to try." My voice shook with emotion.

Callie glared at me, her eyes filled with hatred. I had taken an opposing side and she didn't like it. I once more wondered about her relationship with Katherine. Callie seemed possessive of Katherine, jealous of her relationship with me. I suspected at some point there would be a showdown between the two of us. With whom would Katherine side? Me, her surrogate daughter, or Callie, quite possibly her lover?

Katherine gave me a quick smile and pressed my hand. "Suzie, she's right. We need to know. Do you have a breast pump here, something you can use?"

The relief that flooded Suzie's face told me she too wanted to help the baby. "At one point there must have been a nursery or some sort of day care here because I've seen baby supplies in the stockroom in back. There may be a pump and bottles somewhere.

I'll go see if I can find them. And if that doesn't work, we can always try formula like Madison suggested."

I returned to Sarah's side. "Suzie's going to find a breast pump so you can feed him with a bottle."

She clutched her baby closer, closing her eyes with relief.

"Sarah, he has a good chance if you can get him to take your milk. It should have the antibodies he needs to fight the pox."

She sat up straighter. "I'll get him to eat. I have to."

"Press the bottle's nipple against the roof of his mouth. It should express just enough milk for him to swallow. Suzie can show you how to do it."

Sarah pulled the blanket aside, stroked down the length of her baby. "He's so beautiful. Just like Travis. He has to live, Madison. He has to." The look she gave me was feral, filled with possessiveness and determination.

"He has a good chance through you." I saw Suzie coming toward us with a contraption that must have been a breast pump. "I need to go shower. I've been in the field all day. I'll be back tonight, see how you and the baby are doing."

Sarah squeezed my hand then returned her attention to her baby. I said a silent prayer for them both as I left, smiling at Katherine, ignoring Callie's hostile gaze.

When I returned later that evening, I found Sarah sleeping, the baby in a blanket-padded drawer on the floor next to her. I stooped down and touched his satiny cheek, despairing because the blue cast had not abated. If anything, his skin appeared even duskier.

Suzie sat at the desk, writing in a chart, and I settled in the chair next to her. She noticed my concerned look and shook her head. "It may be too early."

"Were you able to feed him?"

"Yes. I found a breast pump and bottles. He managed to take a small amount. We're going to feed him every two hours, see if we can get more of Sarah's antibodies into him. If he doesn't show an appetite, we'll switch to formula and see how he does with that." She touched my hand. "Go home, get some rest. We'll take care of her."

I left, saying a silent prayer baby Travis would defeat the pox, that the world would go on.

I made sure the following day to join the work party Callie had assigned Seth and several of the men to. We trudged in and out of dormitory rooms and classrooms, searching for corpses, clearing each building as we went, showing this by marking a large X in red chalk on the building's entry. This was the second time I had worked closely with the others and I surreptitiously watched them, wondering about their mindset. Did they plan a revolt or to escape? Surely they weren't content with matters as they now stood, locked in their rooms at night, always under guard. I noticed the men were in good shape, all muscular and lean. They didn't converse among themselves or with the deputies standing nearby, who watched over them with intense diligence. In the past, I had made it a point to be outside the campus during the day so had not witnessed the inevitable confrontations when Callie and her crew disarmed and placed under guard any man who had the bad luck to step into Katherine's realm. Surely their feelings over this kind of treatment favored resentment and hostility over passiveness and acceptance.

I eyed the women deputies standing sentinel, rifles slung over their shoulders, watching the men. Even though they were not a threat to me, I resented their presence and wondered what in the world Katherine was doing forcing men into the role of prison camp inmate. Why didn't she just let them go? Why keep them, for heaven's sake, if their presence offended her so? Of course, I knew the real answer was procreation but that factor had not become a reality until Sarah stepped into our camp.

As the morning wore on, Callie showed up from time to time, her hand resting on the grip of her gun, glaring at the men in a threatening manner. I ignored her and pretended not to notice when her eyes settled on me.

At noon, two women brought our lunches to us, made in the college cafeteria where all our meals were prepared. Our commune had been lucky enough to be joined by a chef from Atlanta. Before the pox, she had been nationally known, with her own cable series, and her skills were put to good use trying to develop appealing dishes from canned vegetables, meat and fruit. Still, we were all hopeful our vegetable gardens would be bountiful and add more flavor and selection to our limited food choices. I opened the brown paper bag and sniffed, hoping our chef had developed a new dish, and sighed with disappointment. The taste of tuna fish was growing tiresome.

I watched Seth sit down alone on the steps of the building we had just cleared. I walked up the stairs, cautioning myself not to sit too close to him so as not to draw attention, and chose a place a few steps down and to his left. At Sarah's urgings, I kept up with Seth, waiting for the day he would suddenly disappear, as many of the others did. I had promised myself if this happened, I would roam the countryside until I found his body, proving to myself once and for all my suspicions were based on reality. But Seth was a healthy male, one Katherine had apparently decided to keep in case her procreating plans were placed into effect. I turned my head slightly, glancing at him. He was a handsome young man with sandy-blond hair and brown eyes. Although less than medium height in stature, his musculature proved he had, indeed, reached adulthood. He and Sarah would have made a beautiful couple together. I knew she loved him but did he love her?

I uncapped my bottle of water and took a long drink before throwing my head back as if enjoying the sun and said, in a low voice, "Sarah had her baby."

His hands jumped and he fumbled with his sandwich, managing to catch it before it hit the ground. His low voice drifted to me on the wind. "What'd she have?"

I withdrew my sandwich and a sealed cup of pear chunks from my bag. "A boy. He has the pox."

"Oh, God," he whispered.

"He has a chance. They're giving him Sarah's breast milk. It should help."

"You'll let me know."

"Yes." I lay back on the steps, my face to the sun, absorbing its heat, wishing I were on Boomer, racing across green fields, laughing with delight. I sat up and noticed one of Callie's deputies staring at me. Sandra, the one I thought I heard Seth call *Crazy Eyes* which seemed an appropriate name for her. A woman whose eyes only lit up when someone was in pain or while witnessing or interjecting herself into a physical confrontation. I often wondered if she hadn't been a killer in her previous life, a bully who had now found her niche: a job that could require brutal force at times. I gave her a slight wave and smiled and after a moment she lifted her hand in acknowledgement. I turned my head away from Seth and concentrated on eating my sandwich. Finished, I said, "If you can find a way, you need to escape."

"I told you I won't leave without her."

"You need to. For you. She's safe but you aren't." I didn't wait for a reply as I rose to my feet, wadding up the bag and walking down the steps.

That evening, when I made my daily visit to the infirmary, Sarah's face still held a rosy cast and her eyes glowed with happiness. I knew right away her baby must be improving. "Where is he?" I asked, looking around.

"Suzie's giving him a bath. I wanted to help but she insists I stay in bed one more day."

"Judging your face, I'd say he's doing much better."

"Yes. He's breastfeeding now and managing to keep it down. He still has a blue cast but it's fading. I think he's going to live, Madison."

"Thank God."

"Thank *you*. You were the one who thought of the breast pump."

"I'm sure Suzie would have herself." I didn't tell her I suspected Suzie had already thought of it before I mentioned it but was too cowed by Callie and Katherine to suggest it. Why were these women so passive, why did they accept Katherine's and Callie's proclamations with such lethargy and eagerness to please?

I sat in the chair beside her bed and handed her a book I found in the college's large library, filled with nursery rhymes and fables for young children. She leafed through it, gazing at the bright colors in the illustrations, a smile touching her lips. She placed it in her lap and leaned back. "Thank you, Madison. This means so much."

I nodded, happy for her. I glanced around to make sure we were alone then told her about my conversation with Seth.

Her expression changed from happy to sad, then frustrated. "He has to leave. I'm afraid for him here."

I gave her a curious look.

She lowered her voice to a whisper. "Callie was here earlier and I pretended to be asleep." She hesitated. "She makes me uncomfortable. Scares me, in fact."

"Yes, she has that same effect on me."

"I heard her talking to another woman, one of the deputies, and they were discussing which of the others..." She arched her eyebrows.

"Men," I filled in.

"That's who I thought they were referring to. Anyway, which should remain and which they should dispose of."

I straightened in my seat. "Is that the word they used, *dispose*?"

She nodded.

My thoughts turned to the corpses of men I had found in my ramblings with those neat, small bullet holes in their foreheads. Although I initially tried to tell myself they must have perished while fighting another man or perhaps a band of men, the horror of what had actually happened always flitted through my mind, in fact, had lodged itself so deep into my conscience, I wasn't shocked by this at all. I knew for a certainty this was Callie's doings, along with her deputies, as she so proudly called them. And Katherine, of course, she would be the one issuing the orders. Most of the dead men I had found were older males and looked sickly. Some had been younger, looking to be in their 30s and 40s, and I wondered if they had shown some sort of weakness Katherine would not want instilled into her gene pool.

Sarah watched me process this. "I see this doesn't shock you."

"I suspected as much."

"Do you think they'll do something to Seth? Madison, he needs to get out of here before they decide to..." Her eyes widened and she sat back against the pillow.

I followed her gaze to Katherine, walking toward us with a smile on her face. I smiled back, forcing myself to relax in my seat.

"Well, you two have become quite chummy." The warm tone of Katherine's voice did not quite reach her eyes.

I rose to my feet. "I came to check on the baby. Sarah says he's improving."

"Yes, so I've been told." Katherine's gaze focused on Sarah for a long moment then turned to me. "I understand you worked with the building cleanup crew this morning."

I nodded.

"I was a bit surprised to hear it. Usually you're off traipsing about the countryside on your horse or helping out in the field."

"I thought I'd give Boomer a rest. His gait was off yesterday. I'm not sure if he's pulled a ligament or damaged a hoof." I sighed with frustration. "Really, Katherine, it would be wonderful if a farrier would come into our compound. He needs to be shod in the worst way."

This time her smile lit her eyes. "You worry so about that horse, Madison. I'm sure he's fine." She patted my arm in a consoling manner.

"I hope so. I don't think I could stand it if I lost him. Speaking of which, I need to go check on him, give him some feed for being a good boy." I hugged Katherine and waved at Sarah as I walked away.

CHAPTER 5

The next morning, I saddled Boomer and rode out of the compound, hoping to assuage Katherine's unease about my friendship with Sarah. I didn't understand why it would matter to her but sensed the prior evening that for some inexplicable reason she did not agree with the two of us becoming close.

I rode to the ridge overseeing the burial pit and watched as a woman operated a backhoe, covering up the pit with clumps of brown soil while the crew stood around watching, their faces covered with masks, waiting to rake the dirt smooth. A few hundred feet away, another woman worked the controls of another backhoe, digging a burial pit for more bodies. If the past winter had been mild, we would be dealing with desiccated flesh and bones instead of rotting corpses. But the winter had been brutal with weeks of below-freezing weather tempered with violent snow and ice storms. The cold weather had preserved the bodies, kept them intact, delaying total decomposition until the spring thaw and temperatures above freezing. I wondered if we would ever run out of bodies to bury. I hated to think of what lay in the small cities surrounding our campus, the thousands of bodies there decomposing, their flesh eaten by whichever rodents and insects survived.

With a shudder of revulsion, I turned Boomer to the east. It was a glorious day, the sky a beautiful shade of blue, the sun a bright, yellow globe riding its back. The land here rose in gentle green slopes and most of it at one time had been farmland. I could see the Smoky Mountains in the distance glowing purple against the bright sky and wondered how long it would take me to get there by horse. Maybe one day Boomer and I would trek in that direction, carrying a sleeping bag and dry food, just to see.

As always, I checked houses I came across, making sure there were no live persons or animals. I anxiously looked for dogs and cats, hoping their species had not been obliterated altogether. And always another horse, a companion for my own. My mother had been allergic to animal dander so I had not been allowed a pet growing up and I longed for that experience. Boomer had shown me that domesticated animals could be a godsend, something to love and care for, to focus on in this cold, heartless world.

I consulted my map as I went, keeping to the grid pattern I devised when I first began these wanderings. My trek today would take me through what looked to be a small town, more community than city, one known for its white-water rafting and horse trails. I rode down its main street and as always when making my way through a once-thriving town found the silence that greeted me eerie and other worldly. I cast my gaze from side to side and every minute or so glanced behind me, ascertaining no soundless monster followed or lurked nearby, ready to spring at me. I cursed myself, thinking I'd watched too many horror movies before the pox, always in the back of my mind the image of a zombie stumbling after me. Now, all the silence told me was that no person or animal remained in this small town. I murmured to Boomer and he picked up the pace and we raced down the paved street toward the mountains looming in the distance. If Boomer hadn't seen the body lying in the middle of the road, I'm sure we would have gone right over it, trampling it into the asphalt. As it was, he drew up short and pranced around, blowing through his nose, as if offended by the sight. Or maybe it was the odor of decomposition which I could not at that point detect.

The body lay on its stomach, the head turned away, and I couldn't tell if it was alive or dead. I reined Boomer in and hopped off, praying this was not a corpse but rather a living, breathing human. I approached with caution, calling out hello as I drew near, noting the slight frame and long, dark hair. A woman. She didn't respond verbally or change position at my greeting and I gave an inward sigh when the smell reached me. I hadn't seen any fresh corpses dead from the pox in a good while so deduced it must be either a suicide or homicide. I reached out, grabbed her shirt and turned her over. Her limp arm slapped my shin and I jumped back with a breathless squeal. I couldn't help but glance around with embarrassment, hoping no one witnessed my act of cowardice, then reminded myself there was no one left to see it. I returned my attention to the body, gauging her to be close to 30. Her sightless eyes gazed at the sky, a small, round bullet hole pierced her temple. There was little blood. This wasn't the first suicide I had found and I sighed with despair, thinking another life lost when there were so few of us left. Although billions had succumbed to the pox, I was certain hundreds of thousands more had died at their own hands and were continuing to do so, as proven by the woman on the ground and more than our fair share of suicides in our small commune. It seemed once a week Callie and her deputies were carting away another for burial. I knew we all suffered from survival guilt and guessed some just couldn't cope with that or maybe living without their family and friends.

I stared at the woman for a moment, remembering my own mad days after the deaths of my parents, thinking this could so easily have been me. I had come close to doing the same, oh, yes, and if not for Boomer, a companion, a living, breathing being to take care of, I'm sure I would have eventually given in and taken my own life.

I looked around, found the gun by her right hand and picked it up. Hefting it in my palm, I thought it didn't look very big, amazed at the damage it could do. Focusing back on the dead woman, I noticed an ammunition belt wrapped around one shoulder. So she must have had the gun for self-defense and I guess the lifeless world just got to be too much for her. I grabbed hold of the belt and pulled it off, glad the body was fresh enough that decomposition hadn't leaked through her clothes and onto the belt.

Kneeling beside her, I put my fingers over her eyes and tried to close them but they wouldn't stay shut. "I'm sorry this happened to you," I told her before standing and returning to Boomer. I turned the gun over in my hands, studying it, trying to figure out how it worked, making sure to point the barrel away from Boomer and me. I finally discovered how to release the magazine, made sure no bullet was in the chamber, and reloaded it. I tucked it into my saddlebag, along with the ammo belt, deciding I'd figure out what to do with it later. Protocol demanded I turn it over to Callie but the more I thought about it the more I decided

Callie didn't need to know about this gun. Not yet anyway. Besides, on these lonely treks through the countryside, I could very likely encounter danger. It would be good to have a weapon to use. Just in case.

I put my foot in the stirrup but hesitated, wondering if I should try to bury the woman. But where? Paved streets surrounded me and I wasn't strong enough to haul her onto the horse and out of town to a meadow or cleared field. And dragging her behind the horse was not an option. A crow landed in the street and watched me expectantly. The thought of what he wanted made my stomach turn. I picked up a small rock and threw it at him. He flew off with an outraged squawk. I remembered passing a hardware store a block back so walked that way. The door stood open, the windows broken. Why people felt the need to vandalize and ransack stores was beyond me. There was more than enough to go around now. At the end of an aisle, I found what I was looking for and carried it with me, stopping on the way out to pick up several heavy boxes of nails which I placed in a carry basket. When I returned, the crow was back, making its evil way toward her body. I found another rock and chased him away, fighting the urge to shoot him with the gun. The tarp was cumbersome but I managed to get it unwrapped and covered her body with it then lined the tarp with the boxes of nails so the wind wouldn't blow it away and bare her body to scavengers searching for carrion. "I'm sorry but that's the best I can do," I told her.

After saying a silent prayer for her soul, I settled in the saddle and clicked my tongue and we raced out of town. On the outskirts, I spied in the distance a farmhouse sitting on top of a hill, a lovely two-story dwelling painted white, its shutters and metal roof forest-green in color. I made a noise in my throat and Boomer lunged ahead, so surefooted and free, and I once more thanked God for this magnificent animal.

In front of the house, I dismounted, laying the reins across Boomer's back. Spying a fresh mound of grass, he ambled that way and dropped his head to the ground. I stood in the yard for a moment, listening for signs of life, sighing with disappointment when no voices hailed me, no birds sang, no insects twittered, no frogs croaked. I wondered if I would ever get used to such quietness. Well, I supposed I had to an extent. Probably the sound of a human voice or the call of an animal would have had me running away at breakneck speed.

I walked onto the large, wraparound porch, admiring the white wicker furniture, the cushions now moldy and torn from the ravages of a cold, snowy winter. The door was unlocked, as most were these days, and I opened it and stepped inside. A dry, dusty smell with a faint underlying sharpness permeated the house and I suspected there were dead bodies nearby, corpses no longer but merely bones and hair and fingernails. I decided to investigate the second story first and in a large, airy bedroom with dormer windows looking out on the front yard found two of them lying entwined together on the bed, their bones spilling apart from and into one another. I imagined these were the owners of this pretty house, who, realizing they were dying, spent their last moments together.

I circled the room, noting pictures of the two of them everywhere, always laughing, always holding one another. This had been a happy home. A shame it ended like it did.

I turned away, the floor protesting with a loud creak, and thought I heard a low growl. I stopped, wary of a wild animal nearby searching for food. After a few moments, I moved again and once more heard the sound. It seemed to be coming from outside the room, so I stepped into the hallway, looking in each direction, curious where the thing was and if I had enough time to get down the stairs before it attacked me. Although we had not seen much wildlife, I knew bobcats roamed the ridges; we could hear their blood-curdling screams at night. I made my way to the top of the stairway, glancing around, ready to fly down the steps if it came after me. At the top of the stairs, the growl sounded fierce behind me and I turned and would have tumbled down if I hadn't caught myself on the banister. A dog stood close to me, the fur on the back of his neck raised, his teeth bared. I wasn't familiar enough with dogs to determine what breed he was with his short, black fur and blocky face halved with a white marking. His coat was matted and dirty, his ears torn and floppy. Ribs stood out in stark relief against his sides and his long tail drooped with despair.

"Hello," I said in a low voice. "I bet you're as surprised to see me as I am to see you."

He cocked his head at me for a moment before resuming his aggressive stance.

"I won't hurt you, boy. If you'll come with me, I'd like to take you back with me to the compound. I can give you a nice home with plenty of food. Lord knows, grocery stores will have bags of kibble galore for you to eat."

He stopped growling as I talked but remained where he was, easily within lunging distance.

I slid down the wall behind me until I was closer to his level and held out my hand. He poked his head toward it then drew back. I spoke to him in a soft tone, encouraging him to smell my fist. After several tentative darts, he finally touched my knuckles with his nose before quickly withdrawing it. I slowly rose to my feet.

"I'm going down these stairs. If you want to come with me, I'll be glad to have you. You poor thing, you're so thin. If you don't think you can make the trip back home with me, I'll be happy to carry you on the horse." I said all this as I made my way down the stairs, turned sideways, my gaze never leaving him. He watched me go, and when he disappeared from my view, I despaired he had decided to stay.

But when I reached the front door, I looked back and watched as he made his way down the steps, his eyes on me. Curious if the couple in the upstairs bedroom had been his owners, and if so, if there was any food for him, I walked down the hallway to the kitchen in the back of the house. A pantry door stood open and I noticed an empty bag of dried dog food with a ragged hole in the side. Apparently he had found the food for himself. I searched through the pantry, locating several cans of dog food. I finally found a manual opener in a kitchen drawer and opened a couple of cans. I spooned them into a large dog bowl near the door and stepped away after picking up a matching bowl beside it. I found a sealed jug of water in the pantry and poured it into the bowl and placed it beside the food. Waiting to see if he would eat, I retreated to the back door, noting this was where the dog entered and left; a large doggie door had been inserted into the wooden one.

The dog whined with frustration as he watched me, hoping I would leave, I'm sure. After a few moments, hunger got the better of him and he slunk to the bowl and wolfed the food, darting glances at me. Afterward, he drank the entire bowl of water, and when his eyes met mine, I was certain I saw gratitude in his.

"You're very welcome," I said to him. "Now, I've got to be going. If you want to come with me, fine. If not, I'll be back tomorrow to check on you." I opened the door but hesitated. Returning to the pantry, I gathered the remaining cans in my arms, thinking, just in case, and left, walking around the house to the front where Boomer still grazed.

Boomer raised his head and nickered as I dumped the cans into my saddlebag before making my way to the barn. This was the part of the trip I always dreaded – barns usually contained dead animals, horses and cows who had returned to their place of comfort to die. But I had to check. Surely one day I would find another horse or hopefully a bull and milk cow. No matter what we tried, we could not capture the taste of milk from the powdered stuff. Having found the dog uplifted me, gave me hope that at least several species of animals too had been spared. I strode down the middle aisle of the barn, checking each stall, but all were empty, no carcass or live animal left behind.

I walked outside, blinking against the bright sunlight, and noticed a pond downhill from the house. Boomer, sensing water nearby, fell in behind me as I headed that way. After I unsaddled him and removed the bridle from his mouth, he stepped into the pond, lowered his head to the water, and slurped. I cupped some in my hand and splashed it on my face, careful not to get any in my mouth. At the compound, we only drank bottled water. We didn't know if the blue pox virus grew in water or was airborne so were careful about what passed our lips although Boomer didn't seem bothered by water in creeks or springs. I lay back in the sweet-smelling grass, staring at the sky. Hearing movement behind me, I sat up, looking that way. The dog stood close by, watching me.

"Hello," I said. "Did you decide to join us or are you here for the water?"

He ignored me as he stepped over and sniffed at Boomer's legs. Boomer raised his head and gazed down at the dog. They stared at one another for a moment then met nose to nose. Boomer snorted and returned to the water. I laughed at that. The dog glanced my way before going to the opposite side of the pond and stepping in. He swam around for a bit, which I found entertaining, his entire body immersed except his head, sticking up out of the water as he paddled about. He got out and shook himself off before trotting over to us. His tongue lolled and he looked to me to be in better spirits as he panted what looked to be a grin my way. I hoped he would come home with me but didn't want to force him. After all, I was probably the first human he had seen since his owners died.

Boomer stepped away from the pond and plopped down in the grass nearby, a cloud of dust puffing up as he did. He rolled onto his back and scratched himself, his legs in the air. I smiled as I watched him. He rolled onto his side, lunged to his feet, and shook himself off, much as the dog had.

While Boomer nosed the grass, searching for tasty tidbits, I lay on my back, closed my eyes, and enjoyed the feeling of the sun on my face and arms. I felt a shift in the air current nearby and turned my head. The dog lay nearby, his gaze on me. "I won't hurt you. I promise you that," I told him. I closed my eyes once more and kept still, hoping he would get used to me.

As the sun grew stronger, my stomach began to rumble. I rose to my feet, careful not to disturb the dog, dozing near me. He raised his head and watched as I walked over to the saddlebag and retrieved my lunch. I sat near him again, opened the brown paper bag and removed a chicken-salad sandwich. I tore it in half, tossed part to him and ate the other. He gobbled it down before I'd taken the first bite. We shared a small bag of potato chips, the dog eating more than I did. I held the cup of diced peaches out to him to see if he might be interested but he ignored that. Dessert was a Little Debbie oatmeal cake. I split half with the dog once more.

Finished, I got up, dusted my pants off, and picked up my garbage. Tucking it in the saddle bag, I noticed the gun. I drew it out and studied it once more, wondering if I could teach myself to shoot. After digging my empty water bottle out of the saddlebag, I walked to a stump and sat it on top, paced off about 50 feet and aimed the gun. Then remembered the animals. Boomer's grazing had taken him a distance away and the dog looked to be following some sort of odor as he zigzagged up the hill, his nose close to the ground. I hoped the gun wouldn't startle them as I squinted my eyes and squeezed the trigger. The bottle flew into the air and I let out a little shriek of surprise. Boomer startled at the gunshot but didn't become overly agitated. He shot me a dirty look as if to say, keep it down, why don't you, then returned to grazing. The dog paused and glanced my way before putting his nose to the ground once more. For the next hour, after I obliterated my water bottle, I searched the ground for things to shoot off the stump. I was excited I seemed to have a good eye as more times than not I hit my target.

Satisfied I could handle the weapon, I stowed it and the ammo belt away before saddling Boomer. The dog, now lounging near the pond, watched with intensity. I settled myself and picked up the reins, looking at him. "I hope you come with me. If not, I'll come back and check on you tomorrow." I clicked to Boomer and we walked away from the pond and toward the meadow. Glancing back, I noticed the dog wasn't following but simply sat there staring after me. I turned back to the front and told myself not to be too disappointed, he needed to get used to me. Boomer snorted with impatience and I could sense he wanted the lead but I held him back, waiting to see if the dog caught up with us. By the time we reached the foot of the first slope, I heard panting beside me and there he was. "Welcome," I said, with a laugh. "I'll take good care of you and promise you'll have a good life." He looked up at me and I took his lolling tongue to be acquiescence. "I'll love you and never expect anything back from you except your wonderful companionship." With a brief bark, he ran ahead of us. I gave into Boomer's will and we went racing across the slope and down the other side.

No one was at the barn when we returned. I lead Boomer inside, removed his saddle and bridle, and began the process of grooming him. The dog plopped down in the dirt nearby, closed his eyes and dozed. I eyed him from time to time, anxious to take him back to my place, give him a bath and more food. Finished, I poured corn and oats into Boomer's feeding trough and made sure he had plenty of water then opened the gate into the small corral in case he wanted to go outside. By this time, the dog had risen to his feet and watched me as I moved about. I returned to him, knelt down, and held out my hand. This time, he sniffed it without hesitation. "Would you like to come with me?" I knew he probably didn't understand a word I said but hoped he could sense my intent. "I'll give you a bath, brush you down, feed you some good food."

I took his open-mouthed pant to be a yes. After throwing the saddlebag over my shoulder, I turned and trod down the hill toward the small campus and my apartment. The dog followed at first but before long caught up with me and we strode together side-by-side. Our entrance onto the campus was met with great excitement. Word quickly spread that I'd brought back a dog and women gathered around me, admiring him and reaching out toward him. I feared the dog would bolt but he accepted their pats and excited voices as if he deserved it. Darlene, the veterinary tech who helped deliver Sarah's baby, squealed with delight, knelt beside the dog, and hugged him tight. I felt a momentary tenseness, fearing the dog would snap at her. But he didn't shy away or try to run, simply let her hug him.

She looked at me, her face excited and happy. "Oh, he's a beaut. Are you going to keep him?"

"Yes, I'd like to. If he'll have me."

"Can I come see him from time to time?" She looked embarrassed. "I'm sorry, but I love dogs and I miss having one."

"Any time you want, Darlene. I can see he likes you."

She grinned with pleasure. "If you want, I can give him a quick exam when he's up for it. Make sure he's healthy. If there's a vet's office in town, I can get any meds he needs, make sure he's updated on his shots."

I stooped beside her to pet the dog. "That would be great. Thank you." I watched her glowing face, realizing not many of us smiled anymore. It was good to see someone happy. "You know, I just found him and I have no idea what his name is. I've never had a dog before. What would be a good name for him, do you think?"

She held his face between her palms, studying him. He stared at her as if he knew exactly what she was contemplating. Darlene reached out and touched his nose. "I think we should call him Adam. He's the first dog we've seen since the..." Her face fell and I knew her thoughts had gone to the days of the blue pox after she lost her entire family and had wandered alone like most of us, almost out of her mind with grief and terror. If she hadn't found us, I doubt she would have lived long. I don't think any of us would have if we hadn't found one another.

"Adam it is," I said. "That's a wonderful name." I rose to my feet and announced, "Darlene has decided the dog's name will be Adam. What do y'all think?"

Women clapped at the news and Darlene beamed with pleasure.

"I'm going to take him home and give him a bath. Would you like to help me, Darlene? I'm afraid I don't have much experience with pets."

"I'd love it," she said, her eyes glowing.

We left the women, the dog walking proudly between us, Darlene leaning down from time to time to brush her fingers across his back. And for the first time since the pox felled so many of us, I felt a part of something more than myself.

CHAPTER 6

Adam cleaned up rather nicely. He would be a beautiful dog once he gained weight and his fur grew shiny and healthy. After we bathed him, Darlene asked to accompany me to see Sarah. I suggested we take the dog along. I didn't want to leave him so soon, fearing he might become frightened and wander off or one of the women might decide to take him as their pet. Although I knew I was being selfish, I intended to keep Adam for myself. But another, darker fear nagged at my brain, one I tried not to think about. I had heard some of the women complaining lately about the lack of fresh meat and deep down feared they might turn their eyes on Boomer or now Adam. I really wished I could find a hen or two and maybe a rooster on my outings. Fresh eggs would be nice and hopefully we could raise enough chickens to appease those hungry for meat. I had become so used to our basically vegetarian diet, I didn't think I could eat red meat or pork again. I had no desire for it now.

We found Sarah sitting in the chair by her bed, breastfeeding her son. She smiled at us when we entered and she and Darlene spent several moments discussing the baby and how he fared. Having assisted with the delivery, Darlene was fascinated with the infant and asked questions one right after the other. Sarah took it in good measure, though, and answered each one, showing her Travis's tiny toes and fingers, assuring her he had won his battle against the pox. I pulled up a chair and sat nearby, Adam settling himself on the floor beside me. When Darlene wound down from her curiosity over the baby, Sarah smiled as she nodded at the dog.

"Did you find him or did he find you?"

"I found him at a farm nearby. His owners were dead and he was inside, guarding them, I think."

"But how did he stay alive so long if he was indoors?"

"There was a doggie door in the kitchen so he could enter and exit." I rubbed the back of Adam's head and he looked at me, opening his mouth as if smiling.

Darlene sat on the floor beside Adam, laying her hand possessively on his back. "Do you know what this means?" she asked, her eyes gleaming.

I smiled at her.

"If he's alive, there have to be more. Oh, Madison, this is wonderful. I prayed at least God would spare the dogs."

Sarah's eyes met mine. "This is good. And if dogs survived, maybe other domesticated animals did as well. Like cats. I love cats."

"Oh, I really pray so, Sarah."

"And horses," Sarah said. "I heard you have one, that you ride him each day."

"Yes, Boomer. I found him after my parents died. He's been with me ever since."

Sarah smiled. "So it's beginning."

"Beginning?"

"The world is coming back. If there's one..." she waved her hand at Adam "...there will be more. This is wonderful news, Madison."

"I hope so, I truly do."

I heard movement behind me and turned my head. Katherine and Callie entered the infirmary, Katherine smiling, Callie with her usual scowl.

"I had to come see for myself," Katherine said.

I gave her a questioning look.

"I heard about the dog." She knelt down beside him, ran her hand up and down his back. "Oh, he's gorgeous. What do you think, Darlene? Does he have Lab in him?"

"Definitely part-Lab," Darlene said. She studied him for a moment. "Maybe a touch of pit bull with that blocky face."

Katherine glanced at me. "I owned Labs in the past. They're wonderful dogs."

"The best in my opinion," Darlene said.

Adam rolled onto his back and allowed Katherine to scratch his belly, jerking one of his legs along with the movement of her hand. I peeked at Callie, watching Katherine, her eyes and expression now softened, a look of yearning crossing her face. She must have sensed me staring at her because her eyes darted in my direction and she straightened, placing the scowl on her face once more.

Katherine rose to her feet. "I suppose you're claiming ownership."

"Yes. I found him. I'd like to keep him."

She cupped my chin with her hand. "Such a protector. No animal will come to harm with you nearby. I love that about you, Maddie."

I could not help but feel pleased by her compliment and smiled my thanks.

She turned to Sarah. "And how are you and the baby, Sarah?"

"Wonderful. Look, Katherine, he's completely lost the blue cast. He's as normal as any of us."

"Suzie told me he won the battle against the pox. That's good. This proves mankind won't die out with us." She brought her attention back to me. "Madison, when you have a moment, I'd like to sit down with you and talk about a matter."

"Certainly, Katherine. I'll come to your office after dinner if that's all right."

"Perfect. Well, I'm off. There are things Callie and I need to see to." She nodded at Sarah, squeezed Darlene's shoulder and smiled at me before leaving, Callie trailing her like an adoring dog.

Back home, I worked floor planks free in my bedroom closet and stashed the gun and ammunition belt there until I ventured out in the field again. I fed Adam two more cans of dog food and freshened his water bowl then locked him inside my apartment, assuring him I would return soon. He settled down on the couch with a forlorn look and I felt bad for leaving him but knew our temperamental chef would not tolerate a dog in her domain. Before heading to the cafeteria, I detoured to the library to pick out a book to read, returning the one I had just finished. Prior to the pox, I hadn't been much of a reader, preferring outdoor activities to this solitary one. But lately, the majority of my off hours were spent lost in a book, reliving another person's life and circumstances. It helped to keep my mind off what Katherine and Callie were doing with the others and what our future bode.

Our commune always gathered in the college's large cafeteria for the dinner hour which began at six and ended at eight. Katherine's policy of assigning women to jobs she thought they were best suited for was commendable. The kitchen staff kept the commune well-fed with nutritional, well-balanced meals. The cafeteria was always spotless and no one so far had suffered the ill-effects of food poisoning. Although Callie and her deputies were intimidating, they kept our commune in order and rarely were there fights among our denizens or episodes of violence or vandalism. Addiction and drunkenness were obliterated when they disposed of all illegal recreational drugs and alcohol, although at Suzie's insistence, Callie made an exception for rubbing alcohol which would be used for medicinal purposes. Weapons were not permitted except for those sharing law enforcement duties.

The rest of our group was divided between the burial crews, cleanup crews, and gardeners. Although canned food was sustaining, it was not as tasteful and the whole compound longed for the fresh taste of home-grown vegetables and fruits along with herbs and spices to flavor them. Callie and her deputies had raided a garden center in the nearby town of all vegetable packets of seeds and now there were several large gardens in the works. If the produce grew, as we all hoped it would, we would have a bountiful summer and fall with hopefully plenty left over to can for winter.

I appreciated the fact that Katherine had so far excluded me from any specific job duties, giving me leave to ride outside our encampment searching for stragglers looking for a place to live. I knew the fact that Katherine and I were close offered me some sort of protection as well as significance. I often wondered, where would I be without her? She had found me wandering alone and crazy with grief and had taken me under her wing, offering me comfort and companionship. Although I did not agree with her platitudes, I certainly cared for her.

Although the cafeteria was filled to capacity, I managed to find a quiet place at a corner table for two. Someone had taken one of the chairs and placed them at another table, for which I was grateful. I wasn't in the mood for company and besides I now found socializing arduous. I placed my tray down, followed by my book, and settled in the chair. While I ate, I perused the book, anxious to find time to begin the read. Finished, I settled back and looked around the room and for the first time it occurred to me I had no real friends here other than Katherine. But then, again, I had not tried to cultivate any beyond a superficial acquaintance. I had noticed members of our commune fell under two categories: those who sought connections with others, who hungered for friendship and companionship, who blocked the memories of their past lives with a fierce intensity; and those who kept to themselves, kept their grief and loneliness bottled up like hidden treasures to be taken out and studied when alone. I did have Katherine, a mother to me now, and I hoped I would form a tight friendship with Sarah. I missed the closeness of friends, long, lengthy chats with lots of laughter and fun times.

Most of the women in our commune were older and it was a rarity to be joined by a young adult. There were a few others close to my age, in their mid to late 20s, but my life here tended to be an isolated one, riding Boomer during the day and reading in my apartment at night. As the youngest in our commune, I hoped that with the warm season upon us, more would find their way to us. And had any children survived? I knew of none but oh how grand it would be for them to be part of our community.

My mind touched on the meeting with Katherine, curious what she wished to discuss. I handed the tray off to one of the dishwashers, smiling my thanks, and left, heading for Katherine's office. I found her in conference with Callie and tried not to let the irritation show on my face at Callie's presence. I returned Katherine's embrace and sat in the chair across from her desk. Callie remained, a smirk on her face. I knew this would not be good.

Katherine leaned back in her executive seat, studying me. "Tell me, Madison, what do you think of Sarah?"

"I like her a lot. I hope she and I can be friends."

"Well, we may have a bit of a problem with Sarah."

"Why is that?"

"She is insisting the baby stay with her. We can't allow that."

"But he's her baby, Katherine. Of course, he should stay with her."

Katherine glanced at Callie before returning her attention to me. "He's a male child. As you know, Madison, we have a policy in place about the male gender. We certainly don't need nor do we want male children in our community. They're not useful."

"But he's just a child. He needs his mother. He won't live without her."

"He'll be taken care of," Callie said.

I turned and glared at Callie, biting my tongue before retorting, *With what, a gun?*

Katherine spoke, forcing my attention back to her. "Well, perhaps we should reconsider. After all, he will be useful once he's old enough to work." She looked at Callie. The two stared at one another, as if conversing telepathically. After Callie nodded her acquiescence, Katherine continued. "We'll place him with a surrogate mother, one who will not be so bonded with him."

I wondered if she said this to appease me. Would the boy child mysteriously disappear one day? Would I find his body with a bullet hole in the forehead? I leaned toward her. "Katherine, remember what Suzie said, babies need their mother's breast milk for antibodies. Shouldn't you at least let Sarah nurse her baby? It's only natural and I'm sure you don't want to chance him getting sick if he doesn't get the antibodies he needs from his mother."

Katherine rubbed her neck, a sign she was thinking about it. "That is something to consider. I'll talk to Suzie, see how long she thinks he'll need to nurse. We do want him healthy and viable so that one day he can join the men in our compound, the ones we plan to use."

"For procreation?"

"Yes, exactly."

"Katherine, this is wrong. You know it is. This isn't how God made us, one gender to rule over another."

Beside me, Callie fidgeted. "Seems it was that way before, wasn't it? Men ruling women, ruling the world? And look where it got us."

Katherine snorted with disdain. "You can't actually tell me you believe there's a God after all this?" She swept her hand around.

"God didn't cause this. Man did."

She smiled. "Exactly and that's why we mean to see to it that *man* never has control again. Surely you feel the same, Madison. Surely you don't want to entrust your future – again – to the ineptitude of *man*."

Oh, how I longed to be out of there, away from all this. Thinking about my future and what lay ahead for us was maddening, something on which I tried not to dwell.

Katherine raised an eyebrow. "Well?"

"It's just, I don't understand why we can't be a more democratic community."

I ignored Callie's snort of derision.

"And you think we're not?"

"No, Katherine. We're more autocratic than anything else. You're our leader, you tell us what to do, we follow."

"And have I steered you wrong so far, Madison?"

I sat back, feeling defeated. "No, you haven't. But why can't men be a part of this community? Why are they either ostracized or imprisoned?" I cast a dark glance at Callie. "Or escorted out of town and then who knows what happens to them?"

Callie's smirk was arrogant, blameless.

Katherine glanced at Callie then back to me. "Madison, you're a young woman, you haven't lived among men as Callie and I have, as well as most of the other women here. You haven't experienced what we have. Believe me when I say the world will be a much better place without man's manic control."

I had heard this before. "I know, Katherine. You say this constantly."

"And one day you'll agree with me. Until then, as a part of our community, I do hope you'll at least respect our policies and abide by them."

"I have so far, Katherine." Our eyes met. "I owe you my life," I said, my voice faltering. "I love you and I'm trying to go along with what you want. I'm trying very hard not to oppose you in any way."

She gave me a compassionate smile. "You're just a child, Madison. Very much like me when I was your age. You'll see eventually. Until then, all I'm asking is that you trust me to know what's best for us, for our future."

"Of course."

She studied me for a long moment. "I believe you told me your father was a scientist at the CDC in Atlanta?"

"Yes, an epidemiologist, but he wasn't responsible for the release of the pox, Katherine. I told you that."

"Oh, no, child, that's not why I'm asking. Callie and I have been discussing the pox and why so many of our young died from it. Explain your father's theory to Callie. You can certainly do it better than I can."

I turned to face Callie. "Dad told me that the pox is basically an accelerated form of the common cold, a virulent virus the CDC was studying at the behest of the Pentagon. He suspected it was developed for use in germ warfare but didn't know where its origin lay, here in America or another country. As everyone knows by now, it was released into the population by two men, Donners and Hartlett, whom the CDC labeled terrorists after their escape. That's why it was initially called the DH pox."

Callie and Katherine exchanged smiles over this and I knew they shared the same thought: *men!*

"According to Dad, the common cold is not caused by one singular virus but each cold a person has is the result of a different virus. I believe he said that there are over two hundred types of viruses known to cause the common cold and new cold viruses are continually developing. But once a person has a cold caused from a specific virus, they are, in all probability, immune to that virus. As people age, their past illnesses with colds increase their ability to fight future ones because they've virtually run through most of the viruses in their lifetime. Young people are not so immune because they haven't caught all the viruses. That's why older people actually survived the pox over the younger ones, who were in all probability much healthier, the pox being a strain of a cold virus they had probably had at one time in their life."

Callie, for once, showed interest in me over Katherine. She scooted out the chair next to me and sat down. "What about the blue color? What caused that?"

"It's called cyanosis, meaning discoloration of the skin from lack of oxygen. This happens when the blood oxygen levels fall. The circulatory system constricts skin vessels, rerouting more blood to the internal organs. Thus, less blood at the surface, which due to the refraction of light, gives the skin a bluish cast. My dad referred to it as heliotrope cyanosis, which is a term he said was coined during the flu pandemic or Spanish Influenza of 1918, where a person would get the flu and subsequently develop a secondary infection, much like happened here with pneumonia. As the sick person's lungs filled with fluid and he struggled to breathe, his face would turn blue as he died, virtually drowning in his own fluids."

Callie nodded, seeming lost in thought.

"His theory certainly makes sense to me," Katherine said.

"Do you think more young people will join us, Katherine?" I asked. "Sarah is the first I've seen."

"We certainly hope so." Katherine shot Callie a look and straightened in her chair. "The lack of young women certainly bears an influence on what Callie and I have decided."

My skin prickled and a rush of adrenalin shot through my brain. I tried to remain still. "That being?"

"Since Sarah's baby won his battle against the pox, we feel it most prudent to go ahead with our plans for procreation in an effort to increase our community, to continue on, as it were." She leaned toward me, her gaze intent. "We now have 16 women in this community of child-bearing age."

"And what age group is that, Katherine?" My voice was as cold as I felt inside.

"18 to 35. Suzie tells us a woman's chance of miscarrying or having a damaged fetus increases exponentially after that. We're lucky that men continue to produce sperm throughout their lives, so we don't have to worry with the problem of procuring enough young men."

"So I'm part of that 16?"

"Darling, I wish it weren't so, but yes, you're 18 and healthy and certainly fall into the category."

"But you told me not to worry about this. You told me I wouldn't be included."

"I know but Callie and I have been discussing this and we feel it's imperative we begin building our community."

Callie shifted restlessly. "We shouldn't have to defend any policies we make to you, Madison. But Katherine's right. We need to build our forces. We don't know what's going on with the rest of America. Even as we speak, men could be coming together and forming a militia, organizing another corrupt government. From what we've learned so far, we think ours is the largest community in Eastern America and people are coming in every day. If it continues, we may well be the largest in all of America. This is our chance and we have to take it. We need to make sure men don't take control of this country again or ever." Her voice rose as she talked, her face becoming tense as she glared at me as if insisting I understand their reasoning.

Katherine sighed. "I wouldn't ask you, Madison, but there are so few women of childbearing age here."

"So you wish me to procreate?"

"Yes."

"No. I won't do it."

Katherine drew back as if I had slapped her.

Callie glared at me. "You'll do as you're told."

I ignored her and addressed Katherine. "What about disease? Have you thought about that? AIDS, STDs, herpes, things of that nature."

"We've had Suzie test each man's blood and no man with any sort of disease or infection will be placed in the pool. We certainly don't want to chance any of our young women getting sick or contracting any sort of infection or disease."

"And the women, are they tested as well? After all, they could give a disease to the men which they would pass on to the other women."

"Of course they will be tested, Madison. As will you."

I rose to my feet. "This isn't a communist commune or a socialist one. This is America. It should be my choice whether I breed or not. I'm not some farm animal chosen to produce piglets for your dinner table."

Callie lunged out of her seat.

Katherine held up her hand as if to stop her from taking any form of action. "We need your help, Madison. I wouldn't ask you otherwise."

"But I don't want to have a child. I'm too young to even think about it."

"In that other world, yes. But times have changed. It's a different world now, Madison, one we are responsible for and one we have to protect."

I would have told her then I was a virgin but Callie stood nearby and I could imagine the remarks she would make to that. Besides, it wasn't their business. "Katherine, I don't know that I can do that. Please, give me some time before asking me for something so important."

"I can't give you much time, Madison. Our plan is to become the largest, most powerful community in America. We need to start building our citizenship now."

I turned on my heel but Callie put a hand on my forearm, staying me, squeezing hard enough to let me know she meant business.

Behind me, I heard Katherine say, "Let her go, Callie."

I slammed out of the door as Katherine added, "Give her a chance to process this. She'll come around to our way of thinking."

Followed by Callie's chilling voice, "Or I'll make her see the light."

I stopped by the infirmary to see Sarah before going to my apartment. She sat in a rocking chair holding her baby, a small duffle bag on the floor near the bed. When she looked at me, I noticed she had been crying.

I pulled a chair near, sat by her, put my hand on her arm. "I heard, Sarah. I am so sorry."

She shook her head. "They can't do this, Madison."

"I talked to Katherine, told her the baby needs to breastfeed so he can continue to get your antibodies. She's going to talk to Suzie and I think she'll agree he needs to stay with you, at least long enough…"

"They can't take my baby away from me. I'll leave before I let them take him." Her voice edged with hysteria.

I glanced around the room, thankful we were alone. "Have you told them that?" I whispered.

"No. I'm afraid if I do, they'll force me to stay. Imprison me like they do the men."

I couldn't deny this so said nothing.

She brushed a finger along her baby's cheek. "Will you help me, Madison? Will you help Seth?" Her voice was so low, I wasn't sure she had spoken.

I hesitated. What would I do if I got caught? Where would I go? I wouldn't have Katherine's protection anymore, the freedom to ride Boomer all day knowing I had a comfortable bed waiting for me and a clean barn for my horse. I would at the very least be kicked out of the commune, at the worst, killed by Callie. Those neat, round bullet holes flashed into my mind. And then I thought of Seth lying out there, the same wound in his forehead as the others I had found. "If I can," I whispered.

She darted a look at me. "Do you know where they're keeping Seth? I won't leave without him. He'll protect me and the baby."

This I did not doubt. I sat back and thought about it. The college had a small holding area the security force used while they waited for the police to come on campus and make an official arrest. There were three small cells Callie referred to as solitary and I knew some of the men were kept there each night, the rebellious ones or those Callie deemed the most likely to try to escape. The others were imprisoned in a men's dorm with locks on the outside of the doors and the windows barred. The only way to find Seth would be to ask him where they put him at night. I stood, put my hand on her shoulder and squeezed. "I'll see what I can do."

CHAPTER 7

I kept to myself the next few days, riding out early in the morning on Boomer, Adam trotting alongside us, and returning at dusk. I raided the kitchen during off hours, filling my backpack with bottles of water, canned and dried foods, baked breads and pies. Tara, our chef, a woman with a kind soul, seemed to sense my inner struggles and I always found a treat from her wrapped neatly in foil with my name attached, made especially for me.

Katherine kept her distance, making good on her word, allowing me time to consider her plans. And I was grateful for this. I imagined Callie chomping at the bit, anticipating what she would do to me to make me comply.

My thoughts were in a quandary. I loved Katherine. She had helped me, had been there for me, I would not have survived without her. But I did not owe her a child. I was too young to be pregnant, too naïve and immature to be a mother. I hadn't slept with a man, had not experienced love. How callous and cavalier, to have sex simply to produce a child. Why could Katherine not let nature take its course, women and men falling in love, coupling, procreating? But I knew the answer to that: the male gender. She did not want men in our community other than for their manual labor and semen. If not for that, they would not be there. What had happened to her in the other world to make her so bitter against the male population? True, two men, two terrorists, had wreaked this havoc upon the world but not all men should be penalized for it.

At times, I fiercely wished I were lesbian. At least I could love another without fear of recrimination or being ostracized or disbanded or killed. Quite a few women in our commune had paired off with a partner and lived together as if married, an arrangement which was now accepted as the norm in our current world. But my sexual interests dwelt with the male gender and I felt no desire to cohabit with another woman.

Where would I go if Callie kicked me out? There were other communities out there but I didn't know where and didn't have the wherewithal to travel alone for days or weeks or months trying to find them. And when I did, would I fit in any better than here? Here, I had Katherine, our chief, the one who loved me and had saved me, who treated me with respect and as a favored daughter. There, I would be an unknown, a new member without the protection of a leader. I felt weak, ineffectual, angry at myself for not having the backbone to saddle up and leave. But I had been by myself for so long after the pox felled my parents, wandering alone, half-starved, wracked with grief and feeling guilty for somehow surviving this wretched disease. Sleeping wherever I could find a bed without a corpse, fearing every small night sound, crying myself to sleep, scrounging for food from convenience stores and open groceries. Things were easier when I found Boomer trotting down the middle of the interstate one day while I crossed the clogged lanes. I had a friend, a living being other than myself. But still, I longed for human companionship, someone to talk to, to whom I could tell my story. And then I found Katherine and things changed for me. I had a reason to move forward, to go on, someone who would hold me while I grieved the loss of my parents and my former life, someone to guide me to a better place.

I considered and reconsidered and always came to the same endless battle: leave and risk loneliness and danger and possibly a worse place than this or stay and conform to Katherine's dictions and essentially become her puppet.

On my third day during my venture outside the campus, I spied a party of women walking down a two-lane country road and rode toward them, Adam keeping pace. I slowed when I neared, noting three of the four middle-aged women were armed with rifles slung over their shoulders. They stopped when they spied me, watching my approach. A sense of unease traveled through my body at their lack of happiness or curiosity at seeing me, the hungry looks they cast Boomer and Adam. I reined Boomer in but remained astride, noting their grimy, unkempt bodies. What was so hard about keeping one's self clean when there was such an abundance of soap and bath products?

The oldest one – I surmised this because her hair was entirely gray – stared at Adam then Boomer before her eyes met mine. She was short and squat, her face deeply lined around the mouth and eyes. "We ain't had fresh meat since the pox hit," she said in a hillbilly twang.

"No one has," I answered, my inner voice screaming at me to get out of there. But it was my job to find stragglers and lead them back if they were so inclined and perhaps I misread their demeanor. I glanced at the one without a rifle. She looked to be the youngest of the lot and stared off in the distance as if uninterested in the goings-on. I turned my attention back to their leader. "Are you looking for a place to stay? I can take you where we have plenty of food and clean, comfortable quarters."

"I'd rather have me some meat," the red-headed one said. Her body build was thin and wiry, muscles bulging in her upper arms. She stepped toward Adam and he backed away, hackles raised, growling low in his throat. So he felt threatened by them too. This could quickly turn dangerous.

Before I realized it, my gun was in my hand and for a fraction of a second I was thankful I'd placed it in its holster which I'd looped around the saddle horn. "Touch either one and you're dead."

Rifles now pointed at me as the gray-headed woman said, "Get off the horse and walk away. We don't want or need you but we're gonna take them animals."

"Over my dead body."

"That can be arranged," she said in a soft voice. She glanced at the others, a sly grin playing around her mouth. "After all, we ain't exactly virgins when it comes to killing."

The two with rifles grinned. The other turned her back and walked away as if she did not want to be part of this.

"If you want meat, you can follow me to our commune. We have all kinds of meat there."

The dark-blond sneered at me. She seemed the scariest of the lot, with a large, broad build, heavy through the shoulders, arms and legs. "Potted, I bet. Or that processed crap." She shook her head. "Nothing tastes as good as fresh meat."

Gray-hair raised her rifle in the air and pulled the trigger. The sound startled Boomer and he reared on his hind legs, almost throwing me off. I managed to hang on to my horse with one hand, the gun with the other, but just barely. When he brought his feet down, gray-hair was on us, reaching for his bridle.

"Again," I said to Boomer, kicking his flank with my feet and pulling back on the reins. He reared up, his front hooves knocking the woman to the ground, her rifle tumbling out of her hand. "Adam," I screamed, as he attacked the red-headed one, jumping and hitting her chest, knocking her to the ground. I shot at the blond, training her rifle on Adam, and my bullet grazed her arm. She yelped and dropped her firearm. "Go," I yelled to Adam and we raced away. I lay over Boomer's neck, praying we could get away before they could regroup and try to shoot us. A bullet whizzed overhead and I knew if we didn't get out of range fast, my two animal friends would in all likelihood die. But either the women were poor shots or we were too far away as no more bullets pierced the air close by and we escaped unscathed.

We didn't stop running until we were miles away. I reined Boomer in and slid off, noticing the heavy lather on his chest, sides and hips. Adam immediately lay in the grass, panting, his tongue lolling. My body shook so hard I couldn't remain on my feet and collapsed beside him, placing my hand on his side and one on Boomer's leg. "God, I love you guys," I told them and burst into tears.

After we cooled down, I led Boomer and Adam to a nearby stream where they slurped water while I rehydrated with my own supply. I waded into the brook and splashed water on my face, trying to still the tremors that still swept through my body. And knew I would have sacrificed my life for these two animals without hesitation. "No one will ever harm you if I'm around," I promised them. Adam licked my cheek and Boomer nudged my back, their affirmation they heard the promise in my voice. I vowed to report these women to Callie when I returned, knowing she would not want people such as these joining our group, women who handled rifles with ease and did not seem to mind using them against other women.

I followed the stream on the ride back, my thoughts dwelling on the women and those in our community. And I knew I did not owe any loyalty to those who felt they could get what they wanted or dominate others through violence and bloodshed. My mind turned to Seth and Sarah and how I could help them escape our encampment. In mid afternoon, while eating the lunch Tara set aside for me, it became quite clear. I would tell Katherine I would accept her proposal and choose Seth as my mate. From what I gathered, the men were taken to the women's quarters each night with one of Callie's guards placed outside to ensure no harm came to the woman and that the man did not try to flee. I figured after a week or so, the guard placed on me would begin to relax and I could find some way to sneak Seth out the back door. A shiver worked its way up my spine as I considered this. I would be betraying Katherine, the person who saved me from despair, loneliness, isolation. A woman I considered family. For a moment, I desperately longed for my past life which had been sheltered, loved, protected. My problems narcissistically centered around me and were as mundane as what should I wear or where should I go or what should I do that day. If I followed through with this, I would step into another world, one unknown to me, one of betrayal and lies and deceit. I asked myself if I could do it and my mind answered with a resounding yes. What Katherine and Callie were doing was not right and there wasn't much I could do to resist but this one thing was a start. I only prayed I wouldn't get caught.

When I returned, I found Callie in her small office down the hall from Katherine's. She sat behind her desk talking to Sandra, the deputy who seemed more prone to violence than anyone I'd ever met. Callie saw me in the doorway and lifted her eyebrows inquiringly. I stepped inside, ignoring Sandra, and told her about the women I met. Callie straightened as I relayed my tale, occasionally darting a glance at Sandra. She questioned me extensively about exactly where I had run into the women.

"I thought you should know," I told her, "in case they come this way."

Callie nodded, her brow creased in thought. "Not the kind of women we want in the commune," she said more to herself than anyone. "Not if they're sporting rifles and freely use them against another woman." She locked gazes with Sandra.

Sandra placed her hand on her gun, her brown eyes wild and dancing. "I think we ought to go make sure they don't come this way. Stop something before it has a chance to get started."

Angst skittered along my spine. The Callie-Sandra combination could be deadly. "Callie, the one without a rifle wasn't part of that. She never threatened me and, in fact, when the others did, she turned and walked away."

Callie nodded as she rose to her feet. "We'll take that into consideration. Don't worry about your animals. We'll make sure they don't get near them," she said before brushing by me and hurrying out the door.

I watched their retreating forms, wondering if I had done the right thing by telling Callie and what she and Sandra would do if they found them. Then dismissed my unease, thinking those women had admitted to murdering others and were willing to kill and eat Boomer and Adam. They didn't deserve any concern from me.

After dinner that evening, I visited Sarah in her new quarters in the oldest of the women's dormitories. She smiled when she opened the door and invited me in. I stepped inside, glancing around. Sarah had made no effort to make the small apartment hers. I noted it was minimalistic, consisting of a tiny living room, even smaller bedroom, and miniscule kitchen and bath. Stained linoleum covered the floors and the walls were dirty beige with brighter smudges where pictures once hung. I surmised this must be where the freshmen had stayed; I had seen better rooms in other dormitories. Sarah waved me to a tattered dark-green sofa, asking if I'd like something to drink.

"Whatever you're having," I said, settling in and glancing around. I lunged to my feet. "Where's your baby, Sarah?"

She popped her head out of the kitchen. "In the bedroom asleep."

I stepped to the threshold and looked in. Sarah or perhaps Suzie had found a bassinet and placed it in the room beside the twin-sized bed. Travis lay on his back, arms thrown out as if in surrender, looking so angelic and pure. "He's beautiful."

Sarah, beside me, sighed. "Yes, he is."

I turned to her. "I have an idea. Why don't we get our drinks and talk?"

I followed her into the kitchen where Sarah handed me a glass of tea, apologizing for no ice.

"I don't like to drink it with ice anyway," I said as I returned to the living area.

She settled beside me on the couch, giving me an inquiring look.

"Before I tell you, how did you get Katherine to allow you to keep your baby with you?"

"I have you to thank for that. Suzie told me you told Katherine the baby needed to stay with me so I could continue to breastfeed him, giving him my antibodies. When Katherine asked Suzie what she thought, she told her the best thing for the baby and me right now is for me to breastfeed. So I've been given a reprieve. For how long, I don't know. But it's wonderful having him here with me." Her eyes darted toward the bedroom once more and I noted the wistful look on her face.

I nodded as I leaned closer to her and lowered my voice. "Have you heard about Katherine's and Callie's plans for procreation?"

She drew back, a shocked look on her face. "No. But then, I don't go out much. I'm terrified they'll take my baby away."

"They're pairing the women of childbearing age with the men."

Sarah's eyes opened in shock. "Have they placed Seth with anyone?"

"I don't know. I hope not because I'm going to tell Katherine I choose him."

Sarah drew back, her brow furrowed. Before she could speak, I said, "Don't worry, Sarah, I don't intend to sleep with him but I do intend to help y'all escape. They'll bring him to my apartment which should make it easier for him to get away."

Tears sprang to her eyes. "Oh, Madison, do you think it could work?"

"Only one way to find out. I figure I'll give them long enough to think everything is working out fine between us, then I'll find a way to smuggle Seth out of my apartment, have you meet us somewhere, and help the three of you get away."

Her face lit up and this was the first time I detected no hint of fear or anxiousness in her. She clasped my hands and it occurred to me I would miss Sarah once she left. She had become the closest thing to a friend I had in this small commune.

She pulled me into a hug. "Thank you, Madison, thank you so much," she whispered.

"I'm going to tell Katherine tomorrow. I'll drop by afterward and let you know if I'm successful."

I left, glad to be doing something to help my friend. My euphoria slipped away as I realized if I got caught this could be dangerous for me as well as Sarah, Seth and the baby. I vowed to myself I'd be very careful, only take the chance when the time was right.

The following morning, before heading to the stables, I crossed the courtyard and entered the students' building. I found Katherine in her office, alone for once. Forcing a smile on my face, I knocked on the doorjamb.

She glanced up from the paper she had been reading and gave me a guarded smile as she placed her pen aside. "I'm happy to see you, Madison." She scooted her chair back, came around the desk, and hugged me.

I hugged her tight, my thoughts truncated, as always, when it came to my love for her versus my disgust with her policies.

She drew back and studied me. "Callie told me what happened to you yesterday. Are you all right? They didn't hurt you, did they?"

I shook my head. "They wanted Adam and Boomer." I paused, the fear hitting me once more, twisting my stomach in knots. "They wanted them for fresh meat."

Katherine shook her head. "Well, you don't have to worry about that any longer. Callie and Sandra took care of them. They're no longer a threat to your precious animals."

"What about the one without a rifle, the one who walked away? Did they find her?"

Katherine's eyes changed and she glanced away. "They didn't encounter her, only the ones with rifles, and rest assured their killing days are behind them."

I nodded, glad she chose not to tell me what Callie and Sandra had done, thankful for Katherine's concern for my well-being as well as my animal friends. This brought on a pang of guilt that my reason for being here was to betray her. "I've come to talk to you, Katherine."

"I can see by your eyes you have something to say. Sit." She waved me to a chair as she returned to her seat behind the desk.

"I've been thinking about our discussion." I looked out the window behind her. I could not stand to look her in the eyes. "And although I don't want to be involved in what you and Callie have planned, I understand what you're trying to achieve." I returned my gaze to her. "I'll go along with it if you'll let me choose my mate."

"Is there a reason for this? Are you attracted to one of the others?"

"I've never even given them a thought in that regard, to tell you the truth. But if I'm required to have sex with them, I cannot stomach the thought of a different man each time or one that I find repugnant."

Katherine's eyes crinkled at this. "My dear, Madison, it does not surprise me to hear you say that."

I stared at her, waiting.

She regarded me for a long moment. "I take it you've made your choice." This spoken in a low voice.

"Yes. Seth, the one who came in with Sarah."

"And why Seth?"

"He's attractive, well-built, and although a bit short, he's at least taller than me. I would not enjoy making love with a man smaller than I am."

Katherine gave a wry smile. "I quite agree."

"I've worked with him, had short conversations and he seems intelligent enough. I would not want to mate with a man with a low IQ." I stared at her once more. "I want my daughter to be intelligent, strong, healthy, beautiful."

Katherine raised her eyebrows as she leaned back in her chair. "Well, I see you have been thinking about this."

"For three days."

She remained quiet for so long, I grew concerned. "Have you put him with someone else, Katherine?"

"We did, yes, but he refused to cooperate. Callie's had him in solitary, hoping he'll change his mind."

"Offer me to him. I think he will."

Now she eyed me with suspicion. "Is there more to your relationship with him than you're telling me?"

"No, of course not. I kind of got a vibe, I guess you would call it, from him, as if he might be interested. If he says no, then, of course, I'll have to choose someone else."

She picked up her pen, tapped the desk as she thought about it. I waited, watching her. After several long moments, she raised her eyes to mine. "Have you considered Sarah, what she might feel about this? It seemed the two were close when they first came here."

My lie was ready. "I visited Sarah last night and asked her about it. She looks at him more as a brother than possible mate. She agreed with the idea." I hesitated. "I got the feeling she thinks this will help him stay alive."

Katherine gave me a sharp glance. "Why would she think differently?"

"Well, for one, the way Callie places guards around the men, the way she keeps them away from the women. The fact that y'all won't let Sarah see Seth. I'd say she's put things together for herself."

Katherine nodded. "Very well, Madison, if that's what it takes to get you to cooperate, I see no problem with it. I'll speak to Callie today."

"How soon before we begin?"

Her smile was mischievous. "Are you that anxious?"

I shrugged, giving her an embarrassed glance. "It's going to be awkward at first. I'd rather get that behind me and get on with it."

Katherine nodded. "I understand. I'll have Suzie let you know when she needs you for the blood work."

I rose to my feet. "Okay, I'm going to go help the burial crew today. Just let me know when you want us to, um, start."

She waved her hand at me as I walked out the door.

CHAPTER 8

A week later, Callie brought Seth to me at eight in the evening. I opened the door, my eyes widening at his battered face. Callie shoved him inside and I stepped aside before his body collided with mine. I looked back at Callie, glaring at me.

"I'll come back for him at midnight. Be sure you put your time together to good use." With a lecherous grin, she wheeled around and stalked away. I wasn't surprised to see one of her deputies step into my field of vision, her hand going to her gun belt. I got the message.

I closed and locked the door, breaking Callie's rule, but I did not care. She had no right to enter my apartment. My gaze met Seth's. Before he could say anything, I held up my hands. "I don't want to have sex with you, Seth. That's not why I asked for you."

He shoved his hands in his pocket and nodded, waiting for my explanation.

I walked closer to him, dropped my voice to a whisper. "Sarah knows what I'm doing. She wants to leave and I'm going to try to help the three of you escape."

Something flickered in his eyes and I suspected it was a blend of relief and hope. "How is she? How's the baby?"

I smiled at him. "They're both doing well. Her little boy is beautiful."

His stance relaxed as his face brightened. "Good. I've been worried about them."

"Katherine's letting her keep him for now so she can breastfeed. But I'm worried that won't last long."

"But she's safe for now?" he asked, an anxious cast to his eyes.

"Yes, for now. Can I get you anything to drink?" I asked, wondering how much pain he was in. "Tylenol or aspirin? I know that has to hurt."

Seth dropped onto the couch, gingerly touching his lips, swollen and red. "It looks worse than it feels."

Adam, lounging in the chair across from Seth, got down and trotted over, sniffing at his jeans. Seth reached down, scratched his ears. Adam groaned with pleasure.

I sat on the opposite end from him. "Who did this to you?"

"Who do you think?"

"Callie?"

"Yep. Says I need to learn respect." He snorted with disdain, shaking his head. "She cheats, had her puppets hold me while she used her sap on me." His gaze met mine. "There's something terribly wrong here, Madison. I'm surprised you stay."

"I don't have anywhere else to go."

"What will they do to you if they find out you helped us?"

"I don't know. Frankly, I don't care. I promised Sarah I'd help and I intend to do it."

"We need to be careful. Callie and her deputies are incredibly watchful."

"I know. I've been studying their routines, trying to figure out how to do this."

Adam shook his head, jumped onto the couch, and settled between us. Seth and I put our hands on him, rubbing different areas. Adam rolled onto his back, his legs in the air, his face blissful.

"What a pretty boy you are," I cooed at him.

"I miss having a dog. Where'd you find him?"

"A farmhouse about fifteen miles from here. He was inside, guarding over the bodies of his owners. I didn't think he'd come with me but he did." I kissed Adam's head. "Did you see any animals while you were traveling?"

"Saw a doe once, thought I saw a raccoon in a garbage can but wasn't sure." He gave a half-grin. "Didn't investigate in case he might be rabid."

"I haven't seen any cats at all. I found my horse Boomer trotting down the interstate one day but I haven't seen any more horses. No farm animals and I've visited a lot of farms in this area. I'm terrified we're going to lose the animals."

"Maybe not. Winter's just over so we might start to see more now that it's warming up."

I studied him for a moment, gauged he must be in his late 20s to early 30s. A bit old for Sarah, but in this new world, women's choices in picking mates were somewhat limited. "What'd you do before the pox?"

"Worked as an EMT while I attended medical school."

"This new world will need doctors."

"Afraid I don't qualify yet. I got a late start at it after I did a couple of tours in Afghanistan and was nowhere near being finished."

"Still, working as an EMT, you must have some medical knowledge."

"It helped." He settled back on the couch, a hand idly stroking Adam's neck.

"Where are you from, Seth?"

"Chattanooga." He grew quiet for a moment. "The pox took my whole family. I left with a friend who managed to survive but he couldn't handle it. Hung himself one night while I was asleep." He swiped his hand over his face.

I closed my eyes, remembering my own devastation finding myself alone in a world filled with rot and death.

"Found Sarah in Cleveland not far from where I started." A smile flitted across his lips. "She was walking down the middle of the road singing this God-awful song about daisies or something." He sighed. "I don't think I've ever been so happy, seeing her. I thought it was a hallucination at first."

"Where were y'all headed when you came across our community?"

"I'd heard about this campus, how it was so environmentally progressive. So we figured here we might have a better chance of existing, you know, living as comfortably as possible. Hoped there'd be others here too. Sarah was pretty far along and I was terrified she'd have that baby on the road." He shrugged. "Only wish I'd known what was here to greet us before we stepped inside the campus."

"I don't think any of us knew it would be like this," I said.

He gave me a questioning look.

"Katherine wasn't so interested in using men at first. All she told me when I first met her was that she wanted a community without men. Frankly, all I cared about at that time was finding another human being to share my life with."

Seth raised his eyebrows at this. "Why a community without men?"

"She's never talked about it. She was married before and I think it must have been an abusive relationship. At least that's all I can come up with. Anyway, it wasn't until Callie joined us and got close to Katherine that she began to change, to develop these policies and agendas they've put in place concerning men. And as you know, Callie's only too happy to enforce them."

He regarded me with suspicion.

"What?"

He thought for a moment, then, "I'll just say it. Get it out in the open. I'm not being set up here, am I? You're not working in cahoots with Katherine and Callie, are you?"

"Why would they even want you to try to escape, Seth?"

"Gives them a good reason to kill me."

I drew back, surprised. I hadn't thought of that.

"Callie scares me a little. She has a mean look in her eyes." He shook his head. "And that deputy, Sandra, she's crazy with lust to kill or hurt someone. The guys call her Crazy Eyes."

I nodded. "I've seen it too when she's manhandling someone." I studied his battered face. If anyone had witnessed that look, Seth surely had.

"You need to think about this, Madison. Long and hard. They'll probably kill you if they suspect you helped us escape."

"I can only hope Katherine will stop Callie before she gets to me."

I lay my head against Adam's, my hand on his chest, his heart thudding heavily against my palm. I had to ask it, had to know. "There's one thing I don't understand, Seth."

"What's that?" he asked in a low voice.

I raised up to look at him. "Why don't y'all try to escape? I've watched the work details, the way the men are around Callie and her deputies. You all seem so passive, accepting. I don't understand it. It reminds me of a movie I watched once about the

Holocaust, the way the Jewish prisoners just accepted their fate and what was dealt out to them. I didn't understand it then, don't now."

I watched his eyes change, grow darker, angrier. "You don't have any idea what they're doing to us, do you?"

"I'm not sure but I think Callie's killing the older, weaker ones. I've run across a few bodies…"

"They're doing more than that. Anybody so much as says a cross word and they get beat half to death. One guy tried to escape, took off running and they were on him before most of us knew what was happening. Made us watch while they executed him. Shot him through the head."

I drew back, shock coursing through my body. "But that's barbaric. They don't have the right do to that."

Seth gave me a pitying glance. "Oh, Madison, you're too innocent for all this. They don't have the right to do most of what they do but they do it anyway. Because they can."

We were silent awhile, each lost in our own thoughts. Finally I said, "I'll do everything I can to help you and Sarah get out of here."

"Just be careful, Madison. Promise me that."

"I will. Where do you think you'll go, Seth?"

He shrugged with a despondent look. "Have no idea. I heard about a community up near Bristol with both men and women living there. Didn't hear anything negative about it but I don't know that I'll trust any of the communities out there. Not after this." He looked away from me. "Besides, it's probably best not to tell you, in case we do make it out of here."

I nodded my agreement. "Just make sure when you approach a community, you see men and women living and working side by side without one guarding the other with guns." I ruffled Adam's fur. "Or you could go to the farmhouse where I found Adam. Summer's coming on so you wouldn't have to worry about trying to find ways to stay warm. It's a beautiful place, Seth, with its own pond and a well for water. I checked the pantry and it's packed full of food, enough to sustain y'all for awhile. Of course, you'll have to find a store somewhere so you can stock up on baby food when the time comes."

Seth's face brightened. "You don't think they'd find us there?"

"No. Callie and her deputies go toward Knoxville when they're after supplies. I'm the only one that's ever ridden in any other direction that I know of."

I drew a map for Seth to take when they left and we talked about ways to make his and Sarah's escape successful but never arrived at a real plan. We agreed if anything out of the ordinary happened that required the attention of Callie and her deputies, we would take the chance then. In the interim, we would try to come up with a workable plan. I told Seth I'd tell Sarah to stay alert and if anything happened to take the baby and run to the barn where he would meet her.

Callie showed up at midnight, banging on the door. I mussed my hair, told Seth to untuck his shirt, and answered with a feigned flustered look. Her smirk told me she bought our guise. She pushed Seth out the door and led him away.

CHAPTER 9

Our break came faster than I expected and Seth and I were both so stunned we lost precious seconds before we realized what happened. We were lounging on the couch, talking in low voices about our past lives, people we loved, things we missed. Gunshots and shouting in the distance drew our attention and Seth and I stared at one another. When I understood this was our chance, I lunged off the couch and ran to the door. In my excitement, I fumbled with the lock for a moment before disengaging it and opening the door. Darting a glance outside, I caught sight of the backside of the deputy Callie had guarding us heading toward the commotion.

"Hurry." I ran toward the bedroom, kicking off my shoes as I went. "The guard's gone. We have to move fast, we won't have much time."

I pulled my shirt over my head, undid my jeans and slid them down my legs, fighting embarrassment at revealing so much of my body to a man I didn't love. Was grateful I'd taken the time to put on a sports bra that day. "The tape's in the nightstand drawer." I glanced up, caught Seth standing in the doorway watching me. "Move, Seth, now. We don't have much time." I sat down in the middle of the bed, pulling off my socks. He opened the drawer, drew out a roll of neon-pink duct tape. "Bind my legs and my wrists, Seth. Make it look good."

With a nod, he joined me on the bed, unwound the tape and wrapped it around my ankles.

I held out my wrists but before he touched them, said, "Wait." I rolled onto my stomach, put my wrists behind me. "This will make it harder for me and may look more real to them."

He placed tape around my wrists several times then stood off the bed.

I rolled onto my side, speaking in a rush. "If Sarah heard the gunshots, she should be headed toward the barn. She'll meet you there. You remember where to go?"

He shook his head. "I know you drew me a map but tell me again."

"Take the golf cart and follow the gravel road behind the barn. It'll lead you to an access road that connects to the interstate. But don't go onto the interstate. Take the golf cart into the woods, cover it up, then go back to the access road. Where it connects to the interstate, there's a small trail going back into the woods. Follow that trail. It'll take you to a two-lane road. Stay on that road about five miles and you'll see a large sign with a horse on it at the end of a gravel drive. The driveway will take you to the farmhouse. It sits about a mile off the road, on top of a hill so you'll be able to see anyone coming up the road or the drive. There's a loft in the barn you can hide in if someone comes. But I figure they'll think you took the interstate and are long gone and won't put much effort into finding you."

"This is too dangerous for you, knowing where we're going."

I shook my head. "I've got that covered with Sarah. She's leaving me a goodbye note, telling me y'all are going to the commune in Bristol."

He stared at me but didn't say anything.

"Put duct tape over my mouth and go. Now, Seth. You don't have much time."

He leaned toward me, kissed me quickly on the lips. "Thank you, Madison. Thank you so much."

"Kiss Sarah and the baby for me."

"You got it."

"Wait. Get the map out of the nightstand. It's taped to the underside of the top drawer." I watched as he retrieved it. "Whatever you do, don't lose that. If they find it, they'll probably recognize my writing and I'm dead for certain."

He folded it into a tiny square, tucked it deep into his front jeans pocket. "They won't find it." He tore off a strip of duct tape, placed it over my mouth, awkwardly patted me on the head, then turned and ran out the door.

I lay on the bed listening, waiting for a gunshot outside my apartment, the bullet meant for Seth. Several minutes later, I twisted my hands and ankles, trying to make it look like I'd tried to get free. After awhile, I could feel blood trickling from my wrists down my arms; a small price to pay for Seth's and Sarah's freedom. I worked and worked until sweat flowed down my face and my wrists and ankles felt raw and tender. Finally I heard movement in the outer room and looked that way.

Linda, one of Callie's deputies, ran into the bedroom. She drew up short when she spied me trussed on the bed.

I twisted this way and that, mumbling behind the tape covering my mouth. She ran over, yanked it off. It hurt like the devil.

"Ow!" I yelled.

She ignored that. "Where'd he go?"

"You think I know?" I demanded in a belligerent voice. "Help me."

"In a minute." She took the two-way radio out of her pocket and signaled Callie. When she answered, Linda said, "I'm at Madison's. Whoever they had her with is gone."

I could hear Callie swearing then asking where I was.

"She's on the bed bound with duct tape."

When Callie spoke, her voice rang loud and clear. "Cut her free and send her to Katherine's office. I'll meet her there when I get this mess taken care of. I need you to go to Sarah's, make sure she's still here."

"I'm on it." Linda put the radio back in her pocket and pulled out a pocketknife. As she sawed through the tape, she said, "You have any idea why she wants me to check on Sarah?"

I nodded. "They had me paired with Seth, the one Sarah came in with."

"You know where he was headed?"

I gave her a look of disbelief. "Why would he tell me that?"

"Okay." She hesitated, eying me. "You think you can make it to Katherine's on your own or do I need to take you?"

I stood, shaking my head, studying my bleeding wrists and ankles. "First I'm going to the infirmary, see if Suzie can do something about this. It hurts."

"Make sure you meet Callie at Katherine's like she said."

"Okay, sure, soon as I get these bandaged. I don't want an infection to set in."

Linda ran out the door, her mind already on her task.

I got dressed, taking care to slide my jeans on with as little contact as possible with the torn flesh around my ankles, then made my way to the infirmary, my wrists and ankles burning. Suzie was there helping Shelly tend a woman laying on a gurney with a swollen and bruised face. When Suzie saw me, she joined me, holding my hands as she regarded my wrists.

"He bound me with duct tape. I tried to get out of it but it wouldn't budge," I said.

She raised her eyes to mine and I saw that she didn't believe me. She covered this with a quick nod. "Sit down on that gurney over there and I'll bandage them for you."

I slid onto the cot, wincing when my wrist touched the paper cover. Suzie pulled over a stool followed by a table laden with Betadine, Vaseline, gauze pads and tape. She sat down on the stool, placed a towel on my lap, told me to rest my wrist there. I did as she instructed, gritting my teeth as she bathed the raw flesh with Betadine. She gently applied Vaseline and wrapped the wrist in gauze, securing it with the tape. I waited patiently as she went through the same procedure with my other wrist and ankles. Finished, she got to her feet, gathering up the detritus from her treatment.

I nodded my head at the woman on the gurney, moaning and turning her head from side to side as if in agony. Shelly leaned over her, cleaning blood off her face. "Who's that and what happened to her?"

Suzie glanced over. "That is the reason for the gunshots you heard tonight." Our eyes met. "She found her lover with another woman and created quite a commotion, I understand." Suzie sighed. "Callie did the damage." She shook her head. "That woman's going to go too far and kill someone one day." When she turned her gaze to me, I noted the resignation. "Which may happen soon. If she has internal bleeding, there's nothing I can do for her."

I looked at the woman, noted one leg had been placed in a rubber cast, an arm in a sling. Her face was so battered and swollen, it was hard to detect her features. "Suzie, Callie's out of control if she did that."

"Yes, but who's going to stop her?"

I slid off the gurney, approached the woman, and touched her on the shoulder. Shelly gave me an imperceptible nod before gathering up her bloody rags and leaving.

The woman's gaze turned on me, filled with pain.

"Is there anything I can get you?"

"You're Madison," she said with effort and I thought I detected a hint of triumph flash in her eyes.

I was amazed she could talk with her mouth as swollen as it was. Although her words were slurred, I could understand her. "Yes. Can I help you in any way?"

She grimaced before saying, "Oh, honey, you already did."

"I'm sorry?"

Her eyes glittered, and even though I could tell it hurt her to talk, that didn't stop her. "He got away, didn't he?"

"Who?"

"The one they put you with, Sarah's man."

"Yes, he escaped."

"And Sarah?"

"I don't know. Linda's gone to find out." I watched that flicker in her eyes and it dawned on me the woman had an agenda in play. I lowered my voice to a whisper and leaned close to her. "You did that on purpose?" Blood leaked from her mouth and I picked up a towel and wiped her face as gently as I could.

"I sure did. Gave y'all the chance and he took it." She coughed and bloody spittle flew into the air. Once she could breathe, she said, "You helped him, didn't you? I told them you felt like we did and I reckon his escaping is proof enough."

I glanced around, noted Suzie watching us with a wary look. Shelly busied herself jotting notes on a chart, obviously making an effort to ignore us. "Them? Who's them?"

"The ones who don't buy Katherine's propaganda."

I drew back, shocked. My eyes met Suzie's, filled with fear and panic.

Callie charged into the infirmary, a furious look on her face. "What did you do?" she shouted. She rushed over to me and punched me in the stomach. All the air went out of my lungs and I collapsed to the floor, struggling to breathe. Callie kicked me in the side and black dots danced before my eyes. This was the first time anyone had ever assaulted me and I was surprised to find my feelings hurt that she would do this to me. I blinked back tears, vowing I would not cry in front of her.

When Callie drew her foot back again, Suzie stepped between us. "Stop. Now. I won't allow this here."

Callie clenched her fists, breathing heavily. "You did this on purpose," she yelled. "It was all planned between you and her." She gestured toward the woman on the gurney.

Suzie turned to Shelly, watching us with a shocked expression on her face. "Call Katherine, get her over here."

Shelly threw me a panicked look before she rushed over to the desk with the two-way radio.

Suzie helped me sit up, telling me not to panic, that my breath would come back.

Callie paced around, face red, hands fisted, kicking stools and tables out of her way. The woman on the gurney watched her warily.

When Callie finally paused, the woman said, "That girl over there had nothing to do with what happened with me tonight and you know it, Callie." She paused and blood dribbled out of her mouth. When she spoke, her breath came in gasps. "You been looking for a way to get back at her for Katherine loving her like she does and this is what you picked. Well, it ain't gonna work."

"You shut your mouth, you stupid hillbilly," Callie said.

She made a sound that might have been a laugh. "Everybody knows how you feel about Katherine but she don't feel that way toward you. Madison's her family, woman, can't you understand that?"

"Shut up," Callie screamed. She marched toward the woman, a determined look on her face.

I struggled to my feet, lurching toward Callie, intending to stop her, but Suzie beat me there, jerking the gurney away before Callie could reach it. "You need to calm down, Callie. Katherine's on her way."

That seemed to do it for her. Callie drew herself up, stiffly walked over to a chair and plopped into it. "Fine. That's just fine," she said in a low voice.

We waited in silence for several minutes, Suzie and I breathing a sigh of relief when Katherine stepped though the door, looking calm and serene. "I understand we have a problem." Her eyes took in Callie's state of mind, me slightly bent at the waist holding my stomach, Suzie hovering over me.

Katherine hurried over to me. "Are you all right?"

I choked back tears, resisting the urge to throw myself into her arms, be comforted by this woman.

"Callie punched her in the stomach then kicked her." Suzie sent a challenging look Callie's way.

Callie rose to her feet, pointing at me. "Your little girl there helped one of the others escape tonight." When Katherine didn't respond, she said, "Seth, the one that came in with Sarah, the one she insisted we pair her with."

Katherine's brows rose as she turned to me. "Is that true?"

I struggled to straighten up, Suzie helping me, and held out my bandaged wrists. "Does this look like I helped him?"

Suzie said, "She rubbed the skin on her wrists and ankles raw trying to get out of the duct tape he bound her with."

"That's just to throw us off," Callie spat.

Katherine made a shushing motion toward Callie and she stepped back, surprise flickering over her face before her usual sardonic expression slipped back in place.

When Katherine spoke, her voice was gentle, comforting. "Tell me what happened, Madison."

I told her the contrived version: I was asleep, woke up when I realized my hands were being wrapped in duct tape. I tried to escape but Seth overpowered me and wrapped my ankles, then put tape over my mouth. I didn't get free until Linda showed up and cut me loose.

"Where'd he get the duct tape?" Callie said.

I struggled to make my face impassive, guilt-free. "There was some in a drawer in the kitchen. I guess he found it."

"It's all a lie," Callie hissed.

"Shut up," Katherine said.

Callie's face fell. The bully had finally been bullied and I could see she didn't like it.

Linda rushed in, a piece of paper in her hands. She stopped in front of Callie and spoke to her. "She's gone."

Callie clenched her fists. "Damn!"

"Who is gone?" Katherine asked in that calm, cool voice of hers.

"Sarah." Linda held out the piece of paper. "She left this letter for Madison."

"I told you she was in on it," Callie said.

Katherine held out her hand and Linda handed it over. Katherine began to read aloud. "My dearest Madison."

Callie made a noise in her throat and Katherine looked at her. She immediately silenced.

"When you read this," Katherine went on, "I will be gone, hopefully with Seth. We can't stay here, Madison, much as you would like for me and my baby to. Seth and I are a team and we want to be with people who will look upon us as such. I don't know if you're aware of it, but Callie's been killing men they don't want. Seth told me he heard it from some of the others and witnessed her execute a man who tried to escape. I don't doubt it after what she did to Seth."

"Wait a minute," Callie said. "How does she know what Seth said?"

I tried to look contrite. "It's my fault. I passed letters between the two of them."

Katherine gave me a piercing stare.

"They were in love, Katherine. I thought it was, well, romantic."

"And you didn't think to read the letters?" Callie said with a snide look.

"Of course not. It was between them. I thought they were telling each other their feelings. I didn't want to intrude on that."

"Yet you slept with him."

"Sarah wanted that. She didn't want any other woman to mate with him. Besides, it was a way for them to exchange letters."

"That doesn't make sense." Callie gave me a challenging glare. "I bet she never slept with him. For all we know, they could have spent their time together plotting a way for him to escape with Sarah."

Katherine studied me a moment before dropping her gaze to the paper and reading. "I hope you'll forgive me for leaving, Madison. If you ever decide this place isn't right for you, you can find us at the commune I told you about."

Katherine gave me an inquiring look.

"She told me about a community in Bristol where men and women live together."

Katherine nodded before continuing. "I cherish our friendship and hope one day to see you again. I know you love Katherine but encourage you to think about what your future will be if you stay. Love always, Sarah."

Katherine raised her eyes to mine. "You knew nothing about this? That they planned to escape?"

I shook my head. "She was my friend but why would she share that with me, Katherine, knowing my love for you."

Her face softened and I knew she believed me.

Callie charged forward. "You're going to believe that crap?" she said to Katherine.

"Why wouldn't I, Callie? Madison has never given us any reason to doubt her veracity."

Callie pointed her finger at Katherine. "You got a blind spot when it comes to that girl. You let her gallivant around here, do what she wants, never –"

"Enough." Katherine's voice was hard, forceful. "Madison follows the rules, doesn't cause trouble, and has gone along with this procreation policy you insisted she be part of. Don't question me about her or the way I treat her, Callie. This is my community and if you don't stop this foolishness you will be replaced."

A hurt look flashed into Callie's eyes for a second, replaced by anger with such speed I questioned whether I had actually seen it or not. Without responding, she turned on her heel and left.

Katherine pulled me into a hug. "Why don't you go home and get some rest? You obviously are in pain. Shelly, can you give Madison something to make her more comfortable and to help her sleep?"

"Of course," Shelly said, hurrying to a medicine cabinet at the end of the room.

Katherine kissed me on the cheek then pulled Suzie aside and motioned toward the gurney. "Tell me about this woman."

I looked over and noticed the woman's pale countenance, shallow breaths. I prayed she would live, that Callie hadn't caused internal bleeding. But the look on Suzie's face told me she believed otherwise. When I left, Katherine was trying to talk to the woman but she either was unable to respond to her or chose not to.

Even though I took the pill Shelly gave me, I still had a fitful night's sleep. The woman on the gurney kept flashing into my dreams, blood pouring out of her mouth as she told me over and over she did it for me. I would not ask that of anyone, I told myself, wondering why she would sacrifice herself for another person, whether it be me, Seth or Sarah and her baby. Early morning, I finally gave up and took a cold shower, wishing our generators were powerful enough to heat the water. After dropping Adam off with Darlene, I headed toward the infirmary in the guise of letting Suzie rebandage my wounds but to check on the injured woman.

When I stepped into the room, I noticed the gurney was gone. I checked behind curtains, wondering where everyone was. I opened the door to the storage room, a gasp escaping at a sheet-covered body lying on a gurney. I approached it slowly, praying it wasn't the woman who had stood up to Callie beneath the sheet, knowing it was. Movement behind me and I whirled around. Suzie stood in the doorway, looking more flustered than I had ever seen her.

She answered my unspoken question with a nod. "It's her. She died early this morning."

"Have you told Katherine?"

"I just came from there."

"Is she going to do anything about Callie? Charge her for murder, have her arrested?"

"I don't know, Madison, she didn't say." She put her hand on my arm and drew me out of the room, softly closing the door behind us. "Let me have a look at your wrists and ankles."

"Suzie, this is wrong," I said as she gestured for me to sit in a chair.

She didn't respond as she busied herself unwrapping the bandages.

"Suzie?"

She looked at me with grave concern. "Madison, for your own safety, you need to watch yourself, learn to curb your tongue."

This shocked me. "But Callie killed that woman, Suzie. Something should be done about her."

"You don't know the circumstances, what provoked it. Callie may have been in the right."

"Suzie."

She shook her head and held up her hands. "I want to stay here. I have nowhere else to go and the thought of being back out there, alone..." She sighed. "I have friends here. I like what I'm doing, I like helping people. I may not agree with some of the policies in place but I like this community. I feel safe here, needed. Don't pull me into your little rebellion. I won't be a part of that."

"What rebellion? I know nothing of a rebellion."

She studied me with serious eyes. "Madison, whether you realize it or not, people watch your actions, they listen to what you say. They know that although you're close to Katherine, you don't always follow her protocols. They see that you don't agree with some of the things she and Callie have deemed are best."

"You mean the others?"

"Yes."

"So I'm not the only one who doesn't agree."

Suzie's eyes grew wary. "I'm not saying that. Just realize what you're saying or doing before you open your mouth or do it. Understand how it could be perceived. And maybe you should think about whether you actually want to stay here or not, whether it's safe for you to stay here."

I drew back. "Are you telling me I'm in danger?"

She took my hands in hers, gripping them. "I'm saying there are some who might not feel about you as Katherine does. Some who like the policies in place, don't want to see them challenged by anyone."

"You're talking about Callie."

"Not just Callie."

"You think I need to keep my opinions to myself, not even voice them to Katherine?"

She looked into my eyes. "Yes."

"Even though Callie killed someone."

"Yes, Madison, even then. Whether you know it or not, Katherine protects you because she loves you. It's best if you just go along and don't cause problems for her." She hesitated for a moment. "Think about how much worse off we'd be if someone like Callie were in charge. At least we have Katherine to rein her in."

I mulled this over as she treated my wrists and ankles, thanking her before I left. At the door, I turned back. "What was her name?"

Suzie glanced up. I looked toward the storage room door.

"Oh. Macy Connors. She was from a small town in Kentucky, I think."

"She told me she did it to help Seth escape," I said in a low voice. "Can you believe that, Suzie? Giving up her life for that?"

Suzie studied me for a long moment. "Yes, I can believe it," she said before turning her back, dismissing me.

I crossed over to the student building, for once aware of those around me. Some smiled and seemed friendly enough, although others watched me with a guarded look. In a few, I detected outright hostility. What had I done to incur their wrath, I wondered. I paused on the steps outside the building, mulling over what Suzie said. Maybe I could accomplish more if I simply seemed to go along with Katherine's and Callie's policies. It seemed I only had one ally, albeit a powerful one, but how long would she tolerate my constant challenges before considering me a hindrance or possible threat? Before Callie convinced her of such?

I ran into Linda, coming out of the building as I entered. She stopped and asked how I fared. When I assured her I was fine, she told me one of the others had also escaped. I allowed the shock I felt to show on my face. It hadn't occurred to me someone else would take advantage of Macy's outburst. Relief quickly washed through me and I turned away, nodding my head, not wanting Linda to witness this. This worked better for me, if one of the others had fled when Seth did, perhaps casting a cloud over any involvement I might have had.

When I stepped into Katherine's office, she had her chair turned toward the window behind her, staring out, lost in thought.

"Katherine?" I asked softly.

She turned and for a brief moment I caught the wariness in her eyes before she smiled and they grew warm. "Madison. How are you today?"

"Fine." I stepped closer and hugged her when she rose from her chair.

"Oh, that's nice," she said. "I'm not used to you being the one to initiate hugs."

This stunned me. Had I been that cold, that distant? "I'm sorry, Katherine. I can't seem to get past what's happened to us." I sat down in the chair across from her desk. "I love you, Katherine. I don't think I tell you enough, but you're the only family I have." Tears sprang to my eyes.

"Oh, my dear, Madison, I love you too."

"And I won't question you again over what you're doing, what you have planned for us."

"You're young. It's only natural you question those in authority."

I nodded but couldn't stop myself from pursuing the woman on the gurney. "She died, you know."

Katherine's gaze would not meet mine. "Yes, I heard."

"Callie did that, she killed her."

"Callie tells a different story, backed up by her deputies."

I nodded. I figured as much. "It's just, I've never been hit by anyone before and even worse never seen such violence done to a person as had been done to her."

"Oh, sweetie, you grew up in a well-protected environment and I'm sure witnessing such atrocities is terrifying. But it's a cruel world we now live in, Madison, you have to accept that, and at times there are things that will happen you may not agree with but I hope you'll trust me enough to understand I'm doing what I think is best."

"Such as believing Callie and letting her continue on."

Our eyes met. "Callie keeps everything under control. She's an essential part of this community."

"She scares me. I think she hates me."

"No, I'm certain she doesn't. I think she may be a bit jealous of our relationship but it's nothing to worry about."

A bit jealous. Oh, it was more than that. Even I knew that. But I smiled instead and said, "Sure."

She settled back, a look of relief flitting across her face. "What are your plans for the day?"

I decided to ingratiate myself further. "I thought I'd try to track Seth and Sarah if you want me to." Of course, I had no intention of finding them but Katherine didn't need to know that.

She studied me for a long moment. "That's not necessary. I'm sure they're far gone by now."

I wondered if Katherine suspected I was part of the unrest among our community. It seemed I somehow had become involved in something I had no idea was going on. How many of the women in this community felt as I did? How many had been encouraged by Seth's escape? This brought on another question.

"Linda said another one of the others escaped. Do you know who?"

"Yes, a man we had paired with Lucy."

I tried to place Lucy. "Do I know her? That name doesn't sound familiar."

"She works with the gardening group."

A Hispanic woman in her early 30s with ebony hair and dark, soulful eyes. "She didn't get hurt, did she? I mean, he didn't hurt her when he escaped?"

"She didn't suffer the injuries you did but she seems traumatized. Callie's with her now, interrogating her."

"About what?"

"We need to know if she helped him escape or was simply like you..." another of those long stares "...unfortunately in the wrong place at the wrong time."

I bit my tongue. Why in the world would she let Callie interrogate the woman? Callie would probably use Gestapo tactics to get the answers she wanted.

Katherine sat back. "I do have one question for you, Madison."

"Sure," I said, trying to relay confidence I did not feel.

"When you told me you wanted to be paired with Seth, you said Sarah didn't object because she looked upon him as a brother."

I inwardly sighed. When would the lies ever end? "Yes, that's what she told me at the time. It wasn't until after Seth and I, um, began that she told me the real reason she wanted me to be paired with him, so they could send messages to one another through me."

"Yet you slept with him."

"Isn't that what you wanted? My goal was to please you, Katherine, to do as you asked, and Seth apparently didn't have a problem having sex with me. I didn't think it would do any harm to pass letters from one to the other but apparently that backfired on me."

Katherine contemplated this for a long moment then nodded. "Everyone here has a job and maybe it's time you were assigned one. What do you think suits you best?"

"Riding Boomer, checking outside our community, looking for stragglers, things such as that."

"We have Callie and her deputies for that."

"But they don't venture out as far as I do. It's warming up, and like you said, more people should be heading this way. I'd like to find them, bring them to you."

She thought about that for a moment. "For now until I can think of a better job for you."

"Of course," I said in a stilted voice, disappointed at the prospect that my freedom might soon be compromised. I bade her farewell and headed out to collect Adam. My sweet dog pranced alongside me as I made my way to the barn, seeming to know we were going to venture out. He loved these outings, running ahead, exploring, yet always keeping Boomer and me in sight. He and the horse had become good buddies and surprised me with their affection for one another. I had noticed the looks some of the women gave both the horse and dog and had begun thinking they might not be safe here. I had become used to canned foods but some still bemoaned the fact that we did not have fresh meat to eat. I wondered, if I weren't Katherine's protégé, what would have become of my two four-legged friends.

Once Boomer was saddled, we headed in the opposite direction from where Seth and Sarah had gone. Prickling on the back of my neck told me I was being watched and I suspected it was one of Callie's minions, hoping I'd lead them straight to the escapees. I figured I'd wait until I was no longer under suspicion before I made my way to the farmhouse to ascertain they arrived safely. I wondered where the other man had gone and hoped he had gotten away. I prayed Callie wouldn't hurt Lucy. And began to wonder if this world would be any better than the previous one.

CHAPTER 10

Over the next few weeks, I made daily forays into the countryside, searching for people looking for a place to live. The first week, I came across a small party of women, all middle-aged and weak with hunger and fatigue, and was happy to escort them back to our community. I didn't tell them about Katherine's policies, figuring they'd learn soon enough. I had begun to notice that familiar faces I used to see on a daily basis were no longer present and suspected some of the women were leaving our community. But as Katherine had predicted, the trickle toward our commune soon became a steady stream and I stayed busy leading women back there. When I encountered groups with men, I diverted them north toward Bristol, Tennessee, where Seth had heard there was a democratic commune filled with males and females. Katherine seemed happy with my discoveries and didn't mention assigning me a job and I hoped this meant she was content with what I had chosen for myself or maybe had simply forgotten our discussion. Daily, far enough away that the community would not hear, I set up targets and practiced with the gun I had found. When my ammunition grew low, I would ride into one of the many small towns in the area in search of a gun shop or department store and take what I needed.

After a month, I decided it would be safe enough to go to the farmhouse to check on Seth, Sarah and the baby. I intended to leave Boomer and Adam with them. Although I told myself I had become paranoid over the animals' safety, I did not miss the hungry looks some of the women gave them. Though the thought of leaving them behind filled me with pain, I could not chance their lives. It had gotten to the point where Adam and I slept with

Boomer in his stable at night in case anyone got the idea to try to harm the horse.

I rode out early that morning, heading south, finally circling around to the east, following the trail in the woods, making my way toward the farmhouse. Adam seemed to know he was going home as he ran ahead of me, turning back at times to give me a joyous smile before continuing on. I reined Boomer in at the driveway and circled around, looking in each direction for spying eyes. With a joyful bark, Adam lunged ahead, tearing up the driveway, and I felt sad for him, knowing he would be disappointed his former owners would not be there to greet him. Boomer followed the dog at a fast pace and I peered ahead, feeling a great sense of relief when Seth stepped out onto the wraparound porch. He smiled and waved and I answered his greeting in kind, thankful they had made it safely here. I watched as Seth stooped down to pet Adam, cavorting around his feet.

Seth came down the steps as I hopped off Boomer and caught me up in a hug, twirling me around. I laughed when he set me down and stepped back to get a good look at him. He had filled out nicely, his body hard and muscular and very male. Sarah had made a good choice.

"You have any problems getting here?" I asked as I unsaddled then unbridled Boomer and set him free to graze on the thick green grass.

"Nope. It was slow going with the baby but no one followed us. What about you? Did they suspect anything?"

"Callie did but I don't think Katherine believed her."

"We can't thank you enough for your help, Madison. I'd probably be dead by now if it weren't for you."

I waved that away, impatient to see my friend. "How are Sarah and the baby? Are they here?"

He laughed. "They're in the kitchen. Come on in."

I followed Seth into the house, Adam bounding ahead, barking a greeting. Sarah stood in the doorway of the kitchen and smiled with delight when she saw me. We hugged one another, both speaking at once, tears streaming down our faces. Seth walked over to the table where some sort of carrier sat, filled with a small human form. He unstrapped the tot and carried him over to us, as proud as if he were the baby's biological father. I made admiring comments about how much Travis had grown and how healthy he looked, ignoring their attempts to thank me.

We finally settled down around the kitchen table, Seth with the baby in his arms, Sarah sitting close to him, their legs slightly touching. Love and happiness were thick in the air and for a brief moment I envied them their relationship.

They recounted their uneventful trip to the house and I told them what happened after they left. Seth was surprised but happy to learn another one of the men had escaped. I grew ashamed that I had not found out the man's name so I could relay this information to him. Seth and Sarah seemed saddened by Callie's actions and that nothing had been done to her for murdering Macy but Seth was heartened that there were women in our commune who did not agree with Katherine's and Callie's policies.

"I think Callie's had someone watching me so I waited until I was fairly sure she'd lost interest before I came here," I said. "Have you had any visitors or intruders?"

Seth and Sarah shook their heads in unison.

"It's been quiet here. Perfect place to stay, really," Seth said. "I can see anyone on the road before they even know this house is here. So far, those that pass by don't turn up the drive but just keep on going."

"That's good. Have you seen any animals yet?"

Seth grinned. "Got something I want to show you." With a wink toward Sarah, he handed the baby to her and stepped out of the room.

"What?" I asked.

"You'll see," she said with a sly grin.

Seth came through the door holding a puppy in his hands. She had blonde fur and brown eyes and looked to also have Lab in her.

My hands flew to my mouth. "Oh."

"I found her in the barn one day," he said. "So starved she could barely stand. We've been taking care of her and I think she's going to make it."

"She?" I looked around. "Where's Adam? He'll love having a companion."

Our gazes darted around but Adam was nowhere to be found. "I think I know," I said, rising to my feet.

I walked up the stairs and into the bedroom where I'd found the two bodies. Adam sat at the foot of the neatly-made bed, his eyes on the places where his owners had rested. I sat down beside him and stroked his fur, tears stinging my eyes. "I'm so sorry, Adam. I know you loved them very much and I'm sure they loved you the same."

He looked at me and whined and I could feel his pain. "Come downstairs, boy, we have a surprise for you." I got up and touched his collar, encouraging him to come with me. With reluctance, he followed me down the stairs and into the kitchen. When he spied the pup, he went to her, sniffing and nudging. Still weakened, her response to him was not energetic but she seemed happy to have another dog around her, licking his face and waving her tail. Adam looked at me and wagged his tail and I knew he was happy over this.

I sat on the floor beside them, petting the dogs. "How old do you think she is?"

Seth shook his head. "I'm thinking maybe six months, not much more than that."

"So she was born after the pox."

"Had to have been."

I clapped my hands with delight. "So newborn animals can survive as well. Oh, this is wonderful."

Sarah reached over and grasped my hand, tears shining in her eyes. So the living world just might endure after all.

I sat in the chair, silent for a moment. "I want to leave Boomer and Adam here with y'all, if you don't mind."

Sarah squeezed my hand. "Oh, Madison, I know how you love them both."

I swallowed past the lump in my throat, ignored the nascent tears stinging my eyes. "It's killing me to do it but some of the women are making comments about wanting fresh meat and I don't trust them, Sarah. I couldn't stand it if anything happened to either one."

Seth patted me on the shoulder. "They'll be safe here."

"Do you know how to care for a horse?"

"I do," Sarah said. "We had horses when I was a child. I'll take good care of both of them, I promise you that."

"And you'll hide them if anyone comes? I don't want someone to kill them for food or take them with them."

"I swear, no one will get them," Seth said in a firm tone and I could tell by his set face this meant something to him. "It's the least we can do to thank you for helping us." His face brightened. "And maybe Adam and Eve..." he darted a look at the dogs. "We couldn't think of a better name for her to go with Adam. Maybe they'll breed and we'll have all kinds of puppies running around here."

I smiled with appreciation. "If so, I'd like to take one back to Darlene. She was a veterinary tech before and loves dogs." Then remembered the reason I had decided to leave my furry friends behind and said, "Maybe not."

Sarah touched my arm. "Why don't you stay, Madison? You don't have to go back there."

I shook my head. "I can't jeopardize your safety. Anyone else, they probably wouldn't think twice about it but Katherine would be worried about me. She'd send out a search party and Callie would volunteer to head that party simply so she could find me and make sure I never return."

"She feels that strongly about you?"

"I think she does, Sarah. When she looks at me, I see nothing but hatred in her eyes." I forced myself to smile. "Let's talk about other things. Tell me about your life here."

My visit with my friends passed too quickly. After we ate a quick lunch Sarah put together, I told them I needed to leave. It would be a long walk back to the commune.

Sarah and Seth exchanged a smile. "I've got something else I'd like to show you," Seth said.

"Another animal?" I asked, excitement evident in my voice.

"Of a different kind maybe. Come on." He took my hand and led me to the barn, Sarah following with the baby in her arms.

Seth opened the barn doors, crossed the dirt floor, and pulled a large tarp off an unknown object.

"Oh," I said, staring at it.

"You know how to ride one?"

I shook my head, running my hands over the shiny chrome and black leather on the small motorcycle. "Is it hard?"

"You ever ridden a mountain bike?"

"Uh-huh."

"Easy as pie, then. Come on outside. I'll show you."

"Wait. Are you giving this to me?"

"Since you're giving us Boomer, it's only fair. That way, you can visit more often, not worry so much about travel time. Besides, there's a larger one I can use if I need it."

"It's a deal." I could barely control my excitement as Seth rolled the motorcycle out of the barn and onto the drive. Straddling the bike, he showed me how to give it gas, change gears and use the hand brake. Afterwards, he had me sit behind him while he rode around the property surrounding the house, then got off and told me to try it. I had a bit of a problem at first with the gears but by the end of an hour I'd gotten the hang of it and was racing alongside the gravel driveway and into the yard with confidence.

I braked to a stop and put the kickstand down, happy at my success.

"Oh, wait, there's something else." Sarah handed Travis over to Seth and raced into the house. She returned with a bright, neon-pink helmet. "For you, Madison. I think pink is your color."

I laughed with delight as I strapped on the helmet. My gaze landed on Boomer, grazing nearby, Adam and the pup on the porch watching us. I burst into tears.

"Oh," Sarah said, pulling me into a hug. "I'm so sorry, Madison."

"I can't bear the thought of leaving them," I said into her shoulder, tears soaking her shirt.

Seth, standing silently beside us, put his hand on my shoulder. "We'll take good care of them but you should visit often. I know they'll miss you."

"And we will too," Sarah said.

I pulled away from her embrace, embarrassed at my display of emotion, realizing I had held too much in for too long. "I'll just go say bye and then I better leave," I told them.

I walked onto the porch, knelt beside Adam, hugged him, kissed the top of his head. He gave me a sad look. I suspected he knew he wouldn't be going back with me. "You'll have a happy life here again," I told him. "Boomer, another dog to play with, Seth and Sarah to look after you. And a baby to protect." Adam whined and nudged me with his nose. I kissed him again. "It's for the best, buddy. I'll be back to see you soon."

With one last pat, I left him behind and walked onto the yard to Boomer. The horse raised his head and looked at me as if asking if I were ready to go. "You'll stay here with Adam, Boomer," I told him, tears streaming down my face. "It's safe and Seth and Sarah will see that you're well fed and comfortable." Boomer nickered and I buried my face in his neck, stroking that long, elegant muscle, giving into my grief. Cried out, I stepped back and kissed him between the ears. With one last stroke, I turned my back on him but could hear Boomer following me. I looked at Seth and Sarah, standing close, holding hands. "Maybe we should put him in the barn until I leave."

Seth nodded. "Afterward, I'll keep him in that corral behind the barn. It's hidden from the road and there's plenty of grass for grazing."

"If you can find a co-op, get some oats for him. He likes having oats at night. And be sure to keep his water fresh. He's a great horse." I swallowed hard, my throat burning, nose running, tears streaming.

"We'll take good care of him, Madison." Sarah hugged me once more. "But please, come visit us at least once or twice a week. You have the motorcycle and it won't be a long trip for you anymore."

I nodded, watching as Sarah expertly looped the lead rope around Boomer's neck then led him to the barn. "We have oats here from before," she said over her shoulder.

"Make sure it's not moldy," I called after her.

"It's still in unopened bags," Seth said, "but I'll check to make sure it's good."

Seth and I stared at each other for a long moment. "Take care of them."

He nodded. "I'll protect them with my life."

"Do you need a gun?"

"Found some in the house."

"You know how to use them?"

He gave me a look. "I was a soldier in Afghanistan, kiddo. I think I can handle a gun."

"Oh, yeah, I forgot about that." I opened my saddlebag, extracted my own gun, tucked it into the back of my jeans.

Seth's eyebrows arched with surprise. He grinned at me. "There's a lot more to you than meets the eyes."

I smiled at what I perceived to be mock admiration in his voice as I threw the saddlebag over my seat. "Kiss Sarah for me." I bussed him on the cheek before putting on my helmet and straddling the cycle. I started it and without looking at him raced down the drive and onto the road, tears rolling down my cheeks.

A mile away, I pulled off the road, got off the motorcycle and collapsed to my knees, crying with grief. Would I ever see them again? Were they truly safe? Could I have done more for my friends, human and animal?

Once under control, I returned to the commune in well under an hour. Instead of storing the motorcycle in the barn, I decided to take it to my small apartment house and chain it there to keep it safe. I stopped on the outskirts of the campus and stowed the gun in the small satchel attached to the bike. Women stopped and stared at me as I passed but I ignored them, feeling nothing but hatred and loathing for a group that forced me to give up the two things that meant more to me than my own life.

At dinner, I sat alone, startling when Katherine pulled out a seat and sat beside me. She gently reached over, stroked my cheek. I looked up at her and noted the shock registering on her face. It seemed my swollen eyes and red nose gave me away.

"What happened, Madison? Are you all right?" Concern showed in her eyes and I felt remorse for the seed of hatred I could feel germinating for her.

"I lost them."

"I heard you came in on a motorcycle. What happened to the horse and dog?"

Horse and dog? They had names! "They ran off. I was eating lunch in a meadow when we heard what sounded like gunshots. Boomer bolted and took off and Adam chased after him. I looked and looked for them but couldn't find them." I hesitated, shocked at how easy it was to lie so convincingly. I suppose my teary state helped in that regard.

"I can have Callie put together a search party for them if you'd like."

I stared at her. Was she sincere? I shook my head. "No. It's probably better. I hope they find a place to themselves. Some of the women here kept talking about wanting fresh meat and I didn't like the way they looked at them. They're probably safer away from here."

"Oh, Madison, you know I would never have condoned that."

"Yes, but once the deed was done, what could you have done to protect them?" My voice rang with bitterness. I pushed back from the table. "I'm sorry, Katherine. I'm not feeling well. I think I'll go home."

I walked to my apartment in the twilight, lost in thoughts, and didn't see Callie standing beside the motorcycle until I almost collided with her. I stepped back, glad the gloaming hid my expression from her.

She ran her hand over the leather seat. "Nice bike."

Panic traced through me. Had she opened the compartment, seen the gun? "What do you want, Callie?"

"Where'd you find it?"

"On the road, abandoned."

"The horse and dog?"

"Ran off."

She nodded. "Probably for the best."

"Probably." I coughed when my voice cracked.

"Well, for what it's worth, I'm sorry about that."

"Thank you."

"Who taught you how to ride a bike?"

"My dad, when I was younger." Another lie. And so convincing!

"My dad too." She patted my helmet, sitting on the seat. "Well, just be careful and be sure to wear your helmet." She gave me a whimsical smile. "It's the law, you know."

"I will."

She nodded, adding before she left, "I chained it for you. Don't want anybody stealing it. Here's the key." She pressed it into my hand, briefly squeezing. "Goodnight, Madison."

I watched her walk away, wondering why she would do something so thoughtful for someone she seemed to hate so much.

I mounted my motorcycle each day and rode out, searching for wanderers looking for a place to stay. As the warm months progressed, so did the number of people seeking refuge, the greater percentage of which were middle-aged and elderly women. As before, I directed the men to another commune but guided those women who were interested back to Katherine who teased me I should be renamed the Pied Piper. I began to despair at the lack of women of child-bearing age and knew before long Katherine would be on me again about mating with one of the others. But I continued to hold my tongue with regard to her policies and even at times could manage to be civil to Callie. I was more affectionate with Katherine, something she seemed to appreciate and which I found not as unpleasant as I thought it would be. I ignored any talk about the others but knew at some point I would be forced to make a decision; be part of the life of this dictatorial community where men were either enslaved or killed, or leave. And if I left, Callie would pursue me with a vengeance simply to make sure I never returned.

At least twice a week I visited Seth and Sarah and my two animal friends, who seemed happy and content in their new home. Adam and the pup were inseparable and spent a good deal of time hanging around Boomer as if guarding him from some unknown danger. My times with them were happy and stress-free and I always dreaded my return to the commune. But I would not endanger their lives simply because I was so unhappy with my own.

And when Katherine approached me about the procreation program, I had no recourse but to agree to it, although insisting I once again be allowed to choose my mate. She gave me a speculative glance as she leaned back in her chair. "Since the episode with Seth and Sarah, Callie and I have revamped our procreation policy as a means to protect our females."

Apprehension skittered up my spine. "What do you mean?"

"We don't think it's a good idea to constantly pair one man and one woman. We're rotating the men among the women."

I sat straighter in my seat. "Why?"

"Well, it's apparent you and Seth were friends of some sort." She held her hands up when I started to protest. "After all, Madison, you passed notes from him to Sarah and in doing so perhaps helped him escape or at least make plans to escape with Sarah."

"I did it for Sarah, Katherine. Seth had nothing to do with it."

"Perhaps. In any event, you in a sense collaborated with him, something we certainly don't want occurring between our women and the others."

"How many men are you talking about?"

"Six to ten. Depending on the rotation plan Callie has in place."

"For how long?"

"I'm not sure what you mean, Madison."

"One night per man or a week with him?"

"One night."

"I won't do it. I can't." Panic rode my voice.

Katherine gave me a hard look. "And why not?"

A blush crept up my face. I forced myself to look at her. "Because I was a virgin with Seth. I don't have much experience with men. I don't want to be put out there like a prostitute, having sex with a different man each night. I can't bear the thought of it." My voice broke. "I'll leave," I added. "I'll go live somewhere else if you want that from me."

Katherine sighed. "I didn't know you felt so strongly about this." She thought for a moment. "Let me speak with Callie. Perhaps we'll start with one man and see how that goes."

"Thank you, Katherine, thank you so much," I said with relief.

A couple of days later, I rode onto the compound and noticed a small group of people gathered in what we had begun to term the town square, a small four-cornered lawn in front of the building housing Katherine's offices. I moved closer, curious to see who had joined us now. Callie and her deputies surrounded a young man, surely no more than twenty, who glared at them under drawn brows. He was tall, well over six feet, and well-built with wide shoulders, muscular arms and thighs, a narrow waist and long legs. His black hair lay long and shaggy against his collar. His eyes were the color of moss and very intense. I felt a tug inside my abdomen, a feeling I had never experienced before, and realized with a shock that I was attracted to him. I watched as Callie and her deputies struggled with the man, trying to handcuff him. It took all of them to do it and I admired his unwillingness to go passively with them. As they passed me, practically dragging him, for a brief moment our eyes met and my heart fluttered. Yes, actually fluttered at the look he gave me. I caught my hands reaching out to him and quickly returned them to my sides. Well. Perhaps my answer lay with him. I would not sleep with him but surely his hostility toward his captors would be enough to convince him to go along with my deception. I would choose him as my mate and hope that he would be my co-conspirator, at least until I could figure out what to do.

I went to Katherine's office the next morning. "I've decided," I said in the doorway, and waited for her to catch up to what I was talking about.

After a brief moment, she smiled. "Oh, that's good, Madison. And with whom did you decide you want to mate?"

"The one Callie brought in yesterday. I don't know his name."

Katherine frowned. "We're having a bit of a problem with him. It would be better if you choose another one of the others."

"No, I want him. He's tall, good-looking, strong, an excellent biological specimen for procreation purposes."

Katherine barked a laugh. "You sound so scientific."

I shrugged. "A way my father would have put it, perhaps." I paused, thinking of him, wondering what he would think of this convoluted world. As a scientist, I'm sure he would have been a bit fascinated, but as a man and father, horrified.

Katherine leaned back in her chair. "Yes, he certainly is a viable candidate when you consider those attributes." She nodded. "I'll speak with Callie, see if she can convince him to get with the program."

Or he'd die otherwise, I thought but didn't voice.

She leaned back in her chair and smiled. "Have you heard?"

Heard what? The only time I stayed within the commune was to help with the clearance but I never interacted with the deputies guarding the others. I had begun to look upon them as

Callie's minions, there to do her dirty deed. During meal times, I usually ate alone. At times I would say hello to Suzie or Darlene or Shelly if I saw them but never spoke with them for any length of time. I forced a smile on my face. "Must be good news."

"We have two pregnancies now." She laughed at the surprised look on my face. "Yes, two."

"Who?"

"Tonya and Hannah. Suzie did the pregnancy test on both this past week and both were positive. After dinner tonight, we're having a celebration at the cafeteria. I hope you'll be there."

My lips seemed frozen but I managed to tilt them upward. "Of course I'll be there. I'm happy for them. Are they excited?"

Katherine gave me a wary look. "Why wouldn't they be?"

"Well, we don't have a doctor here, Katherine. That does concern me, you know."

"Suzie and her team did a wonderful job with Sarah. I don't think they or you have anything to worry about."

"You're right. I just meant if there were complications or anything."

"We should be fine. One of the women in the group you brought in last week was a midwife in her former life. I'm sure if anything out of the ordinary occurs, she'll know what to do."

Former life, I thought. Had all that had happened before the pox been whittled down to that simple term? I mentally sighed, thinking, yes, that's exactly what it was.

And that night, I left the cafeteria without eating, telling Katherine I had a stomachache, claiming the chicken salad sandwich I ate at lunch must have soured. And tried not to overthink the look Katherine gave me, as if she detected the lie and knew the reason behind it. But I could not tolerate the joyous sense of celebration that permeated the atmosphere, which seemed contrived, forced. I noticed several women also chose to leave, slipping out quietly, without drawing attention to themselves, and wondered if they were part of the group that did not agree with Katherine's policies.

CHAPTER 11

Five nights later, Callie escorted the young man I had requested to my apartment. When I answered the door, she stood behind him, her eyes never leaving his arms and hands. Without looking at me, she said, "Here he is. I'll come back for him at midnight." She raised her eyes to mine. "If he gives you any trouble, yell out. Sandra's right outside the door and she'll take care of him." Her eyes narrowed and her lips tightened. "If he gets away, it'll be worse for you than last time. I'll make sure of that." She pushed him into the apartment, reached forward, grabbed the door handle and pulled it closed. I listened as she slid the bolt home on the other side. A new addition since Seth escaped.

I made sure to lock the deadbolt, my message to her if I couldn't get out, she couldn't get in until I let her. I turned back to him. We stared at one another for a long moment. I could feel my face going red. This was so very awkward.

He stepped toward me and I backed away. I imagined the fresh bruise on his temple wasn't accidental. "Just so you know, I'm not sleeping with you," he said, his voice hard, his eyes cold. "I don't care if they kill me for that."

Relief washed through me at that and I didn't bother hiding it. I could see my reaction surprised him. This was quickly replaced by embarrassment and a rejected feeling. Was I that unattractive? I tried not to let those thoughts show.

"I don't want to sleep with you, either. They're crazy for thinking this."

He nodded his agreement.

I retreated to the couch, picked up my book, and pretended to read. He prowled around, a restless expression on his face. I surreptitiously watched him, ignoring that tug of attraction I had felt before. He was a magnificent specimen, tall and broadly built. The contrast between his dark hair and dark-green eyes was stunning. When he glanced my way, I buried my nose in the book, pretending indifference, although suspected he knew otherwise. I spoke when I noticed him studying the balcony.

"Can't get out that way. They put grillwork over the door." Another addition since Seth got away. It didn't escape my notice that mine was the first to be installed.

His eyes fell on me, reminding me of moss on rocks in a stream in a deep, dark forest. "Any other way to get out of here?"

"I wish."

"Would you tell me if there were?"

"Of course I would."

"So you're saying you're not agreeable with this?" He swept his arm between the two of us.

"I just live here. I'm not ready to have a baby and I really don't want to be pregnant. I'm only going along with this to keep Callie from getting suspicious."

"Callie, the crazy gendarme in charge."

"The very one."

He cast a wary look my way. "I've seen you with—what's the name of the one they call the leader? Katherine?"

"She brought me here."

He stopped in front of an overstuffed chair, studied it for a moment then plopped down. "So, what are we gonna do for four hours?"

"You can do what you want. I'm reading." To illustrate this, I picked up my book and turned a page.

He drummed his fingers on the chair rest. I glanced up, caught him watching me. "What?"

"How old are you?"

I tried not to look at my shapeless body; instead, lifted my chin with indignation. "Eighteen. How old are you?"

One side of his mouth quirked. "Twenty."

"Man of the world, no doubt."

He smiled at that. He had a nice smile, kind of lopsided on his face, which I found very appealing.

We stared at one another. He looked away. "So, are you part of..." he hesitated as if unsure what to say, "...this?"

"I'm not sure what you mean."

He lunged to his feet, paced to the sliding glass doors, stared at the iron grillwork. "What they're doing here."

I remained silent.

"Listen, I'm not stupid. It's pretty easy to figure out. There aren't any old guys here or sickly ones. They're doing something to them, getting rid of them. There's talk they're killing them. And the ones that are left they're imprisoning for manual labor and their damned stud pool."

I put my book aside. "I'm not part of it, I don't agree with it."

He studied my face as if checking for veracity.

"It's Katherine's and Callie's idea. They blame man for the destruction of the populace, mean to see man never has control again."

He snorted.

"I agree. It's ridiculous but listen to it long enough and it makes sense. Through their propaganda, they've managed to convince the women here that they're right, it's our turn now, we have the power." I shrugged. "After all, we outnumber y'all practically two to one."

"God help us," he muttered.

"Amen to that."

His lips twitched. He settled back in the chair. "You from this part of the country?"

I shook my head. "My family lived in Atlanta. My dad worked for the CDC there."

He cocked an eyebrow my way. "He one of those idiots that released the virus?"

My face grew hot. "Of course not. He was an epidemiologist, one of the ones trying to save us from it. He's dead, by the way, along with my mother."

His eyes softened before pain flitted through them. "I'm sorry to hear that. So are mine."

We regarded one another for a long moment. "Did any of your family make it through?" I asked in a low voice.

"Nope. Lost everyone. What about you?"

"Same here."

He drummed his fingers on the arm of the chair, glanced out the glass doors. "So, did you have a boyfriend before man so deviously destroyed the world?"

I didn't miss the ironic tone to his voice but chose to ignore it. "No. I wish now I had."

He cocked his head. "Yeah? Why's that?"

I wasn't about to let him know I was a virgin. Not yet, if ever. "I was in college, away from home, didn't have time to cultivate close friendships before all this crap started."

He studied me for a long moment. "I find that hard to believe, you know. You're too pretty not to have had guys all over you."

Was he being facetious? I ducked my head so he wouldn't see my blush. "What about you? Did you have a girlfriend?"

I glanced up as his eyes came back to me, sad and filled with pain. "Yeah. I was engaged. We were going to get married after college."

"I'm sorry."

He waved a hand in the air. "We all lost people we loved."

My thoughts swept back to my childhood, back when my mother and father were happy together and all seemed right with the world. Before he started working for the CDC, before he became so caught up in his work nothing else existed. He had died at his lab, frantically trying to find a cure for the pox, to save humankind. If my mother had lived, I don't know if she would ever have forgiven him for abandoning her when she needed him most.

When he moved, I startled, having forgotten he was there. He stood at the bookshelf, studying the books and assorted board games. He pulled out the Scrabble box. When my eyes met his, he smiled and held it up. "You play?"

"Haven't in years but I remember how."

"Good. Let's play. It will help pass the time."

He put the game on the coffee table, leaned toward me, extending his hand. "I'm Jonah, by the way. Jonah McMahan."

I returned his shake, hesitating at the heat from his palm, the answering vibration in my own. "Madison Belleu." I paused after saying my last name. It had been so long since I had spoken the word, it felt awkward rolling off my tongue. "Nice to meet you."

Playing Scrabble helped break the tension between us. The first couple of games were stilted, almost formal. By the third, we were aware of the other's lexis ability so began challenging one another. Eventually we were laughing together, enjoying the game. In those few short hours, I forgot about the world outside, my worries over staying or leaving, what Callie was doing to the men she escorted out of town.

Until someone pounded on the door at midnight. I sighed. "Callie."

Jonah stood up and stretched. "How do you want to play this?"

I threw the tiles and their holders into the box, stuffed it under the couch. "What do you mean?"

"Did we do it or not?" His eyes seemed lighter, not so weighted down with annoyance or pain. He laughed at my grimace. "It's your choice. But if we don't, they'll place me with someone else."

Callie banged again and I called out, "Just a minute, I'm getting dressed."

Our eyes met. "That way?"

I nodded. "Yes. At least we both feel the same about this. I don't want to chance it with anyone else."

He lightly chucked me under the chin as if I were his younger sister. "Good choice. I agree." He walked away, opened the door, gave Callie a victorious grin. "I could have used a few more hours," he said as he strode out the door.

Callie leaned her head in. "You okay?"

I couldn't meet her gaze. "I'm fine. I'll see you tomorrow."

For the next several weeks, except during my menses, Callie escorted Jonah to my apartment, locked us in together, and came back several hours later to collect him. While together, we played Scrabble, card games, read aloud to one another, and eventually began to talk about our lives before the pox. I was intrigued to learn Jonah wanted to be a veterinarian, something I had seriously considered. I told him about finding Boomer and Adam and smiled at the excitement he showed at this bit of news.

When he asked what happened to them, I stuck to the same story I told Katherine. Maybe one day I would tell him about Seth and Sarah and how I helped them escape but not now, not like this.

I liked to watch him, the way his facial expression always seemed so somber and stern yet his eyes gave away his moods, feelings, emotions. He came from a large family and told glorious anecdotes about his childhood with his siblings and the pranks they played on one another. As a single child, I had no such memories and encouraged him each night to tell me another story.

Slowly I began to realize I was becoming fiercely attracted to him. He stood a good six inches higher than me with a broad build but now so thin that the angle of his cheekbones dominated his face and I could see his ribs push against his t-shirt when he breathed. He assured me they were giving him enough to eat but I knew they worked the men like farm animals with few leisure times and his caloric intake probably did not match his output. So I made sure to squirrel away fruits and desserts which I gave to him each night, watching as he seemed to inhale them. His black hair was long and shaggy, his eyes that beautiful moss color. I wondered what it would be like to kiss his wide mouth, feel his large hands on my body. I had never felt like this toward a man and found it exciting and stimulating. My dreams were now filled with the two of us engaged in eroticisms together, a new experience for me. I would wake, drenched with sweat, my heart pounding, my body aching for his touch. During the day, I would count the hours until I saw him. When Callie delivered him, I had to refrain from reaching out, touching him, glad he was still alive and I could spend the next several hours with him. I cut down my soirees outside the community to two or three days a week and began working with the clearing group once more simply to be near him. As I worked, I watched him peripherally, the way the muscles in his body moved, the set of his jaw, hoping to catch that fierce, intense gaze of his. And when his eyes met mine, my heart would lurch and my breath would quicken and I could not turn my gaze from his until he released me. I had once watched a cat hypnotize a bird, fascinated that the bird seemed frozen in place, slightly swaying as the cat held it with its gaze, and now knew I was the prey and he the hunter and it thrilled me. I never spoke to him or sought interaction with him, well aware Callie and her deputies would be alert for any sign I might be friendly with him, but always, always, I would catch him giving me a look as if he knew exactly what I was doing.

But alone together, he treated me like a kid sister, which I found irritating once I knew my feelings for him went beyond friendship. After all, what could I offer? My chestnut-colored hair fell straight and thick down my back; my dark-brown eyes seemed too large for my face. Tall, thin, and angular, I knew my body did not offer a woman's soft curves or cushiony feel but I yearned for him to want to touch me as I did him. I missed him terribly when I was menstruating and realized with a jolt that he was my only close friend here.

Alone, in the dark, after he had gone, I would replay our time together, fantasize about what might have been. In the early morning hours, I began to wake from the same nightmare: I was alone, riding Boomer across the fields beyond the campus and came across a man's body. When I dismounted, I leaned over to look into the face and found myself staring into Jonah's beautiful eyes, glazed and staring into nothingness.

When Katherine questioned me about Jonah, I assured her we were having sex and all was well but suspected if something didn't happen soon, they would place me with another man. She and Callie were frantic to add to their stockpile of people and demanded all the single women of child-bearing age who entered the compound agree to their procreation policy. So far, none had refused their request. Most seemed relieved to have found a safe harbor and I thought they would have agreed to anything in order to be able to remain. If anyone refused, I was certain Callie would in all probability personally escort them out of town but I wondered if she would actually leave them at the border or take their lives.

After two months, Callie found me at a job site and ordered me to accompany her to Katherine's office. I knew this had to be about Jonah and me. It seemed each week Katherine was announcing another pregnancy, and as the youngest, she for some inexplicable reason felt I should have no problem becoming impregnated.

We found Katherine at her desk working on policies for the commune which she seemed proud to call a constitution. I briefly wondered if I were in some sort of nightmare that didn't have an end. Katherine smiled when she saw me, motioning me to sit in the chair in front of her desk. Callie stood near the door as if guarding it in case I wanted to escape.

Katherine sat back in her chair, studying me. "How are you, darling?"

I smiled simply to force a chipper tone into my voice. "Great. Couldn't be better. As I'm sure you know, we've cleared the first two quadrants and hope to have the next done by the end of the week."

"Yes, I know, and our little community looks so much better, doesn't it?"

"Sure smells a lot better," Callie muttered.

Katherine sent a chilling glare her way. "And how are things with Jonah?"

"Fine, Katherine. No problem."

She leaned toward me. "You are sleeping with him, aren't you?"

I struggled not to squirm in my seat. "Of course. Why would you ask that?"

"It's been almost three months. You're not pregnant."

"Oh, really, Katherine, that isn't enough time." She frowned at my defiance. "I've been reading up on the subject and have learned it can take as long as a year, you know. Besides, with all the pressure you two are putting us under, it's a wonder any one of us can conceive. That's all we think about, and to be honest about it, I'm a little sick of gauging whether or not I make you happy by my next period."

Katherine seemed to consider my words. With a sigh, she said, "Well, you're right, it can take awhile, but you're so healthy, I thought you would be one of the first to become impregnated."

"Apparently not."

Her eyes narrowed. "How often do you have sex?"

I looked away, my face reddening. "Every time we're together." I returned my gaze to her. "Isn't that what you want?"

"Of course, dear. But maybe we should consider placing you with someone else."

I lowered my eyes so she could not see my panic. "Of all the men you have here, Jonah's the only one I would consider. He's close to my age and in good health. He meets the physical and mental requirements necessary to ensure my daughter is strong and intelligent."

Callie snorted. "Since when does she get to make the decisions?"

Katherine shot a cold glance her way before turning back to me. "You do find it pleasurable, I hope."

"At this point, it's a chore I need to do to keep you two from kicking my ass out of here."

Katherine looked shocked at this. "Madison, dear, I love you. I would never ask you to leave our home."

I rose to my feet. "I'm not so sure about that. Not anymore." I turned on my heel and walked over to the door. Callie barred my way. I stared at her, waiting for her to give way. She looked at Katherine and, apparently receiving the signal, stepped aside.

That night, seething with anger, I told Jonah about my conversation with Katherine. He watched me pace around, throwing my hands in the air, restless with frustration.

"Maybe we should just do it."

I stopped pacing and glared at him. "What the hell? I thought you didn't want to do it. Besides, I won't sleep with someone who isn't attracted to me or doesn't have feelings for me."

He stepped closer. "And what if I do?"

"Do what?"

"Have feelings for you. Feel attracted to you."

I studied his eyes. They were warm, affectionate. "Don't lie to me, Jonah."

"I'm not lying." He reached out, traced my cheek with one finger. "Listen, I know you don't feel the same for me, I don't expect that." He shrugged. "After all, I'm one of the others."

I waved this off. "You know I don't believe that crap."

"Still, you're part of the community. I'm not. I'm here for one reason only. But I do care about you, Madison. You're my friend. I've gotten to know you over the past couple of months, and I started having feelings for you that first night."

I tried not to gape. "But you treat me like a kid sister."

"I've been trying to treat you like my kid sister. I got to tell you, it gets harder each time I'm with you."

Oh, how I yearned to pull him to me, kiss that beautiful mouth. I almost did until one lone thought entered my mind. "I don't want to get pregnant."

"I don't want to impregnate you, at least, not unless we were married or committed to one another." He paused. "And away from here." He clasped my hands in his. "At least tell me you have some sort of feeling for me, Madison. It's killing me not knowing how you feel about me."

I squeezed his hands. "Oh, I've had feelings for you for a good while, Jonah. I didn't know you felt the same for me."

I went into his arms and we finally shared a kiss. By the time we broke apart, I felt as if my body were awakening from a long sleep as tingles swept across my spine, an electric sensation flared in my lower abdomen, raced into my legs.

We stared into one another's eyes. His seemed lit, as if with deep pleasure. Or that's what I hoped.

"What are we going to do?" I whispered.

"It's your choice."

"I don't want to get pregnant."

"Then we won't go all the way. There are other ways to make love, you know."

But I wanted to go all the way. I didn't want to be a virgin anymore.

He led me toward the bedroom. I pulled back. He turned to me with a questioning look in his eyes. "What?"

"I'm a virgin. I've never had intercourse before."

He watched me for a moment. "That's okay. Like I said, we won't do that."

"No. I want to, Jonah. I want to make love to you. I've wanted that for awhile now."

"Oh. Well. Don't get me wrong. I want that too, but what if you get pregnant?"

"I'll sneak into the campus drugstore tomorrow and get condoms."

He smiled. "Great idea. And for tonight, I guess, we'll just indulge in some heavy foreplay."

I smiled back. But later, after he was gone, as I lay in bed, my body for once relaxed and content, the thought niggled at my brain that perhaps Jonah had his own agenda in play here. If I declared my love for him, he would, of course, expect me to want to help him escape. I stared down at my body, wondering what he would see in someone like me. And decided yes, indeed, that must be it. I debated taking this thing with him forward and decided I would, only for my own pleasure. After all, after tonight, I could not go back to before. And we would see how it played out.

The next day, I made a trip to the campus drugstore, thankful no one lurked inside. I strolled through the aisles looking for the condoms, my face flaming red. I snatched the first package I saw off the shelf and stuffed it deep into the pocket of my jeans, grabbed a bottle of Pepto Bismol on my way out the door in case I met anyone and they were curious why I was there. As I stepped outside, squinting my eyes against the bright sun, a voice spoke behind me.

"What are you doing here?"

Callie! I spun around, a grimace on my face, thankful I'd had the foresight to take the bottle of Pepto Bismol I held out for her to see. "Got a stomachache, thought I'd see if this would help."

She studied me for a long moment. "You sure that's all you were after in there?"

My eyebrows pulled together. "Are you questioning my reason for going in a drugstore, Callie?"

She shrugged. "I'm curious why you came here. I'm sure Suzie has something in the infirmary that could help you."

"She stays so busy, I didn't want to bother her. This always worked for me. If it doesn't, I'll go see her."

Callie watched me for a moment longer then said as she turned, "Make sure you check the expiration date on that medicine. We've had some women get sick from taking meds that were expired."

"Will do." I spun around and headed toward my bike, noting as I walked the top of the brightly-colored condom pack peeking out of my jeans pocket.

And that night, after we made love, lying in each other's arms, I feared I would do anything for him, whether he loved me or not.

The following weeks passed in a haze of days filled with combing the countryside on my motorcycle searching for stragglers or visiting Seth and Sarah and my animal friends, and nights filled with such heat I feared my body would ignite. Days longing for him, nights quenching that hunger. But a small part of me waited, knowing the words would be spoken by him before long: help me escape. And then what would I do? Would he want me to go with him or would he leave me behind, a means to an end no longer needed? Discarded as though garbage? When he whispered love words to me, I wanted to believe them but always, always, that seed of doubt germinating and growing strong during the times I wasn't with him, so strong that at times I hated him and wished I'd never seen him. But when he was there, oh, no other thoughts but my love and need for him.

CHAPTER 12

I stood at the barred window, the night's breeze chilling my nude body. Closing my eyes, I breathed deep, my mind in turmoil.

I turned around and my gaze met his in the dark. We stared at one another for a long moment.

"God, you're so beautiful," he said.

Oh, if only I could believe you, I thought.

He got out of bed and came toward me. I watched him, that fine, hard masculine body moving with a panther's grace, the male part of him which only moments before seemed so large and so pleasing now so soft and insignificant. Heat traveled my body and I felt a grabbing sensation in my lower abdomen. I clenched my fists, only to keep from reaching out to him.

He put his hand on my neck, drew me toward him. "Come here. You've got goose bumps."

I allowed the embrace for a moment before moving away. He watched me, a curious expression on his face. But he remained taciturn, turning back to the bed and sitting upon it, his back against the headboard. He picked up a cigarette pack from the nightstand and shook out a cigarette. He looked at me, held it up and said in a low voice, "Thanks for this." I nodded. It thrilled me to be able to provide him with things he could not obtain for himself. He lit the cigarette, the flame highlighting that angular face, those dark-green eyes. Seven minutes. That's exactly how long it took him to smoke one, how long it would be before his hands were on me once more.

I prowled the room, picking up things, running my fingertips over them, liking the tactile sensations.

I glanced up and met his gaze once more. "Is it always like this?" I asked, setting down the carved figurine I had been tracing.

He smiled but his lips did not part. After a moment, he said, in a low voice, "No. At least, not for me."

I picked up the figurine once more, noticed somewhat ironically it was a man and woman, legs and arms entwined, lips meeting. "You're my first but you know that. I didn't know if it was this…" I searched for the right word "…intense." I looked at him once more. "Between other men and women."

He shook his head. "I can only answer for myself."

My body ached for him already, although we had made love only moments before and soft throbs still pulsed throughout my body. My fingers yearned to trace the muscles of his chest, stroke him, feel him. Put my mouth on his, taste him. I watched him take a final puff of the cigarette and put it out in the crystal ashtray on the nightstand.

He watched me as he exhaled smoke through his nose. "I look at you and I'm on fire," he said in a low voice. "I can't stop thinking about you. I can't keep from touching you. Sometimes it's agony."

With a sigh, I went into his arms, pressed my mouth against his. "God help me," I said, before losing myself in his body.

And afterward, the words I'd been waiting and dreading to hear, whispered into my ear while his hands moved over my body. "Help me escape, Madison."

I froze and he pulled back, stiff and rigid.

His eyes met mine. "What?"

I lunged off the bed, began to get dressed.

"What, Madison? What is it?" He got to his feet, approached me.

I held my hands in front of my body, warding him off. "Don't talk to me. Don't say another word. Not for the rest of the night."

He picked up his clothes and began to dress. I walked through the living area into the kitchen and stared at the clock. Another hour before Callie came. I debated alerting her but decided not to. She would know something was wrong and I wasn't about to face questions from Callie or Katherine tonight. Not until I figured this out.

I made hot tea for myself then decided it would only be polite to make tea for Jonah too. I stepped back into the living room where he sat on the sofa ramrod straight, his face impassive.

"Thanks," he said in a rough voice when I handed the cup to him.

I sat in the armchair across from him. He took a sip before placing the tea on the coffee table between us. Leaned forward, stared into my face. I looked away.

"Look, Madison, I'm sorry I said that, okay? It's not fair to put you in that position. Forget I said it."

I wanted to throw the tea at him. How could I ever forget it? Saying it while we made love made the act itself ersatz, inferior. Not an act of love, an act of using. A means to an end kept repeating itself over and over in my mind. "You shouldn't have," I said. "Not while…" I looked down, trying to hide the furious blush riding my face.

He sighed. "You're right. It just slipped out. I've wanted to say it before but thought you'd think I was using you. And I'm not. I promise you that. I love you, Maddie. I want you to leave with me."

My head jerked up at that. "And then what? Leave me behind when you think you're safe? They'll kill me if I help you escape, Jonah."

"I would never leave you behind, Madison, never place your life in jeopardy. I want a life with you, I want us to be together." He grew quiet for a moment then added in a low voice, "Besides, you did it once before."

"Who told you that?"

He stared at me. "Don't you know how the men see you? They think of you as their savior. They know you helped two others escape along with a woman and her baby. They know you don't agree with the policies of this community any more than I do. You've told me that yourself."

"Katherine saved me. I owe her."

"Not your life. You don't owe her that."

I turned and glanced at the clock once more. Thirty minutes.

"What the hell are you going to do, Madison? Stay here and mate with whomever they tell you to until you're pregnant? Bear children year after year after year so they can build numbers? What's their plan anyway? To have a community large enough to take over all the other communities out there? To rule the country? Rule the world?"

Thoughts I'd had myself although I chose not to tell him that.

"I love you, Maddie. More than anyone. I want you with me. But I'll tell you something. Even if you don't help me escape, I'll do it one way or the other or die trying."

I got up, went into my bedroom and closed the door. And only when I heard Callie knock on the door, heard it close behind Jonah did I allow the tears to come.

The next day, I headed out early on the motorcycle. I debated going to see Seth and Sarah but changed my mind. I needed to decide what to do about Jonah. Of course, I wouldn't turn him in to Katherine and Callie but did I want to help him? A huge part of me hoped he was telling me the truth when he said he wanted me to go with him but I wasn't assured this was what he truly wanted. After all, he had loved before, had been engaged. How could his feelings for me compare to someone he wanted to marry and be with for the rest of his life, a woman he may still be grieving? Having been a virgin and never in love, I had nothing to compare him to, no standard baseline. I snorted at that thought, wondering what my scientific father would have thought of me using those words when speaking of love.

I stopped for lunch at a park in the small city near our community college. I had grown so accustomed to being alone with only silence for company that the sound of voices startled me. I jumped to my feet, looking around. They sounded like they were coming from a small ridgeline near the border of the park. Thinking it may be stragglers looking for a community to call home, I walked that way. When I heard Callie's angry voice, I knelt down and crept forward, curious what she could be doing out here. Hiding behind a conglomeration of large rocks, I peeked through a slender space between two abutted against one another. Callie and Sandra, the deputy Seth called Crazy Eyes, were standing over one of the others, an older man who looked too frail to be doing what they were forcing him to. Why in the world were they making him dig a hole, I wondered, until I saw Callie snatch the shovel out of his hand and shove him in the shallow opening in the ground. A grave, I thought, just as Callie pulled her gun and shot him. I watched in horror as his head flew back and blood and bits of flesh and brain exploded into the air. Stifling a scream, I ducked behind the rock just as Callie's head shot up. God help me if she found me here. I waited for her to search for me but after a few moments heard nothing but dirt hitting the ground. I peeked between the rocks again and saw Callie and Sandra filling in the grave. So it was Callie doing the shooting, after all. My stomach rolled at the vision of all those dead bodies I'd come across in my ramblings, all those neat bullet holes in their foreheads.

Another voice, one I recognized but I couldn't see her. I took the chance, raised my head and watched Katherine approach Callie, saying something to her, paying about as much attention to the hole in the earth and the dead man crumpled there as she would have to an ant crossing her trail. The wind shifted and her voice drifted toward me. "I thought I told you to bury them deep," she said, kicking at the man's foot, still at ground level.

"It's deep enough," Callie said, a belligerent look on her face.

Katherine picked up the shovel. "I don't want Madison finding any more bodies, Callie. She already suspects you're killing the others. We don't need any sort of confirmation of the fact, do we?" She shoved the shovel at Callie, who stepped back.

"Why do you protect her?" Callie shouted. "You treat her like she's fragile, can't take the truth. When are you going to tell her, Katherine?"

Katherine glared at her for a moment. "We need young people, how many times do I have to tell you that? Madison is young, healthy, and of child-bearing age. We need her. So, I'll tell her when she's ready to hear it. Until then, do what I say." She turned on her heel and strolled off.

Callie glanced around and I ducked out of sight.

I sat down, sick at my stomach. Did I want to live in this world they had created where sick and infirm men were put down like livestock? Where they had no reason for existing other than as manual labor and semen producers? Where young women were coveted for their ability to bear children? I slid down to the ground, wrapping my arms around my body. What was I doing here? What was the point of living like this?

When it grew dark, I forced myself up and returned to the cycle, my decision made. I wouldn't just help Jonah escape, I would help the others. At least if I were going to die, it would mean something.

That night, after Callie left, I told Jonah I would help him and the others get away. "But that's all," I added. "Once you're free, you can go your way, I'll go mine."

His mouth set in a thin line. "Where will you go?"

I shrugged. "I'm not sure." I didn't want him to know I had decided to make my way to Seth's and Sarah's, stay with them until I made up my mind what I wanted to do.

Jonah touched my hand. "I wish you'd come with me."

I shook my head as I returned to my chair and picked up my book. I ignored him the rest of the evening as he prowled around my small space, running his hands through his hair, glancing at me. I could sense his turmoil, knew he wanted to talk to me, but I wasn't ready for that. I needed to get past the hurt first.

The next week passed in a dreary haze. I made my motorcycle sorties during the day and almost always ran into single or multiple stragglers, mostly women. I noticed with despair there were very few of child-bearing age and none under the age of 25. I understood Katherine's desire to have children but it was not for the right reason, to ensure man survived. She had a more devious plot in mind, to breed girl children, make sure women attained and retained power. The nights passed in fevered dreams, always of the man in the grave, reaching out to me, begging me to help him, grasping my ankle with his bony hands, dragging me into the grave with him. And at night, when Jonah joined me, I kept my distance, pretending to ignore him for the most part, but always, always, my body yearning, on fire for his touch.

Finally, one night, Jonah sat on the couch across from me and leaned forward, staring at me.

I glanced up. "What?"

"Apparently you don't want to talk about us, so let's talk about the escape. If you want to help us, we need to make a plan."

I put the book aside. "What do you have in mind?"

"I don't know. The best time would be when they've got us all on work detail, create some kind of diversion, long enough to overcome our guards, take their weapons, and run."

"That might work." Despite myself, my interest was piqued. "Do they give you any kind of schedule so you know what you're going to be doing beforehand?"

"No. But some jobs, as you know, take days to complete. We've finished clearing out the buildings on campus and are almost finished with the roads and houses beyond the campus. I heard Callie tell one of the deputies they're going to put us on street detail in town next, clearing stalled cars off the roads."

"That's perfect. You'll all be outside."

He nodded. "It'll be easier to get away."

"You'll need to give me a heads up before you decide to escape so I can be there. I can't be with the cleanup crew every day or Callie and Katherine will get suspicious. They're used to me off campus looking for stragglers to lead back here."

He stared at me. Was that panic I saw in his eyes? "You don't need to be there. We can get away without you having to be there."

"I have to be, Jonah."

"No, it's too dangerous. You might get hurt."

"I'll get hurt if I don't escape when you do."

His mouth tightened.

"Callie will, of course, link me to you. She'll make sure I pay the price afterward."

He cursed in a low voice. When he looked at me, his eyes darkened. "If it has to be that way, I want you to go with me, Madison. I love you. I think we need to stay together."

I picked up the book and ignored him.

He lunged to his feet. "Why won't you believe me? I admit I asked you at the wrong time but you had to know at some point it would come up."

I glared at him. "Don't go off topic. If you want me to help you escape, we need to finalize a plan so we can enforce it once we have the chance."

"Dammit!" He paced around, shooting me baleful looks. I pretended to be absorbed in the book. Finally he settled in the chair once more. "Okay, we'll get back to that but let me put one thing out there then I won't say another word about it."

I gave him my attention, telling myself, don't believe him, whatever he says don't believe him.

"Madison." His voice dropped, became huskier. I recognized that voice, oh yes, I did. And a shiver swept through me as it reminded me of heated nights, twisting bodies, hot gasps, intense, overwhelming pleasure. Don't think about that, I told myself as he continued. "I loved before you, was engaged to a girl who I thought I'd be with forever. But it wasn't like what I feel for you, it was nowhere near what I feel for you. It's different with you, more intense, more beautiful. Spiritual, I guess. I've always heard we have one true love in our lifetime and my one true love is you."

I cast my eyes away. I couldn't stand the heated look in his, drawing me toward him, willing me to kiss him, give my body to him.

"And if you don't believe me or want to be with me, that's your choice. But know this, Madison, I will protect you, I'll give my life for you if it comes to it."

My gaze met his. "I don't expect anything from you, Jonah, except for you and the others to escape. Can y'all get your hands on any sort of weapons?"

He gaze bore into mine. "That's it? That's all you want to talk about?"

"Yes."

He sat back, closing his eyes. "The only weapons we could possibly get would be the tools they give us to work with or what we take from them."

I nodded. "I found a gun once."

He leaned forward. "Just one?"

"And only because I wasn't looking for it."

"Where is it?"

"Here, in my bedroom."

"Can I see it?"

I put the book aside and walked into the bedroom, lifted up my mattress and retrieved the gun. I stood for a moment, debating whether to remove the bullets then decided I'd chance it. When I returned to the living area, I handed it to him, butt first.

Jonah turned it over in his hand, studying it. He ejected the magazine, saw that it was loaded, darted a look toward me. "Nice Glock. Do you know how to shoot it?"

"Didn't at first but I've practiced a bit. I think I'm pretty good with it."

Jonah nodded. "Looks clean."

"I got a book on how to clean guns from the library and learned how to do it that way."

"Where do you get your ammunition?"

"At a Wal-Mart in Knoxville."

"There any more guns there?"

I shook my head. "It's pretty ransacked. Only thing left is ammo." I watched him dry fire the gun. "Do you know how to shoot?"

"Yeah. My dad was a cop, he taught me. We used to target practice together."

"When I go out now, I'll start searching homes for them, see if I can find anything, smuggle it back here."

"Have you checked the town for a police department or sheriff's department?"

"It's so small, I doubt they'll have both but I'll ride there tomorrow and check it out."

"There'll probably be a small law enforcement building there. They should have guns and ammunition although they'll probably have them locked up but you should be able to get to them."

I nodded. "I think the college had a small police force. There's that building where they detained people, the one Callie uses for the oth—the men. I know they had a security force at the university I attended."

He shook his head. "That's too dangerous. Callie might catch you. Besides, she's probably confiscated for herself and her deputies all the weapons and ammunition there. Look for gun shops. I'm sure there are plenty around this area."

"I'd say so." I wondered why I'd never thought of that. We sat in silence for a few moments. I shifted, said, "How many others are there?"

He gave me a wry smile. "So you think of us by that name too?"

That stunned me. "I wasn't aware I do. I'm sorry if I offended you."

Jonah gave a small shake of his head. "There's about ten of us but that changes constantly."

"What do you mean? I've been routing any men I come across north to the community Seth and Sarah told me about."

He peered into my face, a look of astonishment on his. "Think about it."

"Callie."

His eyebrows drew together. "Callie looks for reasons to kill us. I'm sure if they didn't need us so badly, we'd all be dead."

I didn't doubt that for one moment. "I'll try to get enough weapons for us to use, and once y'all are on the car detail, we'll wait for the right opportunity."

Jonah nodded. "It'd probably be best to wait until we're outside the commune, that way there will be fewer people to deal with once we escape."

"You're right."

He gave me an intense look. "Do you think, if it came to it, that you could shoot someone?"

I pondered this for a moment. "Maybe to injure them, disable them, not to kill. No. I won't be part of that."

"I don't want to be, either."

"What about the others? Are any aggressive enough to want to kill Callie or her deputies?"

Jonah sat back, running his hand through his hair. "Oh, man, they hate her. And that deputy everybody calls Crazy Eyes, the one who likes to hit, we'd all like to get our hands on her."

"But will they kill them? I can't be part of killing, Jonah."

"Not even if it helps us escape? After all, I'm sure they'll be trying to kill us."

"I don't want another person's death on my mind."

He stood. "Yeah? What about all the old or sick men they've killed since I've been here, since *you've* been here? You ever think about that?"

I rose to my feet. "That's all I think about, all I dream about." I walked into the bedroom, closed and locked my door, ignoring his apology.

CHAPTER 13

My daily mission now involved riding to the outlying areas, searching for guns. The next day I visited the sheriff's department of the small city which housed our college campus. The door to the squat, square building was unlocked and I stepped into a dark interior, the smell of death heavy in the air. I pulled my flashlight out of my backpack and shone it around, trying not to stare at the decomposing bodies lying about the main room. What the heck had they all been doing here, I wondered, as I stepped around them and made my way to the hallway at the rear of the room. As I walked down that narrow corridor, the hairs on the back of my neck stirred to attention. Listening for anything out of the ordinary, I paused. What was that? A scratching sound coming from the office to my right. I pushed open the door, listening to it squeak, thinking it sounded ironically like something one would hear in a horror movie. I moved the flashlight beam around the walls and onto the floor. A cat sat astride a body, its snout inside the abdominal cavity. When the light reached it, it raised its head and hissed, something long and twisted hanging from its mouth. I lunged out of the room, choking on bile rising in my throat. I ran down the hallway and out the front door. Standing on the front steps, my hands on my knees, fighting nausea and dizziness, closing my eyes against that horrible image, a thought wiggled its way into my brain. Cats lived! Another sign of life in this apocalyptic world.

I sat down on the steps until I had myself under control and with a deep breath rose to my feet and walked back inside. This time I ignored the sounds from the office and continued on my quest until I came upon a large gun safe in a small utility room. I was surprised to find it wasn't locked and easily opened when I lifted the handle. Inside, neatly lined in a row, stood two rifles and one shotgun. Someone had been here before me; there were at least half a dozen other empty slots. I wondered why a sheriff's office would have a shotgun as I realized these would not do. I couldn't smuggle large weaponry into our commune without being seen. On a shelf above the rifles I found two guns, a revolver and small .22 caliber pistol. Well, beggars couldn't be choosers, I told myself as I took them down and put them on a small table nearby. In a drawer beneath the rifles, I found boxes of ammunition which I stashed in my backpack along with the two guns. I checked other drawers for pistols but found nothing else so closed the door and retreated out of the room. I stopped outside the office with the cat, contemplating luring it out of there and taking it with me. Deciding no, the cat was most likely feral, I continued on, playing my flashlight over the floor, trying to ignore splayed legs and arms, mouths twisted in agony, decaying flesh, the horrible stench of dried blood and feces and vomit.

Outside again, I propped the door to the building open so the cat could get out and took in great gasps of fresh air as I walked to my motorcycle. After securing the backpack in the satchel, I glanced at the building, thinking I should go back and search the bodies for weapons. But the thought of re-entering that place of death, of touching or being near all that horrid, decomposing flesh overwhelmed me to the point that I felt dizzy and sat down hard on the pavement, closing my eyes and telling myself to breathe deep. I leaned my head on my knees, squeezing my eyes shut against the tears blurring my vision. Why did it have to be like this and why was I in this mess? Why couldn't Katherine be more tolerable of men? It would be so much easier to go along with her policies, turn a blind eye to what they were doing to the others but I had traveled that road before and the thought of going back was horrific. But more horrible and terrifying was what lay ahead. Would I be able to help the others escape? Would I get away? What would I do once I had? I had changed my mind about staying with Seth and Sarah. They had their own small family to worry about, they didn't need me adding to that, and besides, I didn't want to place their lives in jeopardy. I had never been alone in my life until the pox and if it hadn't been for Katherine... I owed her so much and was going to repay her by betraying our friendship. And for what? I raised my head. "For freedom," I said out loud.

"Say what?" I heard behind me.

I startled, looking around and lunging to my feet. Three men stood close by, rifles slung over their shoulders, wide grins on their faces. Their clothes, which appeared to be camouflage gear, were streaked with mud, large sweat spots staining beneath the arms and down the fronts of their shirts. Their unshaved faces looked like they hadn't seen soap in years. Dirt was grimed under their fingernails and into the creases of their hands and arms. A vile odor emanated from them and I wondered how they could stand themselves.

"Nothing, just talking to myself." I backed up toward my motorcycle, intending to circle around it so as to place it between me and them. It scared me the way they stared at me, as if they'd had an unbearable thirst for much too long and had finally found something to quench it. I debated pulling my Glock, tucked into my jeans at mid back. But if they had seen it, once my hands moved in that direction, they might take that as an aggressive gesture and pull their rifles. Remembering the guns in the backpack, I groped for the satchel as they advanced toward me.

"Lookit what we got here," the tallest one said. "One hot motorcycle mama. Hey, girl, you one of them Harley's Angels used to ride the streets?" His lips split into a wide grin, revealing stained, decaying teeth.

"No."

He turned his head and spit tobacco juice toward the ground. "What you doing out here, then? You lost, by yourself?" He glanced at his partners and said in a low voice, "Looks like we got us some fresh meat for once, fellas."

They grinned lecherously at him.

Fresh meat? I knew what that meant and chances were I wouldn't be alive by day's end. Or if I was, I wouldn't want to be. I tried to speak but my voice cracked, so I cleared my throat and tried again. "I'm out searching for stragglers, leading them back to our commune."

Only the motorcycle separated us now although they were almost within reaching distance. I backed up another step.

The tallest one spoke again and I assumed he must be the alpha of the group. "You got you a commune?" His eyes lit with interest. "Any women there?"

"It's..." my voice faltered. I swallowed and tried again. "It's mostly women."

He darted a glance toward his two companions whose gazes stayed focused on me. "Got any young ones there, like you?"

I forced my voice to calm. If they could smell fear on me, it would only boost their confidence, their need to dominate. "Plenty. And we're looking for men." I slid my hand inside the satchel, thankful I'd left the backpack unzipped. "You interested? I can take you there."

His eyes glittered with malice. "Oh, girl, we're interested all right. But right now, I think we'd like a taste of what we're gonna get." He lunged for me.

I kicked the bike over against him, pulling the .22 out of the backpack. I aimed it at him as he danced away, cursing. The other two men swung their rifles off their shoulders and pointed them at me. And I knew in that instant if I were going to die, it would be by bullet, not some man slamming his smelly, greasy body into mine.

Alpha gained his balance, his rifle sliding easily into his hand. "Looks like we got us a spitfire, boys. Makes the gittin' more fun." He grinned at me. "Might as well give it up, girl, you got three against one and our ammo's a hell of a lot more powerful than yours. Why, that little thing wouldn't even put a dent in us."

I backed up a step, forcing my arms to remain still, not shake with tension and fear as I gripped the gun with both hands. "Way I see it, I can take out at least one of you before you get me."

"You thinkin' we care if you're alive or not? Shit. Pickin's so slim, we ain't choosey anymore, are we, boys?" He slid a glance at the other two, who nodded their agreement.

The words were out before I could stop them. "You—you rape dead women?" Panic tingled up my spine and my knees felt weak. I fought a sudden urge to urinate.

"Well, now, don't know as I'd call it rape. Haven't heard one protest yet, have we, boys?" He brayed laughter and I knew in that moment he was mentally sick, deranged, an evil presence.

"'Course, we limit ourselves to the ones just starting to thaw, ain't too far gone to give us what we need."

I vaguely wondered why the pox couldn't have taken the bad ones and left the good. God could have at least seen to that when he felt the need to cull humans. Hoping for something to distract them, I darted my eyes this way and that, searching for something, anything. In an effort to buy more time, I gestured to the other two with my gun and said, "What's wrong? They mute or something? I haven't heard either one of them say a word this whole time."

"Nah, they can speak."

"When you give them permission to, I take it."

I watched a glint of anger slide into the shortest man's eyes. So he didn't like having to be follower.

"They can speak whenever they want to." Alpha gave me a defensive look. "Can't you, boys?" He glowered at the other two men.

The skinniest of the troop spoke up. "I got a voice."

"Yeah, 'cause he just gave you permission to, you wimp," I said, surprised at the hatred in my voice.

"Now wait a minute…" Alpha said.

"That's exactly what happened. You told them to speak and he spoke. You gave them permission."

"That ain't what happened." Alpha darted a warning gaze at the other two men but their eyes remained riveted on me. Just look at him, I willed them. Give me a second, that's all I need to pull the trigger. Alpha turned his gaze on me, as if sensing my thoughts. "Don't listen to her, she's trying to get something started here that don't need startin'."

So there had been discord before.

"Now we got us a chance at a real, live woman here, boys. Let's not ruin it, okay?" He glanced from me to them. "She's alive, boys, fresh meat, ought to be good for a few rounds. Hell, for all we know she might be the freshest meat we'll have for a bit." He grinned at me. Skinny snickered and pulled his rifle up. When I glanced at him, Alpha lunged at me, our bodies colliding awkwardly. I stepped back, faltered and fell to the ground, him on top. The .22 flew out of my hands.

Alpha dropped his rifle, grabbed both arms and pinned them behind my back. His fetid breath washed over me. "You ain't so fearless when you ain't got a gun in your hands." He put his mouth on me and I squealed with frustration. I wriggled and squirmed, trying to move my face away from his, my body from underneath. His breath, his body odor were worse than what I had smelled inside the building and I fought the urge to vomit. He bore down harder, pinning my arms to the ground beneath me and I stopped, realizing my Glock, still tucked into my jeans at mid back, was within reach. How could I free my hands to grab it, though? Holding my breath, I kissed back as passionately as I could muster, hoping to distract him, repeating to myself, don't throw up, don't throw up, don't throw up. His body responded immediately and I knew it would only be seconds before he would be inside me. But he would have to let go of my arms so he could use his hand to unzip his pants and free himself and do the same to me. And when his right hand released mine, I twisted my torso, grabbed the gun handle, stuck it in his gut and fired.

Warm blood spurted over my hand.

His eyes widened. "Hunh?" he grunted.

With my other hand, I pulled him closer to me for protection, brought the gun around and shot the other two, now making their way toward us, hitting the skinniest in the chest, the shorter one in the shoulder, amazed my aim was so true with my hand slick with blood. I let go of Alpha and he rolled off of me, screaming. I kicked him away and shot him in his knee, ignoring his wail of agony. Skinny doubled over, holding his chest, gasping for air, while the shorter one dropped his rifle and ran off. I lunged to my feet and watched him go, shooting a bullet in the air over his head to scare him. He yelped and took off faster. I debated placing another bullet in his body but couldn't shoot someone in the back so gave up. I transferred the gun to my left hand, wiped my right on my t-shirt, hating the sticky feel, the coppery smell, thankful none had gotten in my mouth or an open wound. No telling what kind of disease Alpha had. When I looked back at him, he was fumbling around for his rifle. I shot him in the right arm, his dominant one, ignoring his screech of pain. It took all the strength I could muster to step beside each man and pick up their rifles, holding my breath at the stench coming from them, blood mixed with body odor and body waste and adrenaline.

I picked up my motorcycle, balanced it on the kickstand, slid the rifles into the satchel. Stepped back and waited for the screaming to stop. Skinny lay on the ground, moaning, blood bubbles leaking out of his mouth. Alpha finally quieted but gave me a look so malevolent, I could feel it slamming into me with a tangible force.

"In case it has escaped your attention," I said in a voice I didn't recognize as my own, "this is now a woman's world. You men had your chance and screwed it up as only men can do and now it's our turn. We are the power." With a start, I realized I was mouthing Katherine's words. But they never sounded truer than at that moment.

He spat on the ground and I got the message.

I walked over to him and pointed the gun at his forehead. "How many women have you raped and killed?"

"I ain't answering nothin' you ask me." He sounded like a petulant child.

I kicked him in the knee, the one with the bullet wound, and he howled like a wild animal. When he stopped, gasping with pain, I said, "How many women did you rape and kill? Tell me or I'll shoot you in the other knee."

He shook his head several times. "None. Not a one."

When I turned the gun on his partner, Skinny said, "That's a lie. I've watched him kill three different women, raped I don't know how many that were already dead."

"You help him kill them and rape them?" I asked.

He gasped for air several times. "Not the live ones. I raped some of the dead ones, though, enough to keep him from killing me for not participating."

"You're a hair away from being as evil as he is." I strode back to my cycle and straddled it.

"You can't just leave us here," Alpha said in a whiny voice. "We need help."

I paused for a long moment as if considering his request. "I'm going back to our commune. I'll send help your way."

Relief flooded Alpha's face. "I need me a doctor. Y'all got a doctor in your commune, someone can treat bullet wounds?" he panted.

I smiled at him. "Don't worry. I'll make sure they take real good care of you."

"What happened before," he said, "you know we was just funnin' you, right? We weren't gonna do nothin' to you, I swear."

"Oh, I know what you were going to do, no doubt about that." I started the motorcycle and headed home.

On the way out of town, my body shook with such force the motorcycle wove dramatically, threatening to topple over. I finally stopped when I felt I was far enough away that they couldn't see or hear me, stepped off and let the cycle fall to the ground as I sank to my knees. I lay on my side, my knees drawn to my chest, waiting for the trembling to stop. Where had that come from? I had shot those men and didn't feel a bit of remorse for it. You had to, I kept telling myself, and knew this to be true, but I had done it so coldly, so efficiently. Maybe I had changed more than I thought. Maybe this world had begun to harden me like it had Katherine and Callie. Maybe one day I would be like them. The thought made me sick. I forced myself to sit up, breathing deeply as I fought for control. Once the shaking stopped, I fumbled in my backpack for my water bottle, poured water over my hand, stained red from his blood, and scrubbed until it looked clean. I eyed my t-shirt, splotched red with blood, and wished I had something else to put on. If I'd worn a bra, I would have torn the shirt off. But as it was, I had nothing to cover me, so left it on, hating the way the damp material clung to my skin, praying I hadn't suffered a scratch anywhere the bloody fabric touched. Once I stopped shaking, I returned the bottle to my backpack, mounted my motorcycle and rode toward our commune.

On the outskirts, I spied one of Callie's deputies strolling down the street and pulled over to speak to her. Linda, the one who found me trussed after Seth's escape. She eyed the blood on my t-shirt, the rifles sticking out of my saddlebag. Her eyes widened with alarm. "Are you all right?"

I nodded.

"Is that your blood? Did you have an accident?"

"No. This is the blood of a man who tried to…" I couldn't finish the sentence.

She watched me for a moment then said, "I hope you killed him."

"I tried."

She glanced at the rifles. "Those his?"

"His and his two cohorts. I need to turn them over to Callie. Do you know where she is?" I couldn't hide the tremor in my voice and cursed myself for this weakness.

"She's with Katherine over at her office." Linda touched me on the arm. "You sure you're all right?"

"I will be." I gave the cycle gas and headed toward Katherine's office. I dismounted and pulled the rifles out of the saddlebag before slinging my backpack on. I noticed several women pausing in their activities to watch me but ignored them as I stepped into the cool confines of the building. I found Callie and Katherine in Katherine's office, the door closed, discussing something I was sure was secretive and confidential. I rapped on the doorframe before strolling in. Placed the rifles on the desk and watched both women's reactions.

Katherine's eyebrows shot up and her mouth opened slightly.

Callie jumped to her feet. "Where'd you get these?"

"In town. Three men were there, they wanted to rape and kill me but I shot them before they could do anything."

Katherine rushed to my side, her gaze fixated on my t-shirt. "Oh, my dear Maddie. Are you hurt? Did they hurt you?"

"No, I didn't give them the chance."

Callie gave me a curious look. "Did you leave them alive?"

"Yes. Two are too injured to get away but one ran off. He's shot, though, so he shouldn't get very far."

Callie studied me. "Welcome to our world, Maddie," she said with an ironic smile.

I breathed deep. "I thought you might want to go take care of them," I told her.

She stared into my eyes. "Are you saying what I think you are?"

"Yes. They've been raping dead women and the tall one, the one I shot three times, he's raped and killed three live women."

"They told you that?"

"The one with the chest wound told me. He said he's only raped dead women. Either way, they're evil people, they don't deserve to live in this world."

Callie looked at Katherine, who gave a slight nod. "Got you." Callie walked out the door, pulling her walkie-talkie out of her pocket.

Katherine held me at arm's length, her gaze raking over my body. "You're sure you're all right?"

I stepped into her arms, welcoming her embrace, feeling the tremors begin again. "I was so scared, Katherine. They were going to rape me, probably kill me. It's only luck I got away."

She pulled away, placing her hands on either side of my face. "Madison, you're much stronger than you give yourself credit for. I am so sorry this happened to you but so proud of the way you handled it. You're a valued asset to this community, whether you realize it or not."

I sat down in the chair across from her desk. "Callie's going to kill them?"

Katherine sat beside me, took my hand. "Isn't that what you want?"

"Yes." God help me, I did. I wanted exactly that.

After I left Katherine, I went to my apartment, tearing off my clothes as I walked toward the bathroom. I stepped into the shower, ignoring the cold water biting my skin, scrubbed my body and face until they felt raw, and then sat in the stall, my knees drawn up to my chest, my body shivering, letting the tears flow. I kept telling myself Callie would take care of them, they couldn't hurt me or anyone ever again, but that didn't seem satisfactory. Maybe I should have killed them, I thought, shocked that I would even consider that. Drying off, I noticed the caked blood under the fingernails of my right hand. I searched frantically until I found a brush and spent minutes cleaning the blood from beneath. I wanted no part of him attached to me. Anger spiked through me and I found myself hoping Callie made him pay for what he'd done to other women. He did not belong in this world. Once I assured myself no sign of him remained on me, I wadded up the t-shirt and took it outside, dropped it into a metal trash can and set it on fire. As it burned, I retrieved my backpack with the guns and ammunition I had found at the police building and took them inside. Unsure where to hide the firearms, I simply placed them under my mattress for now. As far as I knew, no one else had a key to my apartment so I felt they would be safe there until I could find a better place for them.

At dinner, I searched the cafeteria for any sign of Callie and her deputies. Two were there but the rest were missing and I deduced they must still be in town taking care of things. My mind shied away from the fact that I had been the one to issue the kill order. Although I had told Callie I wanted them dead, I kept telling myself the ultimate decision was hers. But was I any better than Callie or Katherine? The Bible says turn the other cheek but I could not stand the thought of these evil men prowling the countryside, raping and killing women, and committing necrophilia. I wondered what drove them to such behavior. Were they this way before the pox or had something been unleashed in them since that brought them to these violent acts? And why rape and kill when there was such an abundance of women compared to men? They deserved to die, I told myself, but found I had no appetite for food or companionship so returned to my apartment.

That night when Callie brought Jonah to my apartment, she told me she needed to speak to me alone. I stepped outside, closing the door behind me.

Without preamble, she said, "We found them."

"All three?"

"Yes. Followed the blood trail of the one who escaped. He didn't get very far."

"You killed them?"

She gave me a curious look. "Isn't that what you wanted?"

"Yes."

"They're taken care of. You won't need to worry about them anymore."

"Thank you."

She patted my cheek. "You surprised me, kiddo. I didn't think you had it in you." She tilted her head toward the door. "If you don't feel up to it, I can take him back."

I shook my head. "No, it's okay. Maybe he can help me…forget."

She gave me a lecherous look. "Whatever you say." The smile left her face. "Where did you get the gun?"

"The what?"

"The gun you shot them with. We looked around but couldn't find it."

"Oh, that. I was eating lunch on the steps of the sheriff's department and heard sounds coming from inside so went to investigate. Found a cat eating someone." I grimaced at the thought. "I saw the gun on a desk and picked it up, thinking I'd bring it back to you. I still had it in my hands when I stepped outside and found those three men waiting on me." I marveled at how easy lying came to me now.

"What'd you do with it?"

"With what? Oh, the gun. I'm sorry, Callie, but everything's so hazy after I shot them. I guess I dropped it. You didn't see it anywhere?"

"Not at the scene. You bring it home?" Her eyes grew suspicious.

"Why would I need a gun here?" I opened the door. "You're welcome to look if you'd like."

She studied me for a long moment then shrugged. "No. After what you did today, I don't think we've got much to worry about with you." She nodded at me. "Well done, sister."

I watched her leave, relief washing through me she hadn't come inside and discovered my stash of firearms.

When I stepped inside, Jonah eyed me with suspicion. "You and Callie pals now?"

"No." I sat down in my favorite chair and closed my eyes.

"Something happened," he said in a low voice.

I squeezed my eyes but could not stop the flow of tears. What was wrong with me? They hadn't raped me, I hadn't been injured. They're dead because of you, my inner voice whispered. And I did not know whether I was happy for that or saddened by it.

Jonah's warm hand caressed my cheek. "What happened, Madison?" he said, his voice gentle and caring.

Without even thinking about it, I told him, leaving nothing out, not even my statement to Callie that I wanted them dead.

He knelt before me, looking into my eyes. "Are you all right? Did they hurt you?"

"I'm fine. They – he didn't hurt me."

"Maddie, they could have killed you."

"That's why I shot them."

He shook his head. "I'm glad you did. Thank God you'd been practicing with your gun."

The memory of that fear, of those men towering over me, smelling horribly, the ominous, lecherous looks in their eyes flooded through me and I began shaking again.

"Hey," Jonah said, "everything's fine. You're alive, you did the right thing, you saved your life in case it hasn't hit you." He pulled me into his arms, whispering, "Men like that don't deserve to live. I wish I could have killed them for you. If I had been there, I would have."

Needing to confirm there were good men in this world, men worth fighting for, I pressed tighter against him. The thought that I could have died today produced a yearning so fierce it frightened me as I realized I wanted his tender embrace, to feel safe, comforted. To feel alive. I gave into my wants and desires, ignoring my inner voice screaming at me to stop, stop, this was wrong, he couldn't be trusted.

Afterward, he put his hands on either side of my face and kissed me gently. "I love you, Maddie, no matter what happens between us." He drew back and stared into my eyes.

I felt the tears fall, telling myself I was so weak, but could not deny my feelings for him. And so, I pressed my lips to his once again, saying in my mind, I love you too, no matter what happens.

After Callie collected Jonah, I left my apartment and climbed the stairs to a small terrace off the roof, my favorite place during the warm weather. I had placed a lounge chair there, a small table beside it. I reclined on the lounge, staring at the brilliant stars in the ebony sky, my body sated, my mind in turmoil, wishing the two could be in harmony. Hoping to clear my mind, I studied the constellations, marveling at the clarity of the sky. I couldn't remember seeing so many stars before the pox and took a deep breath, luxuriating in the clean, fresh smell. Something positive, after all, had come from this pandemic, something I hoped human kind wouldn't destroy given the chance. But I knew better. It seemed we were destined to repeat the same mistakes we had made before. Born into this world was evil once more and, as before, I feared evil would prevail.

The next morning, I paid a visit to Katherine. She sat in her office, busily writing on a legal pad, smiling when she saw me. She put her pen aside and came around her desk to greet me, hugging me close. I clutched her, comforted by her strength, her understanding. "Sit," she said, waving to the chair across from her desk.

I eased into the chair, watching as she returned to her seat. Our eyes met and Katherine said, "Are you all right?"

I nodded, blocking the image of the man on top of me, his smell, his words. "I'm fine."

"You sure?"

"Yes."

"Do you want to talk about what happened?" she asked in a soft voice.

I shook my head. "I want to talk about why you hate men so much."

Her eyes widened as she straightened in her seat. "After what happened to you yesterday, I imagine you can understand why some of us don't have much respect for the others."

I nodded. "It's just, I wonder if the same thing happened to you or...or worse." I gave her a questioning look and noted her expression had hardened. Perhaps I was treading on sensitive issues. "You don't have to answer me, Katherine. It's something I've wondered about, though, why you and Callie and, well, so many of these women don't respect the male population. Why you think you can do a better job of it than they can."

Katherine sat back in her seat and regarded me for a long moment. "You're so young, Madison, you didn't have a chance to really experience life before the pox hit, not like the rest of us did."

I could not deny this.

Pain flared in her eyes. "Imagine, if you will, a young woman very much like you. Strong, independent, determined to have a career and live a good life. But that is not to be. This young woman goes off to college, like you, but here begins the downfall. She meets a young man and falls in love with him to the point that she allows him to take over her life bit by bit. First by alienating her from her friends, then her family, then suggesting she dress a certain way, act a certain way. He plays mind games with her and it isn't enough he has removed her from important people in her life, he begins to hack away at her self-confidence, her feelings about her self-worth, her intelligence, until she begins to think she is a nothing, a nobody without this man. And when he finally has her under his control, he becomes a monster who is not above using his fists to keep her where he wants her. And this he does freely and willfully and regularly. Imagine trying to escape from a person such as this, who threatens your life and the lives of those you love if you ever leave him. Who is not above placing a loaded gun in your mouth and promising to pull the trigger if you do not do as he wants."

I placed my hand over my mouth, wondering how anyone could live like that.

Her eyes met mine and she nodded as if she knew what I was thinking. "Would you have respect for someone such as this, Madison? Would you want someone like this ruling the world once more?"

"But they're not all like that, Katherine."

"Oh, sweetie, there are too many like that. I'm surprised you even ask the question after what you experienced yesterday." She studied me for a moment. "You wanted Callie to kill them. Tell me why."

"Because they were evil men. They raped and killed women. And they would have continued unless they were stopped. They shouldn't be allowed to exist on earth."

"Exactly. They should not be allowed to exist on this earth. I am beginning to think, Madison, that your God or whatever superior being rules the universe, if there is such a thing, decided maybe it was time for a change, that perhaps women could do a much better job."

"But why can't we have the commune you originally intended, Katherine, with women only? Why bring men into it? Why not just send them on their way?"

Her eyes flashed and her voice turned steely. "Because if we allow them to gain power, what will have changed? What lesson will we have learned? The world will become as it was, with stupid, inept, power-hungry men ruling women who are much more capable than they. From what we've been told from women who join us and what Alice hears on the ham radio, we've become one of the largest communities in America. We're well over a thousand now. By increasing our population, we increase our strength, our power. Callie has already accumulated quite an arsenal and shortly will begin training an army of women to defend our commune. We'll be ready if we're ever threatened or we reach the point where we can take control of this country."

I stared at her eyes, shining with madness, and thought how totally insane she and Callie must be to already be planning such a thing. The world was still new, still healing. And I knew I would never want to be part of a country ruled by Callie and her minions. Gone would be a democracy and in play would be a dictatorship with everyone bending to their rules and regulations. Oh, how Callie would love that, and Katherine, the former anthropologist, what would she think? Could she not see where this would ultimately end? I rose to my feet, thinking I could not be party to this.

Katherine raised her eyebrows in a questioning way.

I forced my face to become neutral, my body to calm. "You've answered my question, Katherine. I'm sorry you had to endure that. No one should have to endure that."

"Well, as I see it, it put me on the road to this, Madison, so every beating I took from that despicable man was worth it. And when you question the policies we have here, the way we treat the others, think of those three men and what they had in mind for you."

My stomach twisted at that. I nodded and left her as quickly as I could, thinking if I stayed too long, I just might start believing she was right.

CHAPTER 14

And back I went into the past routine – searching for survivors during the day while collecting firearms and spending long, heated hours with Jonah in the evenings, telling myself I didn't love him, simply lusted for his body and the physical love he introduced me to. Ignoring his amorous words, shutting out everything but the physical sensation as my body's needs were sated. Treating him as a means to an end. As he treated me, my inner voice would whisper during those times when I had to bite my tongue to keep from speaking love words to him.

Lulled to complacence and, yes, contentment by my life, the night Jonah told me of the planned escape came as a shock although I had been expecting it. We were in bed together, our slick bodies intertwined. My eyes were closed, my body throbbing softly when Jonah whispered in my ear, "Tomorrow."

I drew back with a start, staring at him.

"We'll be working in Canville's main street where we're supposed to finish clearing the road. The past few days, only a couple of deputies have been with us. Callie hasn't been in sight."

I nodded, my mind racing. Could I do this? Did I really want to? Why so soon?

"There's a drugstore right before the bridge going into town. You know it?"

"Yes," I said.

"Can you place the guns inside that building? That's where we eat lunch. I know the door's unlocked because someone broke the glass out and it looks like it's been forced open. Put the guns right inside the door."

"Okay, I can do that. When are you planning to escape?"

"Noon, when we break for lunch. How many guns have you managed to collect?"

My mind couldn't concentrate. "Around eight."

"Are they here?"

"Yes."

"Can I see them?"

I got up, put on a robe, stepped inside my closet and worked several planks free. Jonah joined me, watching as I pulled out a large canvas bag, opened it and began setting the weapons on the floor. He sat beside me, hefting each one, checking the ammo, dry firing them. "Did you get any ammunition?"

I pulled out boxes of bullets and handed them to him.

"You couldn't get any more guns?"

"No. Every gun shop and department store I checked had been ransacked. Katherine told me the other day that Callie is building up an arsenal and I suspect she's responsible for the depletion. I didn't take any of the rifles and shotguns I found because they're too hard to hide and too bulky to transport. I kept to the smaller guns, figuring they'd be easier to stow away."

"Okay. I guess some of us will just have to use whatever we can find."

I leaned against the wall. "Jonah, there's no need for violence. Just show them the guns and I'm sure they'll let you go."

His eyes burned. "Maybe but some of these women are killers. I'm not sure how they'll react."

"I think the only killers are Callie and Sandra."

"The one called Crazy Eyes?"

"Yes. Is she one of the deputies guarding you?"

"No. She hasn't been there lately."

"What time will y'all get there in the morning?"

"We're usually onsite by eight-thirty, nine."

"Okay. I'll get up before dawn and ride out there."

He grasped my arms with his hands. "And then leave, right? You won't stay around, be part of the fight?"

"I hadn't thought of it. I figured I'd be one more person to help."

"No, leave after you plant the guns, Madison. Get away from here if you think Callie will blame this on you. If you don't and you want to, then you should stay."

"I can't stay. Not after this. Callie will know it was me. I'm the only one who ever leaves the compound other than Callie and her deputies. I'm the one she'll zero in on."

"Can we join up later?"

My eyes met his, burning with intensity. "It's better if we don't. I'm not sure—"

"Maddie, I don't want us to be separated. Let's meet up somewhere afterward. I can protect you, keep you safe. I can't stand the thought that something might happen to you out there on your own."

I drew my arms back from his. "I'll be fine. I've managed so far."

"What about those three men? They could have killed you. What if you happen across men like that again?"

"What are the chances, Jonah? I've been all over this region and the majority of people I meet are women. I'll find another band, join up with them, and make my way to another commune."

He put his mouth on mine, kissing me with a fierce passion my body instantly recognized and responded to. I gave into it for a moment then pulled away. "I'll be fine," I said, placing the guns back in the bag and dropping it into its hidey-hole.

Although he tried several times after that to talk me into going with him, I stood my ground, refusing to even discuss it. By the time Callie collected him, Jonah was in a huff. When he heard her knock on the door, he grabbed me by the arms, pulled my body to his, and kissed me with such passion it took my breath away. He drew back, his eyes fierce and intense, and said, "Do what you need to do to stay safe. But know this. I'll find you. I won't let you get away from me. We belong together." He pushed me away from him, opened the door and walked away without a backward glance.

I panicked, realizing this was the last time I would see him. I stepped forward and reached out to him before catching myself and lowering my arms to my side. But it was too late.

Callie leaned in the doorway, nodding to herself as is affirming a suspicion. "Meet me at Katherine's office first thing in the morning."

"What for?"

"We need to talk about you and him, this pairing. Looks to me like there's more going on here than there ought to be. Probably be best all around if we put you in the pool with the other women."

"That's not what we agreed on."

"One day you'll understand the reason we're doing this, Madison. Until then, keep your mouth shut and do what you're told." She slammed the door shut.

I spent a restless night tossing and turning, worried about what I should do the next morning. I decided to ride out at dawn, plant the guns and return to the commune by breakfast, after which I would meet with Katherine and Callie so they wouldn't detect anything suspicious was afoot. I'd readily agree to become part of the pool, knowing Jonah wouldn't be part of our commune anymore and neither would I. After the meeting, I would ride my motorcycle out of our community for the last time. My eyes teared at the pain of losing Katherine but it couldn't be helped. Callie would immediately tie me to the escape and there would be no help for me. Her revenge would be swift and furious.

It took some getting used to the fact that I would not be involved in the escape. I had always taken that for granted. But I would accede to Jonah's wishes and not participate. However, I would be close by watching them, making sure they got away. Making sure he was safe. And praying no one would be hurt.

I finally gave up on getting any sleep and rose at five. I craved a strong cup of coffee but did not want to start my generator, fearful it would alert others I was up so early. But I needed caffeine, so I drank cold tea until my eyes were not so bleary, my mind not so hazy. Once fully alert, I stuffed my backpack with underwear, jeans, t-shirts and socks, cramming as much as I could get in there, realizing there was no real need. Clothes were in plentiful supply at stores all over the country. If I wanted, I would never have to wear the same pair of underwear twice. But for some reason, I felt the need to hang on to my meager wardrobe. At six, when the sky first began to lighten, I removed the canvas bag from the hole in my closet floor, slung it over my shoulder and stole outside where I stowed it in my commodious saddlebag. I returned inside, pulled on a hoodie and tucked my Glock into my jeans at mid back. I looked around my small home, thinking I would miss it. Well, maybe one day I would have a real home, a happy place with a loving family around me along with Boomer and Adam. But I couldn't foresee it. It seemed more like a pipedream to me, something I would perhaps always long for but never achieve.

I unchained the motorcycle and walked beside it as I rolled it out of my small drive and down the road, keeping to the shadows, hoping one of Callie's deputies wouldn't be doing a perimeter stroll and catch me in her sights. But the small commune was quiet, no lights in windows, no signs of people up and stirring about. On the outskirts of the commune, I kicked the cycle into gear, fed it gas and raced away to the small town nearby, watching the sky as I rode turn lemony yellow and pea-green as the sun tipped over the horizon. It looked to be a beautiful day with few clouds and warm air. Please, God, don't let anyone die today, I prayed.

I easily found the drugstore. As Jonah predicted, the door was not locked. I inserted full magazines into the guns before placing them on the floor along with the canvas bag containing more ammunition then backed away, closing the door behind me. I raced back to town, aware the sun was fully up now and our commune would begin to stir to life as the women dressed and began their preparations for the day. On the outskirts, I stepped off the motorcycle and once more walked it back into town, knowing my chances of being discovered were stronger now than earlier. I was near my own home when Callie stepped out of nowhere and stopped me.

She crossed her arms and gave me an inquisitive look. "Where you been?"

I pretended not to see her. "I don't think that's any of your business. I'm free to go about as I wish."

"For the time being." She fell into step beside me. "I'm curious why you left so early. After all, as warden of this commune, it's my business to know if something's going on I need to be aware of."

Warden. Oh, that fit her well. "I couldn't sleep so got up and decided to take a ride. It helps me relax." I winced inside at the defensive tone of my voice.

"Fair enough. You could have said that to start with." She put her hand on my arm, staying me. "Don't forget to come to Katherine's office right after breakfast."

"Of course. That was my plan."

With a nod, she wheeled around and walked away. I pushed my bike toward the cafeteria, my thoughts in turmoil. Had I given away too much last night with that stupid, weak gesture? I chained the motorcycle to a bike stand and headed inside for breakfast. The room was just beginning to fill and I found myself seated at a table with women from our gardening group. They were friendly enough since I'd bought their favor by bringing them seed packets I found along with plants I rescued from nurseries on my journeys throughout the countryside. Their talk centered on when to plant what and how our community garden was faring. I was happy to hear that the tomatoes, squash and zucchini were in plentiful supply. I remembered my mother's zucchini bread with a pain of such angst, I had to force myself to keep from doubling over. I noticed Callie conferring with some of her deputies and it alarmed me when they kept darting glances my way. With a curt nod, Sandra led a troop of three others out of the building, sending me a sidelong look as she passed. Callie left soon after, talking on her walkie-talkie. This was not good. I wished I could get word to Jonah to escape as soon as he got to the site but that would be impossible without giving something away.

My appetite destroyed, I played with the food on my plate while the women talked around me, occasionally offering a comment or smile. Dreading the meeting with Katherine and Callie, I dallied until the cafeteria was almost empty. With a resigned sigh, I gave my tray to one of the dishwashers and left. After unchaining the bike, I kicked it to life and rode the short distance to Katherine's office where I left it unchained by the bike stand. I found Katherine behind her desk, Callie standing by the window. And knew from the looks on their faces something was up.

Katherine returned my hug but her gaze was cool, distant.

I felt a tug at my mid back and glanced around to see Callie holding my gun in the air. "You won't need this," she said.

I cursed myself for not leaving it on the motorcycle. Apparently I hadn't concealed it under my hoodie as well as I thought.

Callie ejected the magazine and placed both on the desk. "I thought you told me you didn't have the gun."

This confused me then I remembered the incident with the three men. "This is one I found later, after that."

Callie cocked an eyebrow. "The policy is only me and my deputies are allowed firearms. You should have turned it in."

"I need protection when I'm riding outside the commune, Callie. That incident proved it. Besides it's not much more of a weapon than a BB gun."

"I'll keep it from now on." Callie gave Katherine what I perceived to be an *I-told-you-so* look. Katherine ignored her.

After I sat in the chair across from Katherine, she glanced at Callie before saying, "You know why you're here?"

"Yes, Callie made that clear last night."

Katherine leaned back in her chair. "Have you established a relationship with this young man?"

What would be the point of lying? I wouldn't be here after today anyway. "Yes. We've become friends."

Katherine's eyebrows rose while Callie shook her head, a smirk on her face.

"You understand we can't continue to pair you with him?" Katherine asked.

"I figured so." Realizing I needed to at least plead my case, otherwise they would definitely know something was going on, I added, "But I don't love him, so what's the problem, Katherine? I've told you before I don't want to feel like a prostitute, having sex with one man after the other until I'm pregnant."

"It's the only way to ensure that what's happened between you and Jonah won't happen with the other women."

"How can it not? How can we not give our bodies to a man and not at least feel something toward him, whether it be repulsion or attraction?"

Katherine looked at Callie, who stepped toward me. "So far, you're the only one in the pool who seems to have a problem with the plan."

"That you know of."

That stopped her. She cocked her head for a moment, as if relaying scenes in her mind. "There would be signs. We'd know."

"I wouldn't be so sure of that."

"Let us worry about that." Katherine darted a meaningful glance toward Callie. "For now, we have no other choice but to put you into the rotation."

"Katherine, I'm only 18 years old. I shouldn't have to be doing this. Can't you see that?"

"Yes, I agree you're young, Madison, and can't see the logic behind what we're doing yet. But one day you will. I promise."

Callie's walkie-talkie squawked and she walked out of the room. Katherine watched her, her forehead lined.

"What's going on?"

She turned her gaze to me. "Callie's checking something suspicious. She should have some information for us."

Us?

Callie stepped back into the room, the smirk back on her face. "Where'd you go this morning?" she asked me again.

"I told you I went for a ride to relax, as if it's any of your business."

She settled in the chair next to me. "You're in love with him, aren't you?"

"What? Who?"

"Jonah. You two looked awful chummy last night."

"How do you expect me to act with someone I just made love with?"

"Yeah, well, it's in my nature to be suspicious. Your strange actions last night and this morning got me thinking, wondering if you weren't up to something. So I had Sandra and a couple of deputies ride out to the clear site where your boyfriend will be working today, check around, see if something had been put there that shouldn't have been. You want to tell us what they found?"

I forced a scowl on my face. "How would I know?"

"You'd know because you placed them there."

"What are you talking about, Callie?" Katherine's voice was harsh.

"Someone placed loaded guns in a building near where the others are working today. In fact, the very one they eat their lunch in front of. Way I see it, the only person who would have done that is sitting right here next to me."

Katherine looked at me. "Madison?" I could hear the pain in her voice, the sense of betrayal.

"I don't know what you're talking about. Those guns were probably there to start with," I said, my voice faltering.

Callie gave a derisive snort. "We always clear an area before we let the others in, make sure there are no weapons they can use. Other than my deputies, the only person to leave this commune is you."

My mind raced, trying to come up with an excuse, a reason those guns were there other than that I had placed them. "Who's to say you or one of your deputies didn't plant them there, Callie? We've all known since day one you don't like me and don't want me here."

Callie shook her head. "Please. If I'd wanted you gone, I could have taken care of you long ago but I respected the fact that you were under Katherine's protection. And how did you repay her? By arming the others so they can get away and in doing so possibly kill a few of us."

I watched Katherine's eyes as she considered all this then realized I had betrayed her, our community. "Why'd you do it?" she said, her voice soft.

What was the point of denying it? I felt so tired, so sick of it all. "Because I love him and I don't think what you're doing here is right. Why can't you just let them go, Katherine? Why keep them imprisoned as slave labor and sex objects? That shouldn't be what you want from this new world."

Callie shifted. "What do you want me to do with her?"

Panic stuttered up my spine at the glee in her voice. I had finally done it. My actions had provided her with a reason to be rid of me. "Do with me? I'll leave and you won't have to worry about me anymore." I started to rise but Callie clamped a hand on my shoulder and forced me back in the chair.

"You'll be staying."

"Let go of me! You don't have the right to keep me here." I tried to shake her hand off but Callie held firm.

Callie turned her gaze to Katherine. "We need to use her, make an example out of her, send a message to the other women this will not be tolerated. Not here in our commune."

"Use me? Katherine. Please. I love you. You love me. We're a family. Don't let her take me. Just let me go. Please."

Katherine would not meet my gaze. "Are you going to the site?" she asked Callie.

"Of course. Thought it'd be fun watching the others try to escape without bullets in their guns. Figured I'd take our girl here with me so she could watch what happens to those who try to escape, see what's in store for her."

I knew then my fate had been decided before I stepped into the room. And when Katherine said, "Take her, then, get her out of my sight," I accepted the fact that my life as well as Jonah's was probably over.

I didn't verbally protest as Callie pulled me to my feet but I did try to get out of her grasp. Callie was too strong and easily overpowered me, pulling my hands behind my back and handcuffing me. "Katherine, please," I said, but she merely turned her chair to the window, her signal to me that she would not help.

Callie shoved me toward the door but I resisted, turning back to Katherine. "I love you, Katherine. I'm sorry I hurt you but I thought it was the right thing."

Katherine did not respond as she continued to stare outside.

Callie pushed me forward, saying, "Too late for pretty words, girlie. You should have thought about this before you decided to do your treacherous deed."

I dug my heels in but my feet only slid on the slick hardwood floor. Callie pulled me out of the building to a jeep idling at the curb. Sandra sat behind the wheel and the look in her eyes confirmed to me there was nothing but danger and pain ahead. Women watched curiously as Callie shoved me into the back seat and climbed in beside Sandra. As the jeep sped out of the commune, I caught hostile looks aimed at me but there were others who seemed upset or concerned. I wished at that moment that I had joined their resistance, become part of it. At least then my life would count for something.

It seemed to take only minutes to reach the site. Sandra braked to a stop on top of the bridge overlooking the road where the men worked. Callie hopped down then yanked me out. I fell to my knees and she jerked me to my feet and shoved me to the edge of the bridge, placing me between her and Sandra. The concrete wall came to our waists and I realized if Jonah looked up, he would see me standing between the two women he hated most, as if I were part of their group.

As if sensing my thoughts, Callie nudged me. "Let the treasoner be looked upon as betrayer by both sides. How do you think your boyfriend's going to feel when he looks up here and sees you standing with us?"

I opened my mouth to speak but something hard pressed into my side. I thought it was a gun at first but when it barely pierced my skin and blood oozed down my side, I knew it to be a knife.

Callie leaned close and whispered in my ear, "You move one inch or call out to them, I'll give the order to kill your lover. And you, well, your death won't be so swift."

Sandra laughed. "You thought you were so smart but we outwitted you. What were you going to do, run off with him? Chances are he would have dumped you as soon as he got clear of us. You chose the wrong side, honey."

A whistle sounded and the men, who had been busy clearing the road, stopped their movements. I glanced toward the sky, noting the sun's position. It was close to noon. Lunch time. So it would end here. I debated throwing myself off the bridge to the tarmac below but knew that would be Jonah's death signal, so stood firm. I watched as the men walked toward the drugstore, not seeming in any great hurry, and knew they had to be sick with anticipation. Some sat on the sidewalk outside the drugstore while others remained standing. An attempt, I was sure, to hide those who would step inside to retrieve the guns. Callie had placed two deputies at the site but I could see more step into view now from their hidden positions behind buildings lining the street and begin to make their way toward the others. A loud commotion as the men balled together then broke apart, holding guns. The deputies, now joined by six others, immediately reacted, drawing their own firearms. I watched as Jonah's mouth moved, establishing himself as leader of this revolt, and wondered what he was saying to them, startling when a gunshot rang out and the man next to Jonah collapsed to the ground. Pandemonium as the men tried to shoot back, stunned expressions crossing their faces when they realized there were no bullets to fell their enemies.

"It's coming," Sandra whispered in my ear, pressing against me. "You stand still and don't say a word and your boyfriend just might live through this. You react in any way, he's dead."

Tears streamed down my cheeks and my nose ran and I could not even move to wipe my face. I bit my tongue to keep from calling out to Jonah as the deputies swarmed the men, waving their guns at them, demanding, I'm sure, they drop their weapons. Several men picked up sticks of wood, things lying about with which to arm themselves, but those men were tasered or maced the minute they brought their arms up. Not one shot rang out and I thought, of course. The gene pool must not suffer. Jonah held up his hands and spoke to the deputy closest to him. She placed her gun at his temple and her mouth moved. He looked up at me and the play of emotions that crossed his face nearly brought me to my knees. Confusion changing to betrayal followed by anger. Sandra and Callie both held me upright between them, Callie hissing between her teeth, "Steady, steady, let him see you." Jonah said something to the men and I could see their stance change from hostile to resigned. The deputies started rounding them up, marching them down the street to the bus waiting to take them to the compound. The injured ones limped along or were supported by the others. Jonah looked back at me once and this time there was no pain or anguish of deceit but a clear look of hatred. I had no doubt he would kill me if he could get to me.

After the bus rumbled off, Callie pushed me toward the jeep. I stumbled, falling forward and hitting my forehead on the door.

Sandra jerked me upright. "She's bleeding. Katherine sees this, you're in a whole world of trouble."

Callie made a snorting sound. "Katherine won't say a word. This is minor compared to what's going to happen to her when we get back." She shoved me into the backseat. I closed my eyes against the blood dripping from my forehead, wishing now I had jumped off the bridge when I had the chance.

When we returned to the commune, I noticed a large mass of women gathered in the square, all facing whatever was occurring in their center. I bent my head to my shoulder and wiped the blood off my face, trying to clear my eyes. My head pounded and my stomach rolled. A sense of apprehension swept through my body and I fought the urge to scream and bolt. I wouldn't get far so what would be the point? I forced myself to remain calm, telling myself I would not show my fear to Callie or Sandra. It would only encourage them.

As Sandra braked to a stop, she shared an ominous glance with Callie before stepping out of the jeep. Callie once more pulled me out and shoved me in front of her. Sandra hurried away, as if on an important mission. Women on the outer edge of the group began to notice us and stepped aside, clearing a path as Callie pushed me toward the square. A loud buzz swept through the crowd, reminding me of a swarm of bees, and heads turned to watch me. Looks of alarm intermingled with those of hatred as the women spoke to one another, commenting on my appearance and whatever was happening in the square. We finally broke free of the crowd and I stopped, shocked. Someone had placed a bandana over Jonah's eyes and tied his arms above his head. He was shirtless.

Callie pulled me close and whispered in my ear. "Watch what we do to him because you're next." I gasped when Sandra joined us, handing over a bullwhip to Callie. I had seen that whip in the barn and wondered what a college campus would do with such an evil-looking thing. No matter now. It was in the hands of someone who would put it to dire use.

"No. You'll kill him." I tried pulling away but Callie held firm.

"Maybe I will and maybe I won't. It's up to you." Callie pushed me toward Sandra, who clamped her hand on my arm and squeezed in warning. Callie began coiling the whip. "You say one word, try to interfere in any way, I'll whip him till he's dead. Stay silent, watch the whipping, act like you're part of us, and he'll live." She winked at Sandra. "Won't be too comfortable but what do we care?" She stared at me for a moment. "Clean her up. Don't want lover boy to think we hurt his girlfriend, do we?"

Sandra laughed, her eyes maniacal, and I could understand why the men called her Crazy Eyes. She pulled me along with her through the crowd as Callie stepped into the square. I searched the faces of those I passed, hoping someone, anyone, would stop this craziness. My gaze was met with either hostility or fear, those who perhaps felt some empathy for my predicament turning away as if they couldn't bear to look at me. I saw the empty bus and noticed most of Callie's deputies guarded the others nearby, forcing them to watch.

"Where's Katherine?" I asked.

Sandra glanced at me. "She's here. She's the one who gave the order. Looks like you're not the golden child anymore, kid. Like I told you before, you picked the wrong side." Another deputy joined us, a packet of wet wipes in her hand. I desperately tried to remember her name. Was it Peggy? Sandra forced me to stand still while the deputy wiped my face clean with the wipes.

"She's gonna have a big bruise tomorrow," she said, as she roughly scrubbed dried blood from my forehead.

Sandra snorted. "She'll have a lot more than that by the time Callie gets through with her."

A loud mumbling zipped through the audience and I looked up. Callie and Katherine stood near Jonah, Callie unfurling the bullwhip. "Please, Peggy, this is barbaric. You can't let her do this." I ignored Sandra, pacing restlessly, looking to be frenzied with anticipation.

"Honey, I can't stop her," Peggy said and a look passed over her face. So they weren't all behind Callie and Sandra.

Once she thought I would be presentable, Sandra pulled me closer to Callie and Katherine, placing me within direct eyeshot of Jonah. When Callie noticed me, she stepped forward and tore the blindfold away. Jonah blinked against the light and when his gaze settled on me, the look of loathing I had seen before, a look I thought I would never receive from him, settled on his face. His lips curled in a snarl. If he could get to me, I had no doubt he would seriously try to harm me. I wished he would.

Sandra, standing close to me, said under her breath, "Keep your mouth shut or he dies. It will be up to you how bad this goes for him. As long as he thinks you're with us, he'll live at least. If you give yourself away, Callie won't stop until he's dead."

Tears began to course down my face and she pinched me. "Stop it. Don't let him see you cry. Don't let him see anything from you but contempt."

Katherine stepped between Jonah and me and raised her hands for quiet. The buzzing sound quickly died down as everyone waited to hear what she would say.

Her gaze roamed the crowd and she raised her voice to be heard. "I've asked you all to gather here this afternoon to witness this punishment."

Jonah twisted his torso, trying to get loose. "You don't have the right to do this," he yelled. "You don't have the right to keep me here. This is America. This is supposed to be a free country."

Katherine shook her head as if she couldn't believe him. "This is not the America you knew. We're in control now. You bow down to us."

"I bow to no one," he screamed at her.

"We'll see about that." She turned her back on him. "Each and every one of you knows what our policy is concerning the others. They are here for two purposes, as a labor force and as a means for procreation so we can build our community." She pointed at Jonah. "Inciting a riot and trying to escape will not be tolerated."

"I'm a human being, not some piece of property," Jonah shouted.

Katherine nodded at Callie, who stepped forward and gagged him with the blindfold.

"The others are here and they too will witness what happens when they try to revolt," Katherine continued.

I glanced at the men, noting their looks of disgust, disbelief. They shifted about restlessly, grumbling to each other, and I hoped with great fervor they would at least try to break away and help Jonah.

For several long moments, Katherine looked over the crowd as if searching for discord, listening for a word of protest, but no one spoke. With a nod, Katherine turned back to Callie. "Proceed."

Callie paced away from Jonah, unfurled the whip, and struck. I screamed when it tore Jonah's flesh, watching as he twisted and jerked, trying to free himself. Sandra clamped a hand over my face and I bit, drawing blood. She cursed, pulled back her fist and punched me in the mouth. My lip split and blood dribbled down my chin. She pushed a gun into my side and said, "Bite me again and I don't care what they do to me, I'll kill you. If you want to live, if you want *him* to live, keep your friggin' mouth shut and watch."

I could hear Jonah's sounds of pain, muffled by the gag. I looked at his muscular back, so very beautiful, now distorted as blood ran from the torn strip of flesh. I could not stop the sound of agony that tore through me. Callie looked at me and smiled before lifting the whip and sending it singing against Jonah's skin. I faltered, fell to my knees but was yanked up by Sandra. "Behave," she hissed as another lash sounded. "Remember what I said." But I knew she lied. They wouldn't save him for me. There was no reason to. They had done their damage, Jonah had bought their scheme. He hated me now. Whether he would live or die had already been decided between Katherine and Callie. I closed my eyes and tried not to hear the whistling sound as the whip made its journey toward Jonah's back, the sound of torn flesh when it struck, Jonah's muffled moans. And when the whip landed the tenth time, tearing flesh and producing more runnels of blood, I knew she would not stop until he was dead and did not care whether I lived or not. I broke away from Sandra and ran for Jonah, hoping to insert my body between his and that damned whip. I heard movement behind me, a rush of air, and pain exploded in my head. I watched the ground come up to meet me before everything went black.

CHAPTER 15

Voices from a distance rang in my ears. I fought against the black darkness, moaning at the sharp shards of pain zapping my brain. A comforting hand smoothed hair from my forehead, a voice whispered in my ear, "Lie still. Don't let them know you're conscious." Suzie. So I must be in the infirmary.

"What's wrong with her?" Callie's voice, hard and impatient.

"She's unconscious. She's either got a concussion or Sandra hit her so hard it caused her brain to bleed and swell. If that's the case, there's no hope for her."

"Is there not a test you can do to determine this?" Katherine asked, and I was relieved to hear a hint of worry in her voice.

"If we had the equipment and enough power, sure. But there's no CT scan here or MRI for imaging."

"So what can we do?"

"Wait and see. That's all I know to do. If she regains consciousness, she'll either be normal or damaged. There's no way to tell until – unless she does."

"I told you not to hurt her," Katherine said, her voice harsh and angry.

Callie answered in a defensive tone. "I thought we agreed. She needs to be made an example of, Katherine. We need to show we have no mercy when it comes to treasonous acts against our community."

"We didn't agree to anything concerning Madison, Callie," Katherine said, her voice cool and calm, tinged with anger.

"Well, you thought it was a great idea to punish her lover for trying to revolt. What the hell's the difference when it comes to her? She's just as much at fault as he is."

"Yes, I agreed to the punishment for him but I didn't know you'd almost kill him. And now, Madison."

"What Sandra did was justified. She broke away from them, was running for him, what did you expect her to do?"

"Restrain her," Katherine shouted.

I flinched inwardly. I had never heard her raise her voice.

"She betrayed us, Katherine. She needs to be punished for what she did."

"Dying isn't punishment enough?"

"If she doesn't die."

"She's young, Callie. We should have factored that into account when we decided to mate her. She's vulnerable, had never been in love before. What happened was only natural. If we had thought this out, we would have realized that."

"In that other world," Callie hissed. "Not in this one."

"She hasn't adapted to this one as easily as we have. It's been hard for her."

"You're defending her? After she left guns – fully loaded guns for them so they could revolt and escape?"

"I'm defending no one. She said she loved him, in what other way would she have acted other than to help the man she loves escape?"

"At our cost."

A long silence and I imagined they were staring at one another.

Finally Katherine said, "I'll be in my office. Suzie, let me know if she comes around." A pause, then, "Callie, I don't want to hear that she has mysteriously died in the infirmary. I'm putting my own guard on her. Once she's awake and responsive, we'll decide how to handle this. Until then, I'd suggest you get back to work."

Angry footsteps marched away and their heavy tread told me it was Callie. A hand squeezed my forearm and I imagined it must be Katherine. Relief swept through my body. I had been given a reprieve. But for how long? And what would they decide to do with me once they knew I would live?

Suzie whispered, "Katherine, she is out of control. She's liable to kill again, you know that."

"Not on my watch," Katherine said. "I expect you'll let me know if Callie shows up here again." More demand than question.

"Of course."

Only when Suzie told me it was safe to open my eyes did I allow my body to relax. She sat on a stool by me in a curtained cubicle.

"Is Jonah…" I couldn't say the word. "Did she…"

Suzie shook her head. "He's alive. In a lot of pain but he'll live unless infection sets in."

"Is anyone else here?" I whispered.

"No, we're alone. But not for long. How are you feeling?"

"My head feels like it's splitting apart. Is that what happened, Sandra hit me?"

"Yes, with her sap. I was worried she might have cracked your skull." Suzie shrugged. "She may very well have. I have no way of determining that other than some very basic tests." She held up her hand. "How many fingers do you see?"

"Two."

She produced a small light and shone it in both eyes, told me to follow her index finger with my eyes and to touch my nose with my index fingers. She returned the light to her pocket. "Your eyes aren't dilated, you're responding well neurologically, so hopefully you'll be all right. You'll have to deal with the headache for a bit, though."

I struggled to sit up. "I need to get out of here."

"That's impossible."

"Why not?"

"If your head's hurting now, it's going to be much worse if you get up and move around. Besides, Katherine has placed a guard outside and I'm sure Callie has several of her deputies watching the building. They're just waiting for it."

A low moaning sound came from the other side of the room. Suzie straightened and looked in that direction.

"Is that him?"

She nodded.

I sat up, immediately regretting that when my head pounded and the room spun. I winced, placing my hands on either side of my head. "How badly did she hurt him?"

Suzie made a disgusted sound. "What do you think? She tore him up. He'll be scarred for life."

My mind flashed to his beautiful body, that long, muscular back, and I felt ill. "Is he conscious?"

"No. I gave him enough pain killers to keep him sedated. He needs to stay as still as possible while he heals."

"Did she hurt any of the others?"

"Not yet. You managed to interrupt her plans when Sandra knocked you out. Everything came to a standstill at that point. I think it brought some semblance of sanity back to all of us. Katherine stepped in and stopped Callie from doing any more damage."

I lay back down and closed my eyes, wishing my head would stop throbbing. "I can't believe Katherine allowed her to do that, Suzie. It's barbaric."

"Although we're not the only ones who see it that way, I'm afraid we're not the ones in charge. Something I warned you about awhile ago."

"But I love him. And they made him think I betrayed him, that I told them what he planned to do."

Suzie pulled a blanket over me. "I guess you'll just have to find a way to let him know otherwise. For now, get some rest." She patted my leg and moved away.

I drifted off, visions of torn flesh and crazy eyes and maniacal laughter dominating my dreams. I was vaguely aware of periodically being prodded, questions thrown at me such as what was my name and where was I. I must have answered correctly because each time I was allowed to return to sleep. When I opened my eyes on my own, the infirmary was dark. I heard soft rustling behind my curtained cubicle and wondered who moved about so carefully. Where was Jonah? If he were awake, would he allow me to talk to him, explain what happened? Oh, his back, that bloody mess. And Suzie said he would be scarred for life. A permanent reminder of my perceived betrayal.

I slowly sat up, pulling the blanket away, and slid my feet to the floor. Once I stood, the walls tilted and the floor seemed to be rising up to meet me. I sat back on the gurney with a gasp. Whoever had been moving around paused when they heard me and I climbed back on the mattress and closed my eyes, pretending to be asleep. The curtain squeaked as it was pulled aside and I slit my eyes to see who had come to check on me. Darlene, the veterinary tech who helped deliver Sarah's baby and had named Adam, stood over me, watching. After several long moments, she squeezed my forearm and whispered, "You're not alone, Madison."

What did she mean by that, I wondered, as I listened to her walk away. Not alone in my rebellion or something else? My brain was muddled, I wasn't sure I could even formulate thoughts clearly, so decided to think about it later. The headache had returned with a vengeance so I stilled my body and calmed my breath, seeking sleep, a way to escape this horrible pain. Before slipping into the dark place that beckoned me like a long-lost relative, I prayed I would die.

Later I heard voices outside my cubicle and awoke with a start. Callie, her voice raised in anger, demanding to see me, Suzie refusing, telling her Katherine had ordered Callie not be allowed anywhere near me. So the rift I had once prayed for had occurred. Over me. Who would be stronger, I thought, who would win this one? Callie, evil and conniving, or Katherine, who meant well but could not see beyond her own damaged past? Another voice, apparently the one Katherine had chosen to guard me, entered the fray, demanding Callie leave. I struggled to place voice with face and finally thought, Mandy. More Katherine's assistant than bodyguard but she was loyal to Katherine, she would do what Katherine asked. Someone jerked the curtain back and I froze, my eyes closed, waiting.

"She's faking," Callie said.

"If she were, I'd know it," Suzie answered her. "You're not supposed to be here, Callie, so go away. Let me take care of her." Suzie's voice came closer, creating a disturbance in the air space near my bed. My IV line jiggled and I knew without looking she would be placing her body between Callie and me in the guise of checking the saline drip line. What did I do to deserve this sort of protection, this sort of friendship?

Callie laughed, low and vengeful. "And when she's well, I get her, Suzie, and she's going to be in worse shape than lover boy over there."

After the door slammed behind Callie, I opened my eyes and whispered, "Thank you."

Suzie pulled her stethoscope from around her neck, bent over me as if listening to my heart and said in a low voice, "When you can move without feeling like you're going to pass out, we've got to find some way to get you away from here. If we don't and Callie gets her hands on you, you're dead."

Our eyes met.

"There's discourse among the women, some supporting you, others Callie. Things are in an uproar. You're not safe here."

"And Jonah?"

"He's safe for now. He's not even conscious so they don't perceive him as a threat."

Later that night, I slid off the gurney and stood for a moment, waiting for the dizziness to pass. Once assured I wasn't going to hit the ground, I moved forward in small steps, listening for signs of life nearby. For the past half-hour, the infirmary had been quiet except for Jonah's deep sleep breaths. I couldn't tell if anyone other than the two of us was here but I had to see him. I slid the curtain aside and peeked about. A lamp glowed in the small office at the end of the room but no one occupied the chair at the desk. Jonah lay on his stomach on a gurney across the room from me, his head turned away. I watched the rise and fall of his back as I approached, telling myself not to give myself away if the sight was too gory. As I drew closer, I squinted my eyes as if to protect them from what I might see. A light that had been left on at the head of his bed shone down on his upper torso. At first I thought bandages had been placed across his back, now blood-red and soaked through. Nearer, I realized I was looking at gaping flesh flayed open by the whip. A moan escaped my lips. His once wide, muscular back had been torn apart and I saw no way it could ever be put back together. Suzie said he would be scarred for life and I did not doubt that for one minute. And I would be next. It surprised me to realize I didn't care. Let Callie kill me.

I reached toward him and caught myself before touching him. "I am so sorry," I whispered.

He stirred at my voice and I stepped back.

"Get away from me," he said, his voice muffled by the pillow.

"I need to talk to you," I said, "explain things."

"Leave me alone." His voice, filled with pain, rang out.

The door to the supply room opened and Suzie rushed toward me. "Shhh, you'll bring the guard."

Tears streamed down my face. "But I want to tell him—"

Voices from outside the room drew nearer.

Suzie steered me away. "There's no time for that. We need to get you out of here. Now. Do you think you can run?"

"I think so. The dizziness isn't so bad now. But, Suzie—"

"Be quiet," she hissed, grabbing clothes off the small desk nearby as she herded me toward my cubicle. "Hurry, get into these." She pulled the curtain closed, turned me around, untied my hospital gown. "Quick, we can't waste any time."

The outer door burst open and footsteps came toward us. "But what about Jonah?" I whispered.

"I'll take care of him. You're the one who's in the most danger now."

A loud clatter sounded nearby and Jonah's voice rose to a roar. Gooseflesh raced up and down my arms, hearing that. The pain he must be feeling! Mandy and Callie's guard's voices drifted away as they talked in low urgent tones. They would probably hurt him as they tried to restrain him.

I turned to go to Jonah but Suzie pulled me back. "Forget about him for now. I'll take care of him, make sure they don't hurt him. But you need to get out of here."

"How should I leave? Is there a back door? Through a window?" I asked as I pulled on jeans.

"No. Callie has the doors watched. We need to find a way to get you past the guard to this room. Once you're clear, go to the roof. It's a small jump to the next building then you can go down the stairs and out that door."

I pulled a t-shirt over my head. "What do I need to do?"

Suzie pushed tennis shoes into my hands. "We'll have to create a diversion."

"Suzie, Callie will kill you if she knows you helped me escape."

"That doesn't matter. You need to get out of here now, Madison."

A loud cry startled us both. Suzie drew the curtain back and I turned to see Jonah, wavering on his feet. Mandy and Sandra, the guard Callie had placed on me, were circling around him, getting into position to take him down. They tracked Jonah lurching around the room, roaring with pain and anger as he spied me and began to make his way toward me. Seeing this, Mandy rushed to my aid, Sandra toward Jonah. When she reached him, he shoved her hard and she landed on her butt. I thought, his back, he just broke open any of those red welts that were healing. He had to be in horrific pain.

Suzie pushed me toward the door, whispering, "Go, go, go," as Mandy hurried toward Sandra, placing herself between me and Jonah. I ran.

The next few moments were lost in panic and angst as I stumbled my way to the roof. Somehow I made it without encountering another person and without even thinking about it jumped to the next building. I lurched down the stairs, holding fast to the handrails to keep from falling, my feet many times missing the steps, thinking it was a miracle I didn't break a bone, and flew out the back door. I stood, breathing in the sweet night air, my head spinning, my stomach rolling. For several long moments, I debated which way to go. My thoughts could not cohese and I began to panic. Then it dawned on me. The quickest way out was by wheels and if it had not been moved my motorcycle was within running distance. I staggered toward the student center, praying Callie hadn't had the forethought to sabotage or relocate it. But it was where I left it, unchained by the bike stand. I crouched beside the motorcycle, searching the area around me. No one lurked nearby and no lights shone inside the building. I mounted the cycle and breathed a sigh of relief when it started. Without regard for the noise it made or that it would alert Callie and the other deputies, I roared down the main street of campus and onto the thoroughfare, thinking, kill me if you want. But if you don't, I'm coming back for Jonah and someone will pay for what you did to him.

I didn't stop the cycle until I reached Seth's and Sarah's front yard. By that time, I was having trouble focusing and my head felt as if it were going to explode. I let the bike fall as I stepped off and collapsed on the ground.

The door opened and Seth came onto the porch. When he saw me, he ran down the steps and knelt beside me. "Madison?" he asked in a low voice.

"Seth? Is she okay?" I heard Sarah speak from the porch.

"Maddie? Can you get up?" His voice, edged with concern, unloosed me. I put my hands over my face and began to sob. "Shit," he said.

I had the sudden urge to bray with laughter over that.

Sarah, beside me now, pulled at my hands. "Madison? Are you hurt? Can you speak? What happened?"

I couldn't answer them. All I could think about was Jonah stumbling around that room, crazy with loathing for me, saving my life through his hatred. Oh, what would they do to him? What would they do to Suzie?

I forced myself to stop crying and sat up straight, wiping my face with my hand. "I have to go back."

"What? Where?" Seth said.

"They have Jonah." I looked at Sarah and the tears started anew. "They whipped him, Sarah. With a bullwhip. They almost killed him. They made him think I did it, that I betrayed him, turned him in. Oh, God, his back. What they did to his back." The world spun around me and I lay back on the ground.

"She's hurt, Seth," Sarah said.

"No, Sarah, I'm fine. I just need to rest a minute. I have to go back. I have to save him. He saved me." Arms wrapped around me and I was lifted into the air. "Put me down, Seth. They'll kill him. I have to help him. I should have thought this through." My words sounded slurred to me and I panicked I couldn't make them understand what I was trying to say.

"They'll kill you, the condition you're in," Seth said, his voice hard and firm. "You can't stand against anyone like this, much less save him."

My stomach rolled and I turned my head away and threw up. Seth waited patiently then began moving again.

"What happened to you? Where are you hurt?"

I fought to stay awake. "Sandra hit me in the back of the head with a sap. I may have a concussion. Seth, put me down, I have to…"

I don't remember him carrying me into the house or what happened next.

CHAPTER 16

I awoke the next morning in a comfortable bed, the sun shining through the window, a gentle breeze lifting the gauzy curtains from the floor. The low purr of a generator rumbled outside the window and the luring smell of coffee drifted up the stairs. A wet tongue licked my arm and I looked down to see Adam, my precious dog, curled up against me. I turned on my side, molding myself around his warm body, buried my face in his fur, and thought, why does everything look and feel so normal when nothing is?

I must have dozed off. When I awoke next, Adam was gone and the room was too warm. I sat up, waiting for the dizziness and nausea to return, but other than a slight headache, I seemed to have improved. I slowly got out of bed, noticing someone – hopefully Sarah – had replaced my clothes with a soft, cotton nightgown, the likes of which my grandmother had worn. I ran my hands down the fabric, the pain of missing her stabbing my heart with a fierceness I didn't think I could stand. A woman who was part of the feminist movement of the 60s, who marched in the Civil Rights movement, served as a nurse in the Vietnam War, who fought her battles through word and deed. I wondered what she would do in my situation. Go save Jonah, of course. She wouldn't even think twice about it.

I found my jeans and top neatly folded on the trunk at the end of the bed. I jerked them on and ran downstairs where I found Seth in the kitchen pouring a cup of coffee. He looked at me and said before I could even voice it, "You're not going anywhere. Not until you've given me a chance to make sure you're not concussed and we've talked about this."

I shook my head.

His eyes traveled over me. "You're a mess, Madison. You don't look like you've eaten in days, your clothes are torn and muddy, and you don't smell so good right now. Go take a shower. After that, we'll talk."

Tears spilled down my cheeks.

"If he's as hurt as you say, they won't do anything to him. If I know Callie and Crazy Eyes, they'll want him conscious and alert for what they have planned for him. You've got time."

With a nod, I turned and went upstairs. In the bathroom, I peeled off my clothes, ashamed at how sweaty I smelled. I noticed the cuts and bruises all over my body, patches of dirt and grime. It despaired me to realize I had been so filthy and was never even aware of it. I sat on the edge of the tub, my mind in turmoil. I needed to go back, to get Jonah out of there, but how? One person could not stand against Callie and her minions. Would they hurt him because of my actions or would Callie wait until he was well enough to withstand more punishment like Seth thought? Talk to Seth and Sarah, my inner voice whispered, and I sighed, thinking this was best. I couldn't think clearly where Jonah was concerned. I needed advice from someone not so subjective. And if they were going to kill Jonah, he would be dead by now. Tears stung my eyes at that and I forced them back, telling myself if he were dead, I'd know it somehow. But he felt alive to me.

I turned on the water and stepped into the shower, hoping the weather had been warm enough to at least keep the water temperature near tepid. Even though goose bumps broke out on my body when I turned on the spray, I forced myself to stay long enough to wash my hair and scrub my body, wincing with pain when I bent over to wash my feet. Feeling refreshed, I dried off, wrapped a towel around me and returned to the bedroom. In a closet, I found a long t-shirt and pair of women's jeans near enough to my size to be wearable. I pulled these on and went downstairs to Seth and Sarah.

Sarah sat in a rocking chair near the window, nursing her baby. She looked up when I stepped into the room and a smile broke across her face. "You look better."

Seth stood at the stove, flipping pancakes on a griddle. "God, anything would be an improvement over the way she looked last night," he said with a wink.

I lightly punched him on the shoulder as I passed by, ignoring his "Ouch".

I knelt down beside Sarah, ran my hand over the baby's downy head. "He's growing."

"Like a weed."

"Kid will eat us out of house and home once he starts on food," Seth growled.

I smiled at him. It was obvious he loved being daddy to a child that was not his.

Adam nudged my hand and I knelt down to pet him, then Eve when she joined us. Both dogs looked to be healthy and happy and were obviously good companions for one another.

Seth set a plate of hotcakes on the table. "You hungry? Think your stomach can take any food?"

I looked around for my backpack. "I have to get back, Seth. I have to help Jonah."

"You can't help anyone if you pass out from hunger." He cocked an eyebrow at me. "You're skinny as a rail. When did you last eat?"

Stunned, I couldn't recall. My face must have registered this.

"That's what I thought. Take time, eat first, and afterwards we'll talk about what we can do."

"I am famished." After I put kibble in Adam's and Eve's bowls, I placed cutlery on the table. Again, thinking this all felt so normal when it so obviously wasn't. The thought of saving Jonah pricked at my brain like a no-seeum pecking at flesh but I forced myself to wait, to talk this over with Seth and Sarah, people I figured were much more rational than I was at that moment, to come up with a plan on how best to help him escape.

During breakfast, Seth and Sarah cast concerned glances at me but waited until I wolfed down a plateful of the pancakes topped with maple syrup. Once I sat back, wiping my mouth, Seth picked up the plate and carried it to the sink. His back to me, he said, "Do you feel up to telling us what happened?"

The food in my stomach, moments before, so pleasurable and comforting, formed a hard, cold lump. I fought the urge to vomit.

Sarah reached over, placed her hand on top of mine. "If it upsets you too much, then don't, Madison." Her voice, so filled with worry and love, brought tears to my eyes.

I squeezed her hand. "I need to tell it, Sarah. I need to figure out what to do."

Seth , trailing his hand across Sarah's upper back, sat down across from me. "Then tell us, Madison. Maybe we can help."

I realized with a start I had never spoken of Jonah to them so began when I first saw him, in the commune square, facing off with Callie and her deputies. The way he made me feel. How we were paired first, the friendship that developed which turned into a romantic relationship. "I love him," I said, my voice breaking. Then on to the night he whispered those dreaded words to me, how I perceived them, the rift between us that couldn't be repaired even when we began to sleep together again. How I helped them plan to get free and how I was caught and forced to reveal myself as the traitor to their escape and the cruel punishment Callie administered while I was made to watch. "And he believed them," I said, my voice low. "He hates me now. Can't stand me. I think he'd kill me if he could." I placed my hands over my face, tried to force myself to calm down.

Seth waited for me to regain my composure. "How bad is he hurt?"

"Suzie says he'll be scarred for life." I sat up straighter. "I have to go back. I have to get him out of there. He caused enough of a distraction last night that gave me a chance to escape. God, why did I do that? I should have stayed, helped him. They'll kill him, Seth, I know they will, after what he did. And poor Suzie, I know Callie will blame her."

Seth reached over and squeezed my shoulder. "Madison, if you had stayed, they would have killed you. You know that."

I burst into tears, feeling so helpless.

"Listen to me. You can't help anyone if you become hysterical. We've got to decide the best thing to do and we can't do that unless you're calm enough to think rationally."

I nodded, wondering when I had become such a crybaby. I didn't think I'd ever cried this much in my entire life. But then, my life before the pox had been so protected, so without upheaval or trauma. I wondered briefly if I could stand to get through this, then thought I had to. For him.

I sat up straight and breathed deep. "I'm going back, Seth, to see if I can help him escape. They will kill him if they haven't already. Callie will want him dead. It gives her the excuse she was looking for."

"Even though he's so hurt?" Sarah said, placing the baby against her shoulder and patting his back.

"That doesn't matter to Callie. She's got Sandra egging her on. And she's broken rank with Katherine. I'm not sure who's in charge now, to be honest. If it's Callie, God help us all."

"What do you plan to do?" Seth asked.

"I don't know really. Ride to the outskirts of the campus, watch for an opening, and when I have it, take it. Go in and get him out."

"You'll need help."

"I won't ask you to risk your life for this, Seth. You have Sarah and the baby. You need to stay and protect them."

Seth turned to Sarah and the two seemed to communicate with their eyes. I watched with interest. Would I ever have that sort of relationship with a man or was I doomed to be on my own, alone, forever?

Sarah gave a slight nod and Seth turned to me. "When do we leave?"

"Seriously, I can't take you with me. What if something happened to you? I could never forgive myself."

Seth gave a beleaguered sigh. "Madison, what they're doing is wrong, and if you're right, if she's going to kill him, then we need to do what we can to get him out of there. And hopefully save the rest of the other men." He scooted his chair back and stood. "I'll go get my guns and some ammo, then we need to head out."

After he left the room, I turned to Sarah. "Please, Sarah, you can't let him do this. He could get hurt. He could get killed."

"And what about you, Madison? You're risking your life to save Jonah. You risked your life to save us." She gazed at me for a long moment and lowered her voice when she spoke. "Ever since we left, I can tell it bothers him he left the other men behind. He feels guilty about that. I think he needs to do this, Madison. But you have to promise me you'll help him after you've rescued Jonah. Help Seth save the others. They're important too."

"Of course I will." A sense of shame suffused my face. My thoughts had only been for Jonah, for getting him out of there. I hadn't even considered the others. And when I helped Seth and Sarah escape, again, I had not thought about the others and what they had been and would continue going through. I stood, leaned over and kissed her on the cheek. "Thank you," I whispered. "Tell Seth I'll be outside."

While Seth made his preparations, I visited Boomer in the meadow behind the barn, with Adam and Eve tagging along. Once nearly emaciated, my horse had filled out nicely, his muscularity in evidence, his beautiful coat shiny and healthy. He greeted me with a familiar nudge and I ran my hand up and down beneath his mane as I talked lovingly to him. God, how I had missed my furry friends. I swore to them that if I made it back, I would be with them for good. Horse and dog eyed me as if they understood every word I said. When I saw Seth standing at the door to the barn, I kissed Boomer between the eyes, knelt down and hugged and kissed Adam, then Eve, and left, not looking back. Please, God, let me come back to them, I prayed as I walked toward Seth.

Seth had loaded his motorcycle with rifles and handguns tucked into deep, spacious saddlebags. He handed me several pistols and I placed them in my own saddlebags, adding another beside the one tucked into my waistband at mid back. I slung a rifle over my shoulder before stepping on the motorcycle.

Seth nodded at me. "You ready?"

I kicked it in gear and we were off, waving to Sarah who stood on the porch, holding a sleeping baby in her arms. Even from a distance, I could see the worry etched onto her face.

We parked the motorcycles at the bottom of a slight rise behind the soccer field of the college campus and walked the rest of the way. We didn't talk as we made our way up the hill. At the top, we hid behind the open bleachers, studying the scene below. Women were once more milled together in the common area, spilling onto the lawns of the surrounding buildings.

"Something's going on," I said to Seth.

He zipped open his backpack and pulled out a pair of binoculars. Put them to his eyes and focused, watching for a moment, his mouth set in a firm line. Without a word he handed it to me. I gasped once I zeroed in on what was transpiring beneath us. Callie and Sandra stood on a wooden platform – who in the world built that I wondered with a crazy sense of disbelief – Jonah between them. Callie looked to be addressing the women below. Even from this distance, I could see the jerky movements of Sandra, knew she was highly agitated and eager for whatever was forthcoming. I spanned across the crowd, searching for Katherine, but didn't find her anywhere. I came back to the platform and there, right behind Callie, Jonah and Sandra stood a line of three deputies, all with rifles slung over their shoulders. None looked too happy at the events on the stage. Another formation of deputies surrounded the others, their guns pointed at the men who milled about restlessly.

"They're going to kill him," I said.

"Looks it."

I turned to Seth and handed the binoculars back. "I'm going down there."

"They'll kill you, Madison. You know that."

"I have to try, Seth. I don't know what else to do."

"I'll go with you and—"

"No, I can't let you do that."

"Let me finish. I'll go with you and break off when we enter the main street. I'll put myself in position on top of the tallest building." He looked over the campus and pointed. "There, the library."

"That should work."

"Okay. I'll go to the roof, play sniper. That's all I know to do."

"It's enough. If they take me down, just get out of there."

"After I get the others out. They're down there watching like everyone else."

"You see where they're at?"

"Yes."

"I'll help you once I get Jonah away from Callie." I rose to my feet and when he stood hugged him hard. "Thank you, friend," I said, before running down the hill.

I hopped on my motorcycle, vaguely aware of Seth, right behind me, kicking his cycle into gear. We raced toward the main street of the campus, sliding to a stop one block down from the nearest cluster of women. I slung another rifle over my shoulder, stuffed another gun into my belt and took off at a run. Seth split apart, heading toward the library. On the outskirts of the women, I strode through, amazed at how easily they parted and let me pass. Aware of increased grumblings, I wasn't sure if they approved of my being there or wanted to kill me. No one challenged me, though, as I stepped between the women in front of the platform and waited for Callie to spy me. Only then did I notice she and Sandra were holding Jonah upright. His hands were tied behind his back and his head slumped forward onto his chest. I couldn't tell if he was conscious or simply so weak he could barely stand.

When Callie noticed me, her eyes gleamed with delight. "I was hoping you'd show up." She slightly inclined her head toward Sandra, who stepped off the platform. Jonah slumped toward the ground and when Callie let him go landed on his side, his head banging into the wood. Before Sandra drew near, I slid the rifle off my shoulder and aimed it at Callie, pulled a pistol from my waistband and pointed it at Sandra. "Anyone touches me, Callie dies." The deputies in the firing squad watched but did not challenge my actions. Some of the ones around the others seemed to become agitated, torn between their desire to protect Callie and to do their duty and keep the men under guard.

Sandra stopped when I spoke and turned to Callie, who seemed to find this amusing. "We're going to kill him either way," she said. "And you right along with him."

"And what's the charge, Callie?"

"For you or him?"

"Does it matter? Whatever you say is trumped up anyway. Isn't it enough that you practically killed him with that whip?"

"He committed another violation after that." Callie's voice rose so the audience could hear her. "As I was saying before I was so rudely interrupted, he is charged with obstruction of justice and aiding and abetting in the escape of a wanted criminal." She looked at me and smiled. "Meaning you."

"He didn't help me escape. He was trying to kill me," I shouted. "I ran to get away from him and you."

"Yet you return to save him."

I glanced around. "Where is Katherine?"

"She can't help you now. She's relinquished all control to me."

I looked at the women. Some gazed at me with sympathy, others with hatred. Some seemed anxious, others agitated by what was occurring in their midst. "If you allow her to kill him and me, you're part of this," I yelled. "She doesn't have the right to commit murder. None of us does."

"Yet they were willing to kill my deputies and me in order to escape," Callie answered, her voice booming over the crowd.

"You don't have the right to imprison them in the first place," I said. "This is America after all. We're all free. Or at least that's what America stands for."

"This is a new America," Callie said. "Women are in control and women will remain in control and we will do all things necessary to ensure that."

"Including murder."

"Yes, if it comes to that."

"Was there a trial, Callie? In less than a day, did you have a trial and find him guilty?"

She debated for a moment before saying, "You might say we had a tribunal."

"Consisting of Callie and Sandra, I'm sure."

Sandra, beside me, snorted. "Isn't that enough?"

"Then me for him," I said to Callie.

Her smile faded. "You're offering yourself in exchange for one of the others?"

"Yes. Let him go. Once he's safe, I'll turn myself over to you. Do what you want with me."

Rumblings among the crowd now. I could sense the tension in the air like static before a storm. Good or bad, I didn't know and didn't dare hope.

Callie seemed to consider this before shaking her head. "Nope. I've got you both so why should I settle for just one?"

"Because I'll kill you if you harm him or Sandra gets too close to me."

Callie looked at Sandra and in a nanosecond I knew they were going to try something. Callie pulled her gun and aimed it at Jonah. At the same moment, Sandra lunged at me. I stepped away, trying to focus on Callie. A shot rang out and I watched a red spot bloom on Callie's forehead before she fell face-forward onto the stage. Thank God for Seth I thought in the fraction of a second before pandemonium broke out. I was pushed and shoved as women jostled around me. It took several seconds before I realized they were forming a barrier around me. Sandra's hands reached through the bodies, trying to get to me, and I backed away, saying to the women around me, "I have to get to Jonah. Keep her away from me." Sandra's shrieks followed me as I made my way to the stage, women surrounding me, shoving Sandra and her followers back. I wondered how long it would be before one of Callie's minions got her hands on me and feared it would only be seconds. I stepped onto the stage and only then remembered the firing squad and the deputies guarding the others. Several of them seemed to be involved in trying to control the men, who were pushing against them, fighting for their freedom. Most, though, simply stood by, their guns in their hands, watching the women.

Linda joined me when she saw me on stage. "What do you need?" she shouted over the crowd.

"I need to get him away. I can't tell who's with Callie and who isn't."

"I think most are with us," she said, kneeling beside Jonah and placing one of his arms around her shoulder. I did the same on the other side and together we dragged him off the rear of the stage and to the bus Callie used to transport the others between job sites.

Once Jonah was safely ensconced inside, I said, "Where are the keys to this bus and the handcuffs to the others?"

"On Callie's belt," Sandra said. "I'll get them." I hurried off the bus, looking for Seth, watching as he jogged toward the others. I hurried over to him, pulling my pistol and joining the fray. With the aid of what seemed to be a great majority of the women, we hustled the others to safety and got them loaded on the bus. Linda appeared at my side, pressing keys into my hands. "Here. Go now. Get them away to safety."

"I have to see Katherine first. Where is she?"

"In her office, I think."

Linda turned away but I pulled her back. "They need a leader right now, Linda. I'm not so sure they'll accept Katherine anymore."

Her gaze held mine for a long moment. "I'll do what I can," she said.

I turned to Seth. "Go, Seth. I'll meet you at the house."

He gave me a questioning look. "I'll be fine. Thanks for helping me. I couldn't have done it without you." I gave him a quick hug and ran toward the student building.

I stepped into the dark building, a sense of urgency tingling down my spine. I found Katherine in her office, sitting in her chair, her eyes closed. Suzie sat near her, her face pale, wearing an expression of extreme agitation.

When Katherine heard movement at the door, she glanced that way and gave a sigh of relief when she saw me. "Thank God," she whispered.

I focused my attention on Suzie. "I've been so worried about you."

Suzie's gaze never left Katherine. "It's a good thing you came. I have a strong feeling we were next on Callie's agenda."

When my eyes met Katherine's, she said in a very small voice, "I'm afraid I created quite the monster, Madison."

"Well, your monster's dead," I replied in a cold tone.

She closed her eyes for a moment, repeating, "Thank God."

Suzie leaned toward her, pressed her hand against her forearm.

It seemed odd how stiff Katherine sat in the chair, the fact that she kept her profile to me. I slowly walked around the desk, gasping when I saw Katherine full-face. The front of her white blouse was stained red and I noted her breathing seemed shallow and unsteady.

Tears prickled my eyes. I knelt beside her, took her hand in mine. "Katherine?" I said, my voice sounding very much like a young child's.

She gave me a wan smile. "It's probably for the best, don't you think? I've allowed so many atrocities to be committed, it's only fair I pay the price."

I looked back at Suzie, who answered my unspoken question with one word: "Callie." She shook her head at my silent inquiry: will she live?

I burst into tears. "But why did she do this?"

"Because she is insane," Katherine breathed.

"Katherine challenged her but Callie was too far gone by then. She shot Katherine to keep her from going outside."

"I'm so sorry, Katherine."

She put her hand on my cheek. "Oh, child, I'm so sorry for what I've put you through. I love you Madison, you're the daughter I never had." She hesitated, and I watched blood bubbling at the inner corners of her lips. "He took that away from me," she said, her eyes distant. "I wanted a child so much and with his fists he made sure I would never be granted that wish."

"You were right to hate him, Katherine," I whispered. "Thank you for being a mother to me. I would not have survived without you."

Her gaze focused on me. "Oh, Madison, you are a survivor, don't you know that yet?" Her eyes glazed and her chest heaved one last breath. I turned to Suzie who shook her head and held her arms out to me.

Once I had myself under control, my thoughts turned to Jonah. I wiped my eyes and pushed hair off my face. "Suzie, there's pandemonium out there. Can you help Linda put a stop to this?"

Her brow furrowed. "I don't know how, Madison."

"Go out there and talk to them. Tell them Katherine's dead at Callie's hand. Help them to heal from this. But whatever you do, learn from this. Remember the community Katherine wanted to form before Callie joined us and convinced her otherwise. We don't have the right to enslave men, to force women to procreate. This isn't some third-world dystopian country. This is America. Remember that. Honor that. Live that."

"I don't know if I can do this by myself."

"You have Linda to help you but no more Callies with their own agenda trying to influence you to their way of thinking."

Suzie stood, a determined look on her face. "I'll go. I'm tired of being afraid of voicing my own thoughts." Her eyes darted toward Katherine then returned to me. "Will you stay, Madison?"

I leaned over and kissed Katherine's cheek, saying a quiet prayer for her soul. "There's no reason to anymore. I'm going to see to Jonah's safety. I don't know where I'll go from there. But that's what I want to concentrate on right now."

"He'll be safe here. I promise you that."

"But I don't think he'll feel safe and it's important he do." I held out my hand to her. "Help them, Suzie. Help this commune get back on the right track."

She placed her hand in mine and we walked outside together. I watched as Suzie took the stage and waited to be noticed. She motioned for Linda to join her and the two women stood side by side, looking proud and powerful. Few of the women were skirmishing now. The deputies who helped Seth and me had taken the guns away from the ones who tried to keep the others here and all stood together with no sign of animosity between them. The exception was Sandra and a few of her deputy friends, in the midst of the women, with disgruntled looks on their faces. I noticed someone had dragged Callie's body off the stage, a red splotch of blood a reminder of what happened to her.

When the uproar died to a low mumbling sound and women had ceased arguing, Suzie raised her voice and spoke. She began by breaking the news of Katherine's death. This was met with wails of protest, denial, sadness. Once this died down, she talked of the beginnings of a different commune, one for women only. No men would be allowed to reside there, none would be used for labor or procreation, she said, and encouraged those who favored a commune with men or to have a relationship with a man to seek refuge elsewhere. Her voice grew stronger as she spoke about a harmonious community of women who would raise their own crops, do their own chores, and live together peacefully and without conflict. I watched the women's faces, noticed the majority nodding along, smiling at times, as Suzie painted for them a perfect world without strife or contention. Some, though, would shake their head or shoot belligerent looks my way while others seemed discomforted by her words, and I imagined these women would not be here tomorrow.

Sandra stepped forward, rudely interrupting Suzie's discourse. "I can't listen to this shit anymore." She turned and pointed at me. "This isn't over, not by a long shot," she yelled then shoved past me and stalked off down the street. Several women followed her, each giving me hostile looks as they passed.

Linda moved as if to follow and Suzie said, "Let her go. We don't need the likes of her." And that seemed to matter more to the women than anything. They began to relax, to clap during her speech, some whistling and cheering. And I knew Suzie now had Katherine's perfect little world without men's interference, a world where Katherine would have been happy without fear of a monster who developed the need to crush her. Suzie went on to announce that in the near future there would be an election for a mayor and board of commissioners to rule over the commune. Democracy would be alive and well here, I thought, as I watched the women accept this, noting the happy looks on their faces.

When I left, most of the women of the commune had gathered around Suzie and Linda, seeming excited and happy at the forthcoming transition.

I started my motorcycle, my mind turning to Jonah's condition, praying he would be alive when I got back to Seth's and Sarah's house. As I rode out of the commune, I kept darting looks around me, searching for Sandra and her cohorts. But I never saw them. Perhaps they had gone in another direction. I hoped they had put the community behind them and would find a place for themselves but feared for the people with whom they might decide to settle.

CHAPTER 17

It took a short while to return to Seth's and Sarah's home and a thrill of anticipation ran though me when I saw the bus sitting in their driveway. I braked to a stop, nodding at several men sitting on the front lawn enjoying the sunshine. Others were gathered in the shade of the porch and I said hello as I passed. One caught my hand and squeezed it. A man who must at one time have been a giant although lean meals and hard work had left its mark on his nearly emaciated body.

"Thank you," he said.

I squeezed back. "Wish I'd done it sooner," was all I could manage as tears gathered in my eyes.

Sarah had opened all the windows in the house and the cool cross-breeze as I walked toward the kitchen was a welcome relief. There I found Seth administering first aid to a man who sat on a kitchen chair gritting his teeth and stoically trying not to cry out as Seth stitched a cut on his arm with a needle and thread. My stomach twisted when it dawned on me there was no anesthesia to deaden the pain. I turned away, motioning to another man standing in the shadows of the room.

Seth noticed me then and flashed a smile my way. "Glad to see you made it back."

"Thanks," I said as I guided the man to sit in the chair I held out for him.

"Everything go okay?"

"Sandra and her bullies left. Katherine's dead." My voice broke and I cleared my throat. "Suzie, she's the nurse practitioner, took control and promised no more men as slaves or using women for procreation."

Seth nodded. "That's a start."

I crossed over to him, touched his arm. "Thank you, Seth."

Seth nodded and I knew the death he caused would be with him for a good while. "Had to be done," was all he said.

I returned to the man in the chair. "What's your name?" I said, startled to realize he was probably close to my age underneath all the dirt and grime covering his chocolate-colored skin. Had they even allowed them to wash lately?

"Micah."

"Are you hurt? What can I do for you?"

He pulled off a boot and gray sock that had once been white. His foot was splotched with purple spots, swollen and blistered.

"What happened?" I said, bending down and lifting it up with care.

"Boots they assigned me don't fit right. Kept rubbing my feet raw, especially this one."

I looked at Seth, watching me.

"There's Epsom salts under the sink. Put some in a deep pan and have him soak his feet. I'll check him when I'm through here."

After I had Micah's feet soaking – his sigh of contentment a welcome sound to me – I asked Seth if I could do anything else.

"You might want to see if they're hungry. If they are—"

"No need to ask," Micah said. "We're starving. They haven't fed us since day before yesterday."

"Easy enough to remedy that." I headed toward the refrigerator. "How many men are you in all?"

"I reckon there's about ten of us." Micah sighed. "Shoot, this sure feels good." Our eyes met. "Thank you for all you did."

I turned my back. "Wish it'd been sooner," I repeated.

"You did good."

I pulled out lettuce and tomatoes, cans of Spam, mayonnaise and a couple of loaves of Sarah's homemade yeast bread and made 20 sandwiches. After serving two to Micah and two to the man being stitched, along with a bowl of potato chips, I put the remaining sixteen on a platter and took that along with a bag of chips to the front porch. I didn't have to ask the men if they were hungry or wanted to eat, they dug into the meal at once. I returned to the kitchen for water bottles and passed those around noting the looks of respect and words of thanks, thinking I did not deserve any of it. I had left them there too long, had let things go on that shouldn't have, had turned a blind eye for no other reason than I didn't want to be concerned or lose the life I had chosen with Katherine. I owed these men a great deal. And the dead ones, I owed them so much more. I knew my inability to rectify that would stay with me for the rest of my life.

In the kitchen, Seth had bandaged the stitches and was now working on Micah's feet.

I couldn't stand it any longer. "Um, Seth, where's Jonah?"

"He's upstairs with Sarah. She's tending his wounds."

"He conscious?"

"No."

Good. At least I could see him. I ran up the stairs and walked down the hall, peeking into rooms as I passed. They had placed Jonah in a guest bedroom at the end of the hall. He lay on his stomach on the bed and Sarah stood over him, gently tending the lash marks on his back. She looked up when I stepped into the room and gave me a quick smile. "I'm so glad you made it back. I was worried."

"How is he?"

"Unconscious. Which is a good thing or he wouldn't be able to bear me treating his wounds."

I stepped closer and almost vomited at the swollen, torn flesh. "It doesn't look like it's healed any."

"I'm sure them manhandling him opened up the wounds. He'll be fine."

"But scarred for life."

"Yes, Seth thinks so."

"Because of me."

"No. Because of Callie."

I stepped to the window and looked out, unable to bear seeing Jonah so injured.

"How did it go?" she said in a low voice.

I told her what happened, trying not to watch as she applied Vaseline to the torn flesh on his back. "Why Vaseline?"

"Seth said it's a good germ killer. I guess we're going to need to find a pharmacy so we can get some drugs. You know, pain killers, possibly antibiotics. Some of these wounds look like they may be becoming infected. I'll have Seth check them when he's finished downstairs."

She stood, stretching her back, her face breaking into a wide smile when Seth stepped into the room. For two young people, they seemed so mature to me. Way beyond my years.

Seth lightly touched her cheek. "Baby's awake."

Sarah groaned. "And probably hungry."

Seth watched her go, giving me a quick smile before turning his attention to Jonah. "So this is your man, huh?"

"Not any longer. He hates me. He'd probably leave if he knew I was here and he could actually get up and walk."

"Maybe someone needs to tell him what really happened."

"What's the point, Seth? He believed them, thought I'd actually betrayed him."

"Is that any different from you believing he asked you to help him escape for the wrong reason?"

I had no answer for that.

Seth probed at the flesh on Jonah's back. "Sarah did a good job. I guess we'll just have to wait and see what happens."

"What if he wakes up, thrashes around? Won't he open the wounds again?"

"We need to keep him as still as we can. I figured I'd head into the next town over and find a pharmacy. He's going to need antibiotics, sedatives, something to help him sleep. Micah needs antibiotics too. His feet are in poor shape."

"Anyone else injured?"

"Some minor infections from lacerations. Nothing major. Nothing that needs a lot of attention."

"Listen, you have all these men here. Why don't I go into town? You tell me what you need and I'll get it for you."

His face cleared. I could see he had been worried about leaving Sarah and the baby. "That's doable. I'll make you a list."

After Seth left, I stared down at Jonah, loving his face, so young and innocent in sleep, grieving the mutilation of his back. He's safe now, I told myself as I leaned down, brushed my mouth across his cheek, watching his lips twitch. "I'm so sorry," I said before leaving.

I chose to go to a town to the north of the house, in the opposite direction of the commune. It was a small resort-like community, one I had visited with my family years ago. I rode my motorcycle down the main street, easily finding a pharmacy. The door wasn't locked – it seemed no doors remained locked these days – and I picked up a basket and strolled down the aisles, checking for supplies on Seth's list. I had to go behind the counter for the antibiotics he wanted and it took a bit of searching to find syringes and needles. Once I had everything I needed, I took the basket outside and packed everything away in my saddlebags. I returned to the pharmacy with my backpack, robbed an aisle of its packages of candy bars and boxes of snacks until my pack couldn't contain anymore. Headed toward the door, I heard a hissing sound and stopped dead in my tracks. Was that a snake? Oh, God, please don't let it be a rattler, I thought as my eyes darted this way and that, trying to find the varmint. A rustling sound came from behind me and I turned, backing toward the door as I searched the floor. Another sound came from the same direction, a faint whimper. Intrigued, I got down on my knees and looked under a stand displaying reading glasses. A small orange and white tabby hissed at me as it backed away.

"Oh, you poor baby," I crooned, reaching my fingers beneath then holding them steady, hoping the kitten would come to me. It took some coaxing and several long moments but he finally eased forward, sniffing at my hand. "I won't hurt you, I promise," I said. "I'll take you to a good home where you'll have plenty to eat and two dogs to play with." The kitten studied me for awhile then apparently decided I could be trusted and stepped into the palm of my hand. I pulled him out and cuddled him against my chest, smiling when he began to purr.

I stowed the cat in one of my saddlebags, apologizing I'd have to shut him in. He settled down as if he'd been in the same situation before. Realizing we didn't have cat food at the house, I returned to the drug store and picked up a bag, placing it beside the cat and closing the compartment. I settled the backpack on my back and headed toward home, surprised to realize I now considered Seth's and Sarah's my place as well.

Seth seemed happy with my purchases and the men attacked the candy like kids eating ice cream. I smiled at the expressions on their faces as they consumed treats they had been denied for so long.

Seth had settled Micah in the living room where he lay back in a recliner, his elevated feet swathed in gauze. His eyes were closed but he opened them when I passed by, the kitten in my hand. Raising up on an elbow, he said, "What you got there?"

I showed him the tabby. "Found him at the drugstore when I went for medicine. Oh, here, I brought you a candy bar."

"Shoot, I ain't had a Snickers in months," he said with a grin. He put the candy beside him and held out his hand. "Can I hold him?"

"You're welcome to." I placed the kitten in his large hand, watched as he brought him to his chest, speaking to him in a low, soothing voice. "I've always loved cats," Micah said with a smile. "Had them my whole life."

"I brought food for him. Let me know when he gets hungry." I patted the purring kitten on the head and went into the kitchen where Sarah stood at the counter chopping lettuce. Seth held the baby in one arm, stirring a pot with the other.

"I found a kitten," I told him, holding up the bag of cat food.

"We're going to have to open up a kennel you keep bringing all these animals home," Seth groused.

Sarah smiled. "Like he doesn't love it."

I sat down at the table. "What are we going to do with all these guys, Seth?"

He handed the baby to me. I sat him in my lap, wiggled my fingers for him, watched as he captured them in his tiny hands.

"I've been talking to them. Once they're feeling up to it, most want to head off, find another community. I told them about the one in Bristol. That's probably where they'll go."

"Good. I'd hate to see them end up at one like ours was."

"Me, too."

"Where are they going to sleep?"

"A lot want to camp under the stars. Some said they'd take the barn. We haven't got any more bedrooms left but I told them some could bunk in the front room and dining room if they wanted."

"What about Jonah? Is he awake?"

"Just checked him. Where's the medicine?"

"In my saddlebag."

"I'll go get it, give him a sedative to keep him asleep. The longer he goes without moving, the better for his back." He handed the spoon to me and left.

Most of the men stayed almost a week, long enough to get food in their bellies and gain some of their strength back. They left together, thanking us for helping them escape and for the hospitality given. I made two trips to a large department store in a town nearby, filled a backpack for each man with food and water which I gave to them. Micah remained behind, his feet still healing. He and the kitten had formed a tight bond and one seemed lost without the other. Adam and Eve were curious about the little cat and would nudge it with their noses only to be rewarded with a hiss and weak smack which they seemed to find amusing. Jonah, of course, remained upstairs, on his stomach for the most part, drugged the great majority of the day. When he would stir to consciousness, Sarah or Seth would be there with soup and water and to help him to the bathroom. I stayed downstairs, afraid if he saw me, he would react as violently as he had at the commune. But always, always, I listened for the sound of his voice, my body reacting, goose bumps breaking out, heat racing from my abdomen to my toes. What would I do when he healed? Where would I go? I had no idea but knew I couldn't stay once he was awake and moving about.

I began to spend more time outdoors on Boomer, riding the countryside, Adam and Eve trailing along. Finding the kitten, which Micah had named Buster, spurred me to search for other animals. As with Eve, a kitten could mean only one thing: its mother had survived the pox. I prowled through barns and homes, inside culverts, and forged deep into wooded areas. I saw several deer, fox, and a great many squirrels scampering about, which was encouraging. And one afternoon, cresting a hill, Boomer drew up short, his nose in the air, sniffing. He made a strange sound in his throat and I glanced wildly around, afraid he had sensed a predator. But in the valley below, I saw what caused his strange behavior. A horse, this one a roan with a dark mane, grazing in an open meadow. Boomer made a squealing sound in his throat and I slid off his back, glad for once I had not saddled him. "Go," I told him, knowing horses were social animals and he wanted to investigate this other one. He galloped away and I sat on the grass on the hill and watched Boomer approach the horse. They squealed at one another for awhile before coming closer. I tensed, praying the horse below was a mare or gelding and not a stallion like Boomer. I did not want my horse injured fighting. But then again, maybe not, if there were no females around to claim. It took awhile for the two horses to become friends and I patiently waited to see what Boomer would do. Would he go off with the other horse or return to me? Please don't leave me, I prayed, smiling when Boomer headed in my direction, the horse trailing him. When they reached me, I was happy to see he had indeed found a filly. Now we could have more horses if the two bred. I ran my hands over the other horse, inspecting her for injuries or inflammation but she seemed to be in good form. She was friendly enough, which told me she had had human contact before. I threw myself over Boomer's back and said, "Let's go home," laughing with delight when he galloped at full speed toward Seth's and Sarah's, the mare following behind.

Seth came out to greet us when we loped onto the front yard, a big smile on his face. "She's a beauty," he said, rubbing her between the eyes.

"I hope you don't mind but Boomer found her and I don't think he's ready to let her go."

"Maybe we'll get lucky and have foals next year," Sarah said, joining us.

"That would be wonderful," I said, imagining a gangly colt running around the corral.

Micah limped out on the porch, the kitten in his hand. "I swear, Maddie, you're a magnet for animals looking for homes."

"I wish." I noticed movement at one of the upstairs windows and glanced up. Jonah stood there, looking down. Our eyes met and I could sense no warmth in his. I jerked my chin toward the window. "He's up."

Seth nodded. "His back's much better. He says he's tired of being drugged all the time so I'm allowing him up for brief periods of time." We began to lead the horses to the barn. "He's still weak, can't remember much of what happened that day you saved him, only knows Callie told him he'd been sentenced to die."

"Thank God you were there that day, Seth. We wouldn't have gotten any of them out if you hadn't have been."

"Oh, I think that crowd would have eventually done something. They were too riled not to."

I let Boomer into the corral, watching as the mare followed. "What shall we call her?"

"You pick, Madison. You found her, you should name her."

I thought about it for a moment. "How about Sinead? I've always loved that name."

Seth grinned. He put his arm around my shoulder as we walked back to the house. "Listen, don't let Jonah being here make you uncomfortable. I've explained to him that Callie and Sandra set you up so that it would look like you betrayed the men. I think he understands that now."

"Maybe. It still has to be hard for him."

"Just let things happen in their own time. Let him deal with all that's happened, get his mind wrapped around it the right way."

"Do I have a choice?"

"Does anyone?"

And that night, as usual, I lay in bed listening for sounds of Jonah, aware when he walked down the hall to the bathroom, clenching the bed sheets to keep myself from going out there, begging him to believe that I had not betrayed him. And when I slept, vivid dreams of making love with Jonah, waking in a sweat, stifling the tears when they came.

The next morning, Jonah joined us for breakfast. Stunned to see him standing in the doorway, I ducked my head and concentrated on shoveling the food on my plate into my mouth. Seth showed him where to sit and dished fried potatoes and onions onto a plate for him. I glanced up, caught Jonah staring at me, and looked away. Again, no warmth in those moss-green eyes which now reminded me of algae covered with ice. Micah, seeming to sense the tension, began relaying humorous tales of his life before the pox. I had begun to think of him as a big, gangly, goofy brother and loved listening to his deep Southern accent. We had all been pleased when Micah asked if he might be allowed to stay for awhile. I personally hoped it would be forever. I watched Jonah out of the corner of my eye, noting the way he shifted his shoulders, as if to relieve the pressure of his shirt from his back.

His movements were stiff, his face rigid with pain. I couldn't bear it. I got up, placed my plate in the sink and headed outside.

I ran to the corral, jumped on Boomer's back and took off, the mare following us. More than a mile away, a wooded ridge between us, I commanded Boomer to stop and slid off. My feet only held me for a bare second before I was on the ground, my face in my hands, bawling like a baby. So he would live but he would hate me. That much was obvious. Well, it was no more than I deserved. After all, hadn't I turned my back on him first when he asked me to help him escape? Hadn't I shown no trust in him first?

I stayed away most of the day, wandering the countryside, stopping at farmhouses and eventually going into subdivisions, always searching for signs of life. Where had everyone gone? Where were their pets, the wild animals in the woods? Perhaps humans hid in fear, afraid I carried the pox with me, and the animals would naturally distrust a stranger.

I watched the sky pinken as the sun made its descent behind the ridge to the west of the house. It was time to go back. I would go in the front door and if Jonah was in the kitchen with the others simply retire to my room. I couldn't avoid him altogether but would as much as I could until I decided what to do, where to go.

After I brushed Boomer and Sinead, I put them in their stalls and fed them oats, our bedtime ritual. Adam and Eve, waiting on me inside the barn door, gave me reproachful looks for leaving without them and I apologized profusely, taking the time to throw a ball for them and ruffle their fur and scratch their tummies. Once forgiven, I eased the front door open and listened. Voices drifted from the kitchen, those of Seth and Sarah and Micah. But would Jonah actually be part of their conversation? He hadn't joined in this morning, not even when Micah's antics brought laughter or smiles. My stomach growled and I decided to chance it.

I stepped into the kitchen and all three looked at me. "What?" I said, going to the sink and washing my hands.

"Never took you for a coward," Micah said, the kitten perched on his shoulder.

"Well, I am," I answered with a petulant look.

Seth squeezed my shoulder. "Give it time, girl. That's all I'm saying."

"Of course. What's for dinner?"

Sarah smiled at me as she set plates on the table. "We missed you."

I watched, counting four. "He's not coming down to dinner?"

She shook her head. "He had a bad day. I think moving around this morning was more painful than he thought it would be."

"He's sleeping," Seth said. "I'll take a plate up after dinner."

I sat on the porch with Micah later, listening to him play a guitar he'd discovered in one of the bedroom closets. He liked the blues and I liked hearing it. Seth and Sarah were in the living room playing with the baby, their voices low and lulling.

When Micah set the guitar aside and pulled the cat from his shoulder, placing it on his lap, I said, "I'm so glad you decided to stay, Micah. We all are."

"I like it here," he said in his beautiful deep-South accent. "Best place I've been so far."

I twisted my hands in my lap. "I'm so sorry it took me so long to help y'all. I should have done it when Seth escaped."

"Oh, darlin', ain't no way you could have helped us all then. We understood. We figured you'd get to us eventually."

I turned to him. "I'm really sorry it happened to you and the others. It was wrong, Micah."

"More wrongs been done to mankind than that, Maddie. You need to let that go and look toward the future."

I sighed. "I think I need to leave," I said in a whisper.

"Because of him?"

"He hates me and I can't blame him."

"He's confused, Maddie. Give him time."

"I don't know."

"You leave, you're giving up on everything. This is where you need to be right now. Let him decide what to do, don't let him drive you away from people you love."

I reached out and took his hand. "I love you all. You're like family to me." My voice broke. "Dammit, I can't stop crying anymore," I said with a laugh.

"You and the rest of us." Micah stood and stretched.

"How are your feet? Still better?"

"Hell, they feel so good I don't even know they're there anymore." He cradled the kitten in his arms. "Come on, Buster, let's go to bed." He ruffled my hair as he left the porch.

A few minutes later, I followed him inside, watching Seth and Sarah with the baby for a moment, thinking there was something good that came out of this after all.

The next morning, I rose at dawn and headed to the kitchen with my backpack, determined to be gone before everyone else got up. I was stuffing it with food to tide me over during the day when I felt movement behind me. I glanced over my shoulder and dropped the backpack in surprise. Jonah stood in the doorway watching me. "How..." my voice broke. I cleared my throat and tried again. "How are you feeling?"

He walked closer, his movements stiff and cautious. "I've been better."

I looked into those beautiful eyes of his and couldn't read them. A sense of despair washed over me. Before, I had always been able to gauge his emotions by his eyes.

His gaze darted to the backpack. "Where are you going?"

"Riding. I've, um, been looking for people, for animals, you know, kind of like what I did back at the...the commune." I cleared my throat again.

He studied me for a moment. I self-consciously tugged at my braid, smoothed the hair around my face.

"Seth told me you were set up, that they wanted me to think you'd betrayed us."

"Yes, that's true. They told me they'd kill you if I didn't go along with their plan. I was next in line for the whip although they didn't want you to know that."

His eyes flared. "But you didn't get it, did you? You managed not to."

"Did Seth tell you what happened?"

"Said you tried to stop them and got knocked out."

"That's true, Jonah. I don't expect you to believe it but it's true."

He considered this. "Probably. Suzie told me the same thing. Said you tried to save my life. So I guess I owe you my gratitude."

I didn't know what to say. The expression on his face belied the sincerity of his words. "Well, I need to get going."

"Don't leave on my account, Madison."

"No, it's not that, it's just, well, I've got to go." Without a backward glance, I shoved the back door open and ran for the barn.

And so the next two weeks went like this. I arose before everyone else, packed my backpack and left for the day. One day, I found three goats at a deserted farm and after much chasing and cursing managed to get a rope around the billy goat's neck, hoping the nanny goats would follow. Adam and Eve didn't help much, nipping at the goats' heels and barking like crazy as they tried to herd them but I couldn't be mad at them for trying to help. We made a fine procession as we returned to the farm, the billy goat trailing the horse and the nanny goats following passively behind, Adam and Eve bringing up the rear, eager to bring them back in line if they wandered off.

Sarah squealed with delight when she saw them. "Now we can have milk and cheese," she declared giving me a hug.

Over her shoulder, I caught Jonah standing in the doorway watching us, his look cold and indifferent.

Another day, I found a large pig rutting in an abandoned garden. Surprisingly, the pig allowed me to pet him and quite willingly tagged along as we made our way back to the farm. Adam and Eve sniffed and nudged the swine, not sure what he was. But he accepted their curiosity and even began to romp with them, throwing his head down and bringing it up, toppling them onto their backs. It felt good to laugh.

"Ham and bacon," Micah said with a wide grin.

I glared at him. "You lay one hand on this pig, I'll kill you. He's a pet."

"Damn, girl, ain't you craving fresh meat? Some good ole protein in your body?"

I blatantly gave his large body the once over. "Looks like it hasn't hurt you any."

He laughed at that.

On one of my outings, I stumbled upon what had once been a petting zoo and was shocked when I came face to face with a llama and sheep, standing side by side staring at me. I approached them with caution, not sure if either animal was aggressive. Adam and Eve circled the two, sniffing at the air, but didn't challenge them and they ignored the two dogs, their gazes focused on me. Apparently used to humans, they passively let me put a rope around each of their necks and lead them back to the farm. Seth and Micah talked nonstop about how to care for the animals and I found I had nothing to add to the discussion. I'd never even seen one in real life before.

And the best day of all, when I found four hens and a rooster rooting around in a barnyard, busily clucking and strutting. I sat down and wondered how in the world I could get them to come with me. Finally, I went inside the chicken coop, found some burlap sacks and ran around the barnyard like a lunatic, Adam and Eve chasing me, having a grand time. I finally managed to snare the poultry. They weren't too happy about the sacks but seemed to settle down on the ride back to our farm.

Seth, Sarah and Micah had gotten into the routine of stopping whatever chore they were engaged in when I rode into the yard to see what I'd managed to snag. When Seth heard the clucking, he gave a delighted whoop. "Eggs. We can have fresh eggs." He took the sacks from my hands and emptied them onto the yard. The fowl gave me peevish looks before strutting around, scratching for food.

Micah joined us. "Good thing we got that chicken coop out back, huh? Come on, let's get these buggers quartered before they take off on us."

And Sarah and I laughed till we cried as we watched Micah and Seth chase the poultry around the yard.

During that time, I managed to ignore the fact that Jonah was always in the background, watching and listening. The few times we ran into one another, he didn't say much and I found myself making up an excuse not to be near him and rushing away. The only meal I took with the family was dinner and when he began to join us I thanked God Seth and Micah dominated the conversation, grilling Jonah about the proper diet and care for our animal menagerie.

And early one morning, like the previous one, I turned from the pantry to see Jonah staring at me. "I need to talk to you," he said.

"Sure. But I'm getting ready to leave—"

"It won't take but a minute." He hesitated. "I'll walk you outside."

He held the door and strolled beside me as I went to the barn. I noticed he didn't hold himself so cautiously anymore and seemed much more limber than before. "Your back's better?"

"A lot. I'm feeling more like my old self." He hesitated. "Well, physically."

"Jonah, I'm glad. I was so worried." I regretted saying that as soon as it left my mouth.

He gave me a look. "I just wanted to let you know I'm leaving today. I won't be here when you get back."

I stopped in surprise. "You don't have to leave. I mean, if it's me, I can leave."

He shook his head. "No, Madison, that's not it." He looked away from me and for the first time I saw pain in his eyes. "I just need to go someplace where I can clear my head. I think I'll head to that commune in Bristol."

I nodded. "That's where the others decided to go."

His mouth tightened. "You still use that word?"

"I didn't mean it that way, Jonah. I meant the other men."

I stared at the ground. I didn't want him to see the gathering tears.

He cleared his throat. "Well, I just wanted to tell you goodbye and God speed, I guess." He spun on his heels and walked away.

I didn't look up until I heard the door shut behind him. "God bless, Jonah," I said, tears falling down my face.

I stayed away until nightfall, and when I returned, Sarah sat in the kitchen waiting for me. When she saw me, she hugged me tight. "I'm so sorry," she whispered.

I choked back a sob. "I love him, Sarah. I did everything wrong with him and because of that I lost him."

"You had no control over what happened, Madison. Like Seth said, give him time. Let him work it out."

I let her appease me, say soothing words to me, but knew in my heart I could have been a better person with him than I had, one more trusting, more willing to believe in him, in what we had.

CHAPTER 18

As the months went by, we settled into our own routine, working in our vegetable and flower gardens, taking care of the animals, becoming a close-knit family, something I was not used to but appreciated more than I could say. We passed the long nights playing Scrabble or Seth would fire up the generator and we would watch DVDs of movies from the past but never horror or apocalyptic ones. We stayed away from those, preferring dramas or comedies. But these movies, even the ones made shortly before the pox, seemed so strange and unrealistic to me, like a dream I might have once had, and I wondered if the world would ever return to that.

At times, I envied the love between Seth and Sarah, and would on occasion catch Micah watching them with the same emotion flaring in his eyes. I knew he had been married before the pox but Micah, although more than willing to share his boyhood stories, never shared his life with his wife. It was obvious he still grieved for her and I prayed one day he would meet a woman who would take her place in his heart. He was a kind, caring man and deserved to be happy. After thinking about this for a good while, I rode into town one day and returned with Darlene under the guise that I wanted her to check our animals to ensure they were healthy and to make sure Eve, who we suspected might be pregnant, actually was. And as I watched interest flare in Micah's eyes when he saw her, the answering glint in Darlene's, I thought what beautiful children they would have.

I rode out at least twice a week, always searching for life, but as the days grew cooler and winter settled in for good, the number I saw diminished. I made monthly visits to the commune, spending time with Suzie and Linda and was glad to see they were happy with their small community, now more of a harmonious group than one devoted to gaining power and numbers. The women in the commune seemed content and willing to live the rest of their lives there.

During the spring, Seth, Micah and I began repairing the fencing around the farm, making sure the animals would be inside and safe rather than outside and prey to predators or someone hunting fresh meat – always a fear of mine. The fencing around the farm yard and corral was wooden, although that surrounding the acreage adjoining the property was barbed wire, an arduous task none of us liked to do, but we had no choice but to fix the parts that had broken down.

One day, the sky blue and bright, the air fresh and crisp, we were on the outskirts of the acreage, just beneath the ridge that rose to the west, when I saw a figure strolling toward us. Obviously a man by the size and set of the shoulders and the way he moved. Something nudged my brain, a sense of familiarity, but I refused to think about who it could possibly be. As he drew nearer, I noticed the dark, shaggy hair which was longer and imagined if I could see the eyes they would be dark-green and piercing. An image of being wrapped around that body rose in my mind and heat traveled through me like steam through a pipe and I dropped my tools. Seth and Micah, noticing this, straightened and looked in the direction of my gaze.

"Well, I'll be damned," Micah said under his breath. He cast a quick smile at me. "Looks like lover boy's returned."

Seth wiped his forehead with the back of his sleeve as he watched Jonah stroll toward us. When he got to us, Seth said "Good to see you back."

Jonah nodded at Seth and Micah. "Good to be back." His eyes when they landed on me were wary and cautious, but was that warmth beneath that carefulness? "Madison," he said, his voice dropping to a husky level. He cleared his throat. "Could I talk to you?"

I glanced at Seth and Micah, grinning at me. "Um, sure."

"If y'all will excuse us," Jonah said in a courteous tone.

Micah punched Seth on the shoulder. "Hell, yeah, we will. Glad you're back, Jonah."

Jonah and I walked side by side to the top of a small rise behind the house. "When'd you get here?" I asked, settling down on the crisp brown grass just now showing tinges of green.

Jonah sat next to me. "Awhile ago. Sarah fed me lunch before she'd tell me where you were."

"That's our Sarah. She's a real mother hen." I laughed slightly.

An awkward silence passed between us. Well, hell, I thought. "Where'd you go, Jonah?"

"To the commune in Bristol."

"And is it everything they said it would be?"

"Everything and more. Men and women work together there, no one's ostracized because of their gender."

"That's the way it should be, Jonah. I'm glad you were a part of that."

"Yeah." He grew silent and I sat waiting for whatever he wanted to say to me. When he spoke, I jumped a bit. "But there was something missing, something it took me awhile to figure out."

"Really?" I turned to him, interested. "And what was that?"

He looked at me and the warmth in his eyes that I had missed so long was back. My body heated at once. Jonah reached out a hand to touch my cheek. "You."

I closed my eyes as I leaned my face into his palm, saying a silent prayer of thanks.

We stayed there on that small piece of land throughout the afternoon, talking, occasionally reaching out and touching one another, tentatively at first, but as the sun began to descend, with a hunger that bordered on desperate.

And when twilight deepened, without saying a word, we got to our feet and, holding hands, moved into the woods bordering the ridge. I lead him to a small, abandoned log home I had found early in my stay here which I found charming and cozy. We smiled at one another as Jonah released my hand and walked onto the wide, wraparound porch and opened the door. He peered inside then nodded at me. I joined him and stepped inside the small house. Jonah took out his lighter and flicked it on, searching until he found a candle. While he lit it, I walked around, opening windows to air it out. Jonah found wood stacked in the fireplace and lit that against the chilly air now sweeping through the cottage. We inspected the house and I thought whoever lived there had loved this place as evidenced by the homemade curtains at the windows, blowing in the slight breeze, the bright colors throughout the living area, bedroom, bath and kitchen, the details given to the dovetailed ceiling, decorative tiles in the kitchen and surrounding the rather large walk-in shower. Although the hardwood floors were dusty, I knew once cleaned they would glisten as if new.

I caught Jonah watching me and smiled at him. "What do you think? Want to spend the night here?" he asked.

I laughed with delight. "I want to live here."

"We can do that too." His face sobered. "That is, if you still want me."

I rushed to him, caressed his face. "Of course I do. I've never wanted anyone else, Jonah. I never will."

And when he kissed me, I had never felt so right about anything in my life.

The night passed too swiftly, and when I woke in the morning on the large king-sized bed in the bright blue bedroom, snuggled against Jonah, tears sprang to my eyes. So it was true. I hadn't dreamed it. He was here. He was mine. And I was his and always would be.

Hunger drove us out of bed and we dressed quickly and walked hand in hand to Seth's and Sarah's place. Jonah stopped me before we stepped into the yard, his eyes searching my face. "Did you mean it?"

I cocked my head at him, unsure what he meant.

"About living in the house we found. Is that what you want?"

I smiled. "Oh, yes, it's beautiful. Just perfect for us, don't you think?"

He leaned forward, kissed me. "Yeah, I do," he said in that husky voice of his that sent tingles up and down my spine.

We found Seth and Sarah sitting around the kitchen table drinking coffee while Micah flipped pancakes on a large griddle, Darlene mixing batter beside him. I smiled when I saw her, thinking it wouldn't be long before she moved in. It seemed she spent more nights here than at the commune.

Micah grinned our way. "Don't have to ask how y'all are feeling, it's written all over your face," he drawled.

I couldn't help the blush that crept up my face, ignoring Micah's laugh.

We told them about the house while we ate. They seemed delighted by this news or perhaps that Jonah was back and I wouldn't be moping around, feeling sorry for myself that I had lost my true love. I was glad it was close by so I could see Seth, Sarah, Micah, Darlene and the baby every day as well as continue to board the horses there. After much discussion, we decided to keep Adam with them since he and Eve were so inseparable but I was promised my pick of the litter when Eve had her pups. Darlene was promised seconds. I couldn't wait for that.

After breakfast, I packed what few items I possessed and moved with Jonah into our new home, proudly showing it to my friends, who seemed to like it as much as I did. And after they left, I cleaned the small cottage while Jonah checked out the propane tank and generator and made sure everything was in working order. We had dinner with our friends, telling them we would go into town for supplies the next day, and returned to our cottage, eager for the night and one another.

The remainder of that fall, Jonah and I saddled up and rode out every day searching for animals in need of a home. Adam usually joined us and I loved those times together. We saw a mother fox with her babies and this was heartening. We would catch sight of rabbits jumping through foliage and squirrels climbing tree trunks and spied a coyote watching us as we rode by. But domesticated animals were rare and we despaired some species may have been destroyed by the pox. When winter descended, spilling ice and snow, we were forced inside but I found this just as enjoyable, sitting by the fire reading, teaching myself how to quilt, snuggled up with Jonah on the couch watching DVD movies depicting the world as it used to be. If the weather permitted, we paid daily visits to our friends, sharing long, comfortable meals and planning our future. We painted walls and hung curtains and made the small cottage our home and for the first time since the pox, my life was filled with light, warmth, love, and I reveled in it.

But at times a sense of foreboding would come over me and a voice in my mind would whisper, this will not last. I would place my body close to Jonah and whisper back, you are wrong.

CHAPTER 19

Spring seemed to take its sweet time settling in for good but I didn't mind. Once the days began to grow warm, we took up our old habit of searching for life. In one house in a nearby town, Jonah found a ham radio and spent most of a day setting it up and teaching himself how to work it. What we learned was disturbing. Men had begun establishing their own communities banning women and those with women only had multiplied and swollen. Communities with both sexes living side by side were small in number and I wondered why this divisive state.

Darlene now lived with Micah at Seth's and Sarah's but ventured to the commune at least twice a week to visit friends and catch up on the latest news. What she heard was disconcerting. Women passing through or joining them told of skirmishes between communities of men and women and one woman said she had heard of a band of women raiders who hunted down and killed any man they came across. So Armageddon wasn't the pox, it was here and it was now.

And it paid us a visit on a beautiful warm day in early May in the guise of Sandra, the one we called Crazy Eyes, and a band of women she had cultivated since her departure from the commune.

Jonah and I were saddling our horses, ready to head out, when we heard shots from the direction of Seth's and Sarah's home. Without speaking, we quickly armed ourselves and ran in that direction. At the edge of the yard, I saw Micah lying face down on the ground. Screeching, I hurried over to him, motioning Jonah on to the house to check on the others. With a great deal of effort, I managed to turn Micah over. When I did, my eyes widened at the blood leaking from a hole in his stomach, the ground turning red around him.

"Sis," he said in that lazy drawl of his.

Another volley of shots from the house and I glanced that way. "You're fine, you're gonna be fine," I assured him, running my hands over his face and down his arm, clutching his hand. I burst into tears.

"Shhh," he said. "It's all right. I ain't afraid of death, not after what we've been through."

"I will not let you die," I said, my voice hard, tearing off my shirt, wadding it up, stuffing it into his wound and applying pressure.

He grunted with pain. "Ah, now, darlin', you don't have any say in the matter." He swallowed and I could tell it took a great deal of effort to talk. "Best get on up to the house. The others are there. It's that Crazy Eyes. She's..." His body relaxed and his mouth went slack.

I had seen enough of death to know there would be no bringing him back. I leaned back on my heels and howled my anger at the heavens. This was my brother, my family, killed because he was simply a man. What kind of world had this become? We had been given the chance to redeem ourselves, to make a better place and instead had created strife and war between the very small number of survivors left.

"She will pay for this," I promised Micah as I leaned down and kissed his cheek. I took his gun and tucked it in my jeans and ran toward the house. "I will kill her," I shouted, a promise I made to myself.

I joined Jonah, taking shelter behind a stack of firewood, and shook my head at his inquisitive look. His face fell. "I'm sorry, Madison."

I bit my lip and swiped my eyes and tried not to think of my friend. "Is it her?"

"It's Crazy Eyes. She's got a band of about five or six, looks like, with her. They're right over there behind the garden shed."

I peeked out and saw a head dart out from behind the large shed. Without thinking, I pointed my gun and shot and watched the woman tumble to the ground. And only felt despair when I realized it was not Crazy Eyes.

"What about Seth and Sarah and Darlene?" I asked, my eyes pinned on the shed.

"I can hear shots coming from the house. They're still in there."

I glanced around the yard and saw dead chickens scattered about. I could hear the pig squealing in the barn and prayed it was only because of fear. I didn't see our goats anywhere. The sheep, llama and two horses were in the corral behind the barn and I hoped they were safe there and that Adam and Eve and the pups were in the house. I looked at Jonah. "What can we do?"

"We need to get around behind them. I'll go first. Cover me." Before I could protest it was too dangerous, he darted across the yard. I waited for another head to poke around and when it did got off a shot but was too late. The woman managed, however, to send a bullet in Jonah's direction but he fell to the ground and rolled behind the large tractor and the bullet missed him.

I leaned against the wood behind me and tried to settle down. My body shook with adrenaline and my mind could not get past the death of my friend. I looked toward the tractor and noticed Jonah motioning for me to join him. I aimed my gun and shot at the shed as I took off, running at a zigzag across the yard, listening to shots being fired all around me. I rolled behind the tractor, placing myself behind the large, rear tire. Jonah nodded at me then took off.

And so it went like this, Jonah, then me darting for cover, managing to dodge their bullets, until we were at an angle to the shed, sheltered behind the barn.

"We can either try to get to the house or try to get to them," Jonah said, his voice rough.

I thought about it. I wanted nothing more than to get my hands on Sandra, tear her heart out of her chest. How many innocent people would die because of her? I feared that in killing Callie, we had unleashed a monster and that monster needed to be stopped.

I ejected my magazine and filled it. "I took out one, so that should leave four, maybe five, right?"

He nodded as he reloaded his gun.

"You go to the house, I'm going after them."

Jonah put his hand on my arm, his gaze holding mine. "No."

"I can't let her get away. And I can't... I won't let her kill you."

"No."

Tears sprang to my eyes. "Please, Jonah, they'll target you first. I stand a better chance."

He kissed me roughly. "I love you, Madison." And before I could respond, he said, "Let's do it," and we came out from behind the barn, shooting toward the shed. I ran that way, stumbling when I realized Jonah stayed with me, had not turned toward the house, and in so doing dodged the bullet that probably would have killed me. I waited patiently for a head to appear from behind the shed and when it did fired off a shot and felt a prickling of satisfaction as another body tumbled. Jonah managed to shoot another woman who fell to the ground howling with pain and then the bullets from the shed abruptly stopped. One or two more pops came from the house and everything went silent. Jonah motioned me to go around one end of the shed, indicating he would go around the other, but just as we separated a jeep blasted out from behind the shed and came right for me, a woman at its wheel, Sandra in the passenger seat, another woman behind her. Jonah jerked me out of its way and I heard a shot and the jeep swerved and I fell down. As the jeep went by, I saw Sandra, her gun pointed at me from an arm red with blood. The woman in the back seat had her gun aimed behind her, I suspected at Jonah, who I was sure was trying to draw attention from me. I ignored them, my eyes locked with Sandra's as I struggled to right myself, waiting for the bullet. But it didn't come and when I managed to get to my knees to shoot her, the jeep was too far away.

Jonah helped me up then pulled me into a hard embrace. "Thank God you're all right," he whispered. I stepped back when I felt blood on his shirt. "It's nothing, just a graze," he assured me.

Seth joined us, out of breath. "Was that..."

"Crazy Eyes," I finished for him. "How are Sarah, Darlene and the baby?"

"They're fine. I hid them in the attic." He hugged Jonah and me. "Damn, I thought for sure they were going to kill you guys."

"Micah's dead," I said and burst into tears.

"Oh, no." Seth stepped back. "Oh, no, not Micah."

Jonah held me as I cried. I barely heard Seth say he was going after Sarah and Darlene and when they joined us could not bear the grief in Darlene's eyes. And instead of me comforting her, she comforted me, and I was so thankful for this strong, caring woman who did not deserve to lose the man she loved in such a horrific, unacceptable way. And I promised myself once more that I would kill Sandra for this and did not mind the cold hardness I felt building inside my body.

Realizing Sandra and her minions could return any moment, I forced myself to focus on a plan. "We need to get out of here," I said.

Seth shook his head. "I need to see to Jonah first. That looks worse than a graze."

My gaze darted to Jonah, deathly pale and swaying. I put an arm around his waist. "Let's get him inside."

Seth helped me guide Jonah into the house and directed him into a kitchen chair. "Y'all should leave," Jonah said in a weak voice. "Get out of here before she comes back."

"She was injured," I told Seth. "Her left arm was completely covered in red. I also saw blood running down her face. She had the chance to shoot me but didn't take it so I think she may have been too injured to aim the gun."

He nodded. "That should buy us some time." He ripped Jonah's shirt off and inspected the wound. "Looks worse than it is but he's lost some blood," he said more to himself than anyone.

"Will he be all right?" I asked, panic starting to build at the thought of a world without Jonah.

"He'll be fine. I'll need to stitch this up and he'll be weak for a bit but it's not life threatening."

I almost fell to my knees with gratitude.

While Seth tended to Jonah's wound, we debated what to do.

"She'll be back to finish what she started," I said. "She won't let this go especially now that she knows I'm here. We need to leave as soon as Jonah's bandaged and feels ready."

Seth shook his head. "She won't be here right away. If she's injured, she'll go somewhere for treatment."

"The commune," Darlene said in a low, choked voice. "It's close. She knows Suzie's there."

"We've got time," Seth said. "While I tend to Jonah, you all start packing. We'll leave first thing in the morning if Jonah's up to it."

I glanced at Sarah, silent through all this. She held Travis close to her body and the sadness in her eyes told me she did not want to leave this place. But we could not stay, none of us. Sandra would be back and she would be after blood. "I'm so sorry, Sarah," I said. "This was such a happy home and I know how much you love it here."

"We'll have one again," she said with a forced smile.

We buried Micah late that afternoon beneath his favorite tree, a huge oak where he had hung a tire swing for the baby when he was old enough. Jonah and Seth made a cross of wood and carved his name onto it, and we each promised Micah he would not be forgotten as they planted it at the head of his grave.

We got little sleep that night, our ears alert for some signal from the dogs that the women had come back. I hoped Sandra's injury had been such that it would delay her long enough for us to get far, far away and had to constantly tamp down a wild sense of panic that she was on her way and we were all going to die.

Early the next morning, after Jonah assured us he felt well enough to travel, we set out with our menagerie of animals, me on horseback, Seth and Darlene riding motorcycles and Sarah driving a four-wheel-drive truck. Jonah sat in the front seat and little Travis rode in a car-seat in back. The bed was laden with supplies and chickens in crates and puppies on blankets. As we made our way toward the purple mountains in the distance, I glanced back at the place where my life had been so happy, knowing it would be a long time before I would feel that way again. I prayed we would find a place to hide until this war building within our country had passed and peace reigned, if ever. But that inner voice I had come to hate whispered, this is not over, not yet. And the cold ball of anger building in my body answered, not until she is dead.

ABOUT THE AUTHOR

CT French is Christy Tillery French, an award-winning, internationally published author whose books cross several genres including mystery, romantic comedy, romantic suspense and action-adventure, and include *The Bodyguard series* as well as several standalones. She is also co-author of *Whistling Woman* (Southern fiction) with her sister Cyndi Tillery Hodges.

If you wish to contact the author:
Email: ctfrench252@aol.com
Website: http://christytilleryfrench.com
Facebook: https://www.facebook.com/christytilleryfrench
Twitter: @ctfrench

www.ingramcontent.com/pod-product-compliance
Lightning Source LLC
Chambersburg PA
CBHW051506170626
46811CB00002B/674